"THREE BULLETS
THROUGH MY BODY.
THEY GOT ME, JACK.
I'M FINISHED."

Single Jack Deems looked down at the shattered body of Young Dave Apperley. "Who did it, Dave? Tell me who did it."

"McGruder, Westover, Mandell . . . the Shodress gang," Apperley whispered.

Slowly Single Jack took the dying man's hand. "Dave," he said, and his voice was deep and sure, "those buzzards are as good as dead. From now on I'll let my gun do the talking!"

Books by Max Brand

Published by POCKET BOOKS

Max Brand

SINGLE JACK

PUBLISHED BY POCKET BOOKS NEW YORK

POCKET BOOKS, a Simon & Schuster division of
GULF & WESTERN CORPORATION
1230 Avenue of the Americas, New York, N.Y. 10020

ISBN: 0-671-83417-7

First Pocket Books printing August, 1953

10 9 8 7 6

CONTENTS

CONTENTS

SINGLE JACK

1. A Man of Steel

There was just enough current sliding down the black face of the East River to keep a bow wave whispering about the prow of the Nancy Lou. The night was still, and close, and the two men on the deck were soothed by the cool lapping of the water. There was peace on the river such as could not be found in the town. The humming voice of Manhattan never died away, and Brooklyn murmured behind them, but these sounds were far away. Closer and more disturbing were the occasional tugs which went grinding by between them and Blackwell's Island; and now a Boston passenger ship, a vision of light and shadow, went by with deeply singing engines. However, on the whole the river was very still, and there was only a background of sound from the cities.

Upon the broad poop of the little yacht sat two men with a bottle of chilled wine, and cigars to pass the warmth of the evening until the night coolness would begin. They sat at ease, rarely stirring, rarely even speaking, and then in half sentences. But the dog which was chained close to the hatch was constantly on the move. Sometimes he strained toward the side of the boat as far as his chain would allow. Sometimes he scratched restlessly at the deck. Again, he lifted a massive head with a bristling ruff of fur around his neck and two short, pointed ears—very like the head of a wolf—and from his throat there issued a deep, wild cry that went ringing across the river.

"Stop him!" said David Apperley, the younger of the two. "Stop him, Andrew. It curdles my blood to hear him!"

"Let Comanche sing." The older brother chuckled. "The poor devil has had no fun since the day I caught him."

I

"Was that fun for him?"

"He chewed up seven out of my twelve dogs; of course it was fun for him."

"Seven out of twelve! What sort of mangy mongrels did you use to chase him?"

"I'll tell you what they were. Big Devils. Old, hardened wolfhounds. Dash of greyhound for speed; dash of mastiff for nerve and jaw power. Two or three of them could handle almost any wolf. But they couldn't handle Comanche. It was a grand mêlée to watch, I can tell you! I was glad when we got the lariats on him. Gad, Dave, he slashed two of those lariats in two as cleanly as though those white teeth of his were a sharp sword!"

"Maybe the rope was old."

"Rope? Rawhide, Dave. Like flexible steel. But those teeth are chilled steel, too! Stop it, Comanche!"

He spoke in the midst of another howl with which the whole body of the big wolf dog was quivering. The effect of his voice was to stop the howl short. Comanche leaped at the speaker until the chain checked him. Then, straining against the broad collar, his teeth snapping, and his eyes green with devilish hatred, he strove to get at his owner.

"Pretty boy, isn't he?" asked Andrew Apperley, leaning forward to watch.

"One of these days, he'll break that rusty chain. And he'll about finish you, Andy."

The other nodded.

"I'll change that chain tomorrow."

"Change the wolf, rather. Larkin has given him up. You promised me if Larkin couldn't train the beast, you'd give up that four-footed murderer. Larkin can handle tigers and panthers, but he admits that he can do nothing with this brute."

"He's rather a bad dog," said the elder brother, nodding. "But suppose that one day I learn the key to his heart. Suppose that he grows to love me as much as he hates me and all men, just now?"

"And what of it, Andrew? Even supposing that you could do what no man could do?"

"What of it? He would be the best bodyguard in the world. And we need bodyguards, out West. I have twenty rustlers who'd be happy fellows if they could sink a bullet between my shoulders. A dog like this—"

"Dog? Confound it, Andrew, he has 'wolf' written all over him!"

"Look at him again. Buffalo wolves are lower and narrower in the hindquarters. And he's splashed with brown. Besides, his whole pelt is finer than a lobo's. And most of all, when I weighed him—though he was thinner, even, than he is now—he tipped the scales at a hundred and fifty pounds. Timber wolves don't grow to that size. No, Dave, there's dog in him. St. Bernard, perhaps."

"I won't argue with you," grumbled David Apperley. "I won't argue with you. You keep waiting for the dog instincts to wake up in him, but dogs don't howl. They bark, and then whine. This beast can only howl and snarl."

"I admit that," said the owner. "But you can't budge me, Dave. I'll never give him up till I find a man who's a better master for him than I am."

David leaned back in his chair, muttering.

"I won't ask you to explain," he said. "Every man has weak spots. And besides, to own a wolf is rather spectacular."

"Don't be nasty about it. As a matter of fact, I don't think that. But he fills my mind's eye. He's a picture that I like to have in front of me as often as I can. Because he's a hero, Dave. Ah, man, if you'd seen him slash his way through that dog pack of mine, you would have loved him! I covered him with my rifle. He knew well enough that that was the finish of him, but instead of slinking away with his tail between his legs, he lifted his head and looked me in the eye as brave as you please, and dared me to do my worst. I couldn't kill him then. I can't kill him now, and he'll go back with me to my own country—"

"Your own country?" echoed Dave coldly.

A little silence fell between them. The Apperleys were of an old family and a good one, and they had been for many generations in New York, growing greater and richer as the city grew. But Andrew had tried his fortunes in the West. An accidental hunting trip showed the country to him, and he had remained in it ever since. This Eastern trip of his was merely to induce his younger brother to come to the new region with him, but to David there was a species of treason in abandoning New York, and he looked upon a shift in the family seat very much as he would have looked upon changing his citizenship. It was a sore topic which had caused many a bitter discussion between them. And so they fell silent.

"The long and short of it," said David at last, "is that you're an enthusiast, old fellow. You believe in that country because you've grown rich there."

"Not a bit! I believe in that country, because it's a country worthy of belief!"

"Half an ounce of culture to the square league!"

"Perhaps not that much. But culture is a luxury, not a necessity to me. If you have the same blood in you, you'll agree with me! However, I'm not trying to persuade you to come West with me, any more than I can persuade you to believe that Comanche is not pure wolf!"

David laughed a little.

"I'll tell you what I'll do," said he. "I'll give you my word to go West with you to your ranch and try to like the wild life there, the instant that I see any man brave enough to put his hand on the head of Comanche—while he's still unmuzzled!"

Once more the silence fell between them. Comanche grew quieter. But now there was a sudden outbreak of clamor from the big square-shouldered building on Blackwell's Island. They knew it was the prison.

A dozen repeating rifles seemed to be at work.

They could hear distant voices calling orders and shouting answers. Then the broad bright eye of a searchlight began to twist back and forth across the black surface of the East River.

4

"Someone has escaped," said Andrew Apperley. "Some poor devil has made a break for it, and he's away, by this time! There goes one of the guard boats!"

They saw a long, shadowy hull splitting the water. A shower of sparks rose from the chimney of the speed boat, and a white wake glistened behind it.

"They've got enough equipment to make it hot for the poor rat," said David, as he and his brother stood together at the side of the little yacht. "Isn't that a Gatling gun forward?"

"That's it, and another of them at the rear."

"And they can shoot faster and straighter than even your Western desperadoes, eh?"

"I don't know," answered Andrew calmly. "I've seen a man fan two Colts so fast that there was just one blur of reports from the beginning to the end! Hello, have they got him?"

The guard boat had veered sharply around and cut up against the current of the tide, throwing a sharp thin bow wave high on each side. They could see the uniformed guards with glistening guns in hand crowding onto the prow of the speed boat.

At the same time, the searchlight of the guard boat and the searchlight from the prison centered on one spot in the river, and the two watchers could plainly see the head of a swimmer who was forging across the current.

"They've got him!" said Andrew Apperley.

"Game devil!" exclaimed David, filled with admiration. "He doesn't let up a stroke. Hello, Andy, is he going to swim right into the path of that passenger ship?"

For now the towering height of a Boston passenger boat appeared slipping down the stream, and to the amazement of the Apperleys, they saw the swimmer turn and head straight across the way of the speeding ship.

"He'll be free, or else die trying!" exclaimed Andrew. "There's a man of steel, Dave. Look, the boat has him! Comanche, you devil, be still!"

For the wolf dog had broken into a furious howling, and

pawed frantically to break loose from his chain. At the same moment, the escaped prisoner swam straight into the path of the speeding boat, and the big ship passed over him.

2. Dog Strain, and Wolf Strain

"He's gone!" said Andrew Apperley. "But it's a dreadful thing to see, brother!"

"A murderer, most likely," said David calmly. "He's taking the medicine from his own hand that he didn't want to take from the law. We can't waste sympathy on such as he probably was. Look at the guard boat running amuck to make sure that he's gone!"

For as the passenger ship passed on, and the waves of her deep wake tossed the little yacht up and down, the guard boat was weaving here and there across the river, searching for the fugitive. Apparently it had no success, and the searchlight from the prison flashed wildly about, sometimes throwing its blinding brightness straight into the eyes of the two brothers who watched.

"What's quieted Comanche?" asked David at last.

He added suddenly: "And where is he? By gad, he's broken the chain!"

There it lay, a snaky length upon the deck. Apparently it had broken off short beside the collar as the big brute strained and tugged at it for liberty.

"Watch the deck!" said Andrew Apperley briskly.

He hurried below. But he came back almost at once with a gloomy face.

"He must have made for the shore," he said. "And that's the last that we'll see of him. He'll go through the city like a streak and get to the open country beyond. I tell you, Dave, that I'd rather have lost ten thousand dollars than that monster. We'll never see his likes again!"

"I've never seen anything that's pleased me more," answered David. "But hadn't we better send in a warning to the shore? A wild wolf running amuck through the streets—"

"It's too late for warnings. Wherever he's headed, he has gone at full speed, and I know what his speed is like. Hello—my word, what's this?"

He pointed with a rigid arm into the darkness of the river, and David, staring in the same direction, saw something swimming slowly in across the tidal drift. He looked again, and it seemed to him that it was a double shadow. It came closer, and now they made sure of the broad head and the pricking ears of Comanche, with a man's body trailing behind him.

"Do you see? Do you see?" gasped Andrew Apperley. "What was it you said about wolf? Did you ever hear of a wolf going into a river to bring out a drowning man? Is that a dog strain, or is it not?"

They ran down to the prow of the boat, for it was in that direction that the laboring Comanche was making, though it seemed doubtful that the strength of his swimming would enable him to cut in across the sharp sweep of the tidal current.

Andrew Apperley jumped down on the mooring rope, and thrusting his hand far out, he managed to catch the scruff of Comanche's mane as the big animal was carried past. He drew in the dog. It was all his strength could manage, with the assistance of David, to pass the exhausted brute up to the deck.

It was an easier task to draw in the man who had been clinging to Comanche. For all the uproar from Blackwell's Island, and all the play of searchlights and the activity of the guard boat had been done for the sake of a slender youth who seemed in his early twenties. Andrew passed him to David, and the latter stretched the half-conscious body on the deck.

The next instant he sprang back with a yell of alarm.

"Andrew! That devil of a wolf nearly got me then, and now he's murdering this man from the river—hold on—no, by the Eternal—"

7

He fell silent, while the older brother, clambering back to the deck, saw a most strange sight.

The rescued man lay at full length, his face turned toward the stars, while he drew each breath with an audible effort. At his head sat Comanche, his legs trembling with weariness but his strength and ferocity rapidly returning.

"By the Eternal!" said Andrew. "He's taking charge!"

"Signal to the guard boat!" said David.

"Not for a million! Turn this poor devil over to the law, after Comanche has saved him from the river? No chance that I'll do that, Dave! But how can we help him with that brute standing over him?"

"I don't know! It's the oddest thing that I've ever known. Makes me dizzy to see it! What happened to the brain of that beast?"

"The dog strain, Dave, the dog strain. In spite of you and the experts, I was right! He's not pure wolf! There, our man from the river is beginning to come to life. He'll pull through. But how could he have missed that ship? It seemed to pass straight over him!"

"He must have dived and swum under the surface until he was clear of it."

The fugitive came swaying to a sitting posture, at which Comanche, with a throat-tearing snarl, crowded closer.

"Look out!" warned Andrew Apperley. "That dog is dangerous, my friend!"

"This dog? Dangerous?" said the man from the river. Then he laughed, weakly, and passed his arm around the neck of Comanche. "Dangerous?" said the fugitive.

And Comanche turned and licked the face of him he had saved! The brothers, filled with wonder and awe, could not speak.

"I'd offer you something," said Andrew, "if I could get it past Comanche."

"You've given me enough," said the other. "I'll have my pins steady under me in a minute, and then I'll cut on for the shore."

"How did that ship happen to miss you?"

"It happened to save me. They were right at my back, yapping that they'd turn the Gatling loose if I didn't give up and let them take me in. But I tried for the big ship and made it! Then I dived."

He closed his eyes. His nostrils quivered as he drew down the deep breaths.

"Swimming is not my game," he said, his eyes still closed. Then he stiffened a little, and rising to his feet, he stepped toward the rail of the boat nearest the shore, but his legs sagged under him.

It was easy to understand what had stirred him, for the guard boat—its captain apparently guessing what had happened—had swept in suddenly straight toward the yacht.

"Do you know my face?" asked the man from the river.

"No," said David Apperley.

"Have you ever heard of Jack Deems?"

"No."

"Think again."

"Hold on now! Not 'Single' Jack Deems!"

"Does that give you the horrors?"

The two brothers were silent.

"I'm going down into the cabin," said the fugitive. "When they come to search the boat, perhaps you'll stave them off. If you do, that means my life. Perhaps you won't. In that case, I'm getting only what's coming to me. At any rate, I'll wait down there!"

No matter what was his fatigue, or how complete his bodily exhaustion, his mind, it was clear, was strong and steady. And he had gained perfect control of his voice before he uttered a word. Yet, when he started down the little hatch, he was reeling and drooping with every step he made. Comanche advanced, growling at his heels, and disappeared behind him.

At the same time, the blinding brightness of the searchlight from the guard boat fell full upon the faces of the two brothers.

9

"Now, Dave," said his brother. "Tell me what to do. Do we try to save this fellow?"

"No, confound him! I don't like the job. Anybody but Single Jack!"

"I never heard of him."

"You never did? I forget that he hasn't been going so very long. Seven or eight years, I suppose, and you've been away more than that! But Single Jack? I tell you, Andy, he kills a man as readily as you or I would kill a chicken!"

"Tush!" said Andrew. "Seven or eight years? He's not more than twenty-two!"

"He began as a boy. Here's the guard boat. Thank goodness we can soon wash our hands of him!"

"Like Pilate?" asked the older brother.

"Why, Andy, what mad stuff are you talking now? Pilate?"

"Well, Dave, I don't pretend to be logical. But I say that I'm not going to give that young rascal up if I can help it! There's something about him that appeals to me!"

"Like the dog strain in your wolf," said David sarcastically, "you like the wolf strain in that man. Well, Andy, you can do the talking, because I'll have no more to do with the game. Single Jack Deems needs hanging, and every good citizen ought to see that he gets it!"

"I'm not a good citizen, then," answered Andrew. "I'm only a man. But by the Eternal, Dave, when a man can win over a dog as he has won over Comanche, there has to be good in him, and a lot of it! His arm around Comanche's neck! Did you see it?"

"Very pretty!" growled David, "but I'll have no more to do with this mess. You handle it by yourself!"

Flinging himself into a chair, he bit off the end of a cigar with an angry click of his teeth.

Andrew cast a single doubtful look back at his brother; then he shrugged his shoulders. For a good many years he had been half brother and half father to this young man, but he had never been so put out as he was on this night.

He threw another look toward the black mouth of the

hatch. Then he turned to face the inquisition from the guard boat, which was sliding smoothly alongside.

3.   A Hunter of Men

"Yacht, ahoy!"

"Hello, guard boat."

"We're coming aboard you. Man a boat hook, forward!"

The low-lying speedster came to a rest, its engine throbbing with impatient power.

"Who's in charge here?"

"I am," said Andrew Apperley.

"A moment ago, one of the men on my ship thought he saw the escaped man swimming toward your boat. Could he have reached you and stowed himself below?"

"No chance for that," said Andrew quietly. "There's no port through which he could have climbed. If he came aboard, he would have had to come across the deck—and we've been here ever since the chase began."

"What is your name, please?"

"Andrew Apperley. This is David Apperley, my brother."

"David Apperley—not the same one that shoots big game. I've read about you, Mr. Apperley!"

He nodded toward David with much admiration.

"Only," he went on, "the man we're looking for is a lot worse than any tiger or lion that you ever have stood up to, Mr. Apperley! Single Jack Deems—you know about him, of course!"

"I've heard about him, but only through the newspapers. And they live by exaggeration, of course."

"They couldn't exaggerate about Deems. He was born to make perfect newspaper copy."

11

"For what crime are they holding him at Blackwell's Island?"

"Nobody seems to know, exactly, but we guess that it has something to do with forgery, on the one hand, and an immigrant scandal on the other. Some people high up have been behind Deems in this!"

"And they were examining Deems?"

"Trying to. As well examine a lizard or a snake, I say. A bullet is the only thing that can get acquainted with what goes on inside of the head of Single Jack! Now they've let him slide through their hands again. They'll sack the warden on account of this job!"

"Has he ever escaped before?"

"They've never held him long enough to bring him to a real trial. He always cuts loose in short order. They had him five times before this, and this makes the sixth time. Everybody thinks that he has something on somebody high up, and that because of that he can get loose each time. But then again, you can't tell. He's just a slippery devil!"

The police sergeant who commanded the boat strolled across the deck of the yacht and paused at the hatch.

"Of course," he said, "Single Jack can make himself almost invisible. He might have slithered across the deck while you were looking the other way. He might be down there now, listening to what I'm saying about him—"

His own suggestion made him step back hastily from the mouth of the hatch.

"Go wherever you like," said Andrew Apperley, "except that if you go below in this boat, you'll be carrying a good deal of risk."

"Risk? Risk?" snapped the sergeant, changing his tone abruptly. "Peters and Swain, get over here. Go down and man the cabin of this boat and see what's what. Look around, you understand!"

Andrew Apperley shrugged his shoulders, while David whispered in the wildest alarm: "What will happen if they find Deems down there? They'll know that we've been sheltering him! They'll make it hard for both of us, Andy!"

"Hush, David! We'll cross that bridge when we come to it. Ah, I thought so!"

For as the valiant Swain and Peters marched down the narrow flight of steps, one behind the other, there arose from the depths of the cabin a most hideous growling and snarling.

Swain and Peters tumbled hastily back to the deck.

"We're looking for a man. There's a lion or something down there!" said one of them.

"What's this, Apperley?" asked the sergeant, whose suspicions seemed to have been growing sharper for some time.

"Nothing," said Andrew, "except the danger that I was trying to tell you about a moment ago, when you wouldn't listen. I say that there's a big dog of mine in that cabin. He broke his chain and skulked down there. And because he's too wild to handle, we'll have to starve him out before we can manage him. He's a ravening devil, Sergeant!"

"Devil, eh? Devil, eh?" snapped the sergeant, growing ugly. "Now, Apperley, no man has a dog that won't come when it's called. I say: Call up that dog of yours at once, because we're going to search that cabin."

"Comanche! Here, boy!" called Andrew obediently.

For answer, out of the unknown darkness beyond the hatch there came forth the same fiendish sound which they had heard before, and even the stolid sergeant shuddered.

"I'd give a good deal to see that dog," said he.

"It's really more wolf than dog," said Andrew. "And a very rare fellow he is. There's the chain which he just broke to get away into the cabin!"

The sergeant picked up the remnant and tested the strength of the links, and examined the broken link, and the state of the steel which had snapped there.

"I would have said," remarked the sergeant, "that even a horse would have a job to break this chain. Did a dog really manage it?"

"He did. A dog that weighs as much as I do!"

The sergeant was impressed. In his soul of souls he was

simply a hunter, and it was only chance which had made him a hunter of men instead of a hunter of beasts.

Now all of the hunting instincts welled up in him and took mastery.

"I *will* see that brute," said he. "I'm coming back here by daylight and have a peek at it. By the way, I suppose that where a brute like that is, there isn't apt to be any stranger lingering about?"

Said Andrew Apperley quietly: "I've seen Comanche kill a mastiff with one slash!"

"Eh? Then what chance would there be for a man that ran into him in the dark?"

"No chance in the world, I suppose."

It seemed that Andrew had certainly won his point, and the sergeant returned to the rail of the boat. But there he lingered, ill at ease.

"I'll tell you what," said he, "I've a bit of a trick that will handle Comanche for you, most probably. It'll drive him out into the open, you can be sure of that. It's a little stink bomb. Won't do a bit of harm, but in half a minute it'll fill that cabin full of smoke, and Comanche will have to come out to breathe fresh air. Then we'll guarantee to handle him for you. Peters and Loren and Gregg, stand by half a dozen of you with ropes, and Swain, go bring me a smoke bomb. One of you open the cabin door—"

"And let that devil of a wolf out at me?" growled the man to whom the sergeant had nodded.

"I'll do it myself," replied the sergeant with perfect cheerfulness.

"Stop him!" gasped David Apperley.

But Andrew was as cool as chilled steel.

"He takes his own chances. It's his own profession. Besides, I don't think that this Single Jack is the sort of man who'll do a murder in the dark, if he can avoid it!"

"What makes you think that?"

"Hush! There he goes. Poor Sergeant! Comanche will rip his throat in two. I can't stand that!"

He jumped up.

"Sergeant, you'll be killed by that dog, I warn you!"

"Why, a man can only die once!" said the sergeant, still cheerfully.

He flung open the cabin door and instantly leaped back to the deck, with a revolver in his hand to cover any advance that might be made upon him.

But there was no response from the depths of the cabin. All was quiet there. The great wolf dog made not so much as a sound.

"It may be creeping out at you now, Sergeant," suggested Andrew Apperley.

"We'll soon have the big fellow," said the sergeant. "Here's the bomb. A moment after I've thrown it into the cabin, that hatchway will seem to be on fire. But don't worry. It'll make nothing but smoke. You couldn't make a fire out of it to save you! Your permission, Apperley?"

"I suppose that I haven't the power to prevent you."

"Not while I'm searching for an escaped prisoner," said the sergeant with an expressive wink. "So if you don't mind, I'll consider that I have your permission to throw this smoke bomb into your cabin, Mr. Apperley."

"I suppose," said Andrew, "that I must give way. It won't do any harm to any of the furniture or hangings in the cabin?"

"Not a whit. There are no acid fumes about the stuff. Nothing but harmless smoke, I assure you. There will be no danger."

The sergeant poised the bomb to toss it lightly into the cabin, but before the bomb could leave his hand a slightly built man, moving as fast and soundlessly as a flying shadow, leaped from the cabin door straight past the sergeant and his men, and dived over the rail. Dived so deep and so far that he did not break the surface of the water again as he came up.

The sergeant cried out in agony. "It's Single Jack. Jerry, you saw right! Get out the dinghy!"

The sergeant did not think of stopping now to ask any further questions as to why the fugitive from justice should have been in the cabin of the Nancy Lou. He was instantly

15

proceeding toward the shore in the direction in which the escaped man had swum.

David and Andrew saw three men leaning on the oars, while the plump form of the sergeant stood in the prow, a revolver in each hand.

4. "Whenever You Give the Word!"

The two brothers watched the boat of the man hunters swing on among the other craft between them and the shore. They saw that the excitement spread like wildfire along the docks.

"How long before they'll have him?" suggested David.

"Never, Dave. They'll never have that lad. Not tonight, at the least! It isn't in them to get him back tonight!"

"Is that instinct which informs you of that?" asked David dryly.

"You may call it instinct, if you wish. But isn't it an odd thing that we haven't heard any more reports from Comanche?"

"Very odd. They're pealing an alarm on that church bell, aren't they? And see the lanterns along the docks. They're leaving nothing undone to catch this fellow!"

"They'll have no luck, however. They'll have no luck, I tell you! Let's go down and take a peek through the open door of that cabin."

"And have that brute spring out and take us by the throats?"

"If he springs out, Dave, he'll do us no harm."

He drew a Colt and held it before him.

"You've seen me shoot with this little gun, old fellow. I won't miss a target as big as the heart of a wolf, if Comanche thinks fit to tackle us!"

"Very well, you go first. I've no desire for that sort of fame, old man!"

David followed in behind his brother.

They went down the steps to the door of the cabin, which stood wide open, and then Andrew threw a lantern's light into the interior and exposed a very odd tableau, indeed! For there lay the great wolf dog stretched upon the floor, with strips of bedding from the bunk used to tie his four legs together, while a bandage around his head securely muzzled and gagged him!

"By heavens," said David, "he managed that job alone! And in silence! But why did he bother to tie up the wolf?"

"I'll tell you, Dave, but you'll laugh at me."

"Try me."

"He knew that when he bolted for freedom, the dog would follow him, and if there were any other people on the deck, Comanche would go for their throats on the way to the waterside. So he made Comanche safe before he made his own bolt for freedom."

"Andy, you'll have Single Jack turned into a saint before long!"

"Well, there's the fact. He tied Comanche. If you can find a better reason for the tying, let me hear it!"

But David was silent, poking grudgingly at the mass of the prostrate beast with the toe of his shoe.

"Look at the green devil showing in his eyes again!" said David. "He's the same Comanche. And I admit that it completely baffles me. How did this fellow manage to do it? And in the first place, how did he ever call Comanche into the water to save him?"

"I wouldn't make so much of a mystery of it as all that! No, there's no use actually inventing difficulties, when there are enough of them already about the thing. But I'll tell you what, old fellow, it simply goes as an added proof of what I've said before cornering Comanche. There's a broad dog strain in him, and the big rascal simply reverted to the dog characteristics when it came to the pinch. How else can you explain it? He hears a commotion, and presently he sees a man in the water, half dead, or more than half dead, and barely able to make any headway against the current, Comanche gets excited.

"The life-saving instinct of his dog ancestors was working in him. Into the water he dived. He worked up to the sinking man, and brought him back to this ship, not because he prized this ship as a place of refuge, but simply because it was the point closest to him."

David listened and nodded.

"All very well," said he. "I admit that you have a touch of logic in that. But at the same time, Andy, I feel that there's something else behind it. There's something infernally mysterious about the whole affair! Such a devil of a dog couldn't have been transformed into a handy pet in two seconds."

"Still, you want to have your little mystery out of this matter. But I tell you, Dave, that mystery isn't needed. Just be logical and look at the facts. I say that the life-saving strain cropped up broad and big in Comanche. He couldn't help jumping in to save Single Jack Deems, and after he had been working for the man—why, Dave, you know that the blackest-hearted of us will love the thing that we've suffered for. You can't explain mother love, for instance, except on the ground that the mother has suffered so much for the life which she has brought into the world. The same with this monster of ours. He couldn't help having affection for a man whose life he had saved."

David listened and nodded.

"You have the logic," he said. "I don't pretend that I would say what I think in a crowd. But at the same time, I feel that there was something peculiar about the whole affair. Very peculiar, Andy. But let it go. We'll put the new chain on him and get him back to the deck before we take the bandages off him. How neatly they're laid on, as if he were taking care to hold the big dog without hurting him! And what a miracle, really, that the wolf dog would let Single Jack handle him in this fashion—no matter how he may have learned to love him! And all in a brief half hour."

He shook his head, and indeed, even the matter-of-fact nature of Andrew was a little shocked by the thought of what had happened. For it considerably transcended the limits of the possible, as we are apt to conceive of that term.

They put the new chain on the wolf dog and returned the animal to its place on the deck, where they fitted a sort of loose muzzle on the great head, and then removed the bonds. In spite of the muzzle, Comanche made a flying slash with his teeth at Andy, and the latter reeled back suddenly, with a shout. Yet there was no harm done, and presently the two brothers were seated side by side on the poop of the yacht, as before.

"Who would think," said David gently, as though afraid to break the quiet which had settled over the river, "that there had been such a crashing and smashing of guns, and sweeping of searchlights, and hooting of horns! It's all as quiet as a grave, now."

"They're not quiet—the hunters, I mean. They're still going along the docks. But they'll never get him again—at least, not tonight."

"I think not," agreed David. "He's not the sort of a fox that can be run twice and caught in the same day. What did you think of him, Andy?"

"I had an odd feeling about him. But that's because I knew that he was Single Jack, of course!"

"I had an odd feeling about him, too. What was yours?"

"It's hard to describe. I'll tell you one part of it. Whenever I glanced at him, he was grave, and he was usually looking away from me. But the instant that I glanced away from him, I felt that he was looking straight at me and smiling, with a sort of superior strength, and understanding, and triumph. However, I haven't been able to describe exactly what I mean. It escapes from the words."

"I think I understand you, though, because I felt something pretty closely related to what you've been talking about. I mean to say, that when I first saw him, before I had heard his name, or so much as dreamed what he might be, I had

19

a very chilly feeling. I mean, when I looked him in the face, I had exactly the feeling that comes over you when you feel that someone is staring at the small of your back—someone dangerous, a man or a beast—it shoots a chill through your spinal marrow, you know."

"Exactly!"

"Well, I felt that when I faced him. Just as though there were two of him—one before me, and one sneaking up behind me!"

"You phrased it just as though you were speaking for me! I had the same sensation, also! But what about his face, old fellow? What did that seem like to you?"

"Why, young—good-looking, rather, I suppose. But I don't remember the features very clearly. They seem to be under a cloud in my memory. Only I know that if I were to see that face anywhere, I'd instantly recognize it!"

David fell silent, musing and nodding to himself.

"I've read something about it. That's been the trouble with Single Jack's crooked career. He would have been the greatest criminal in the world from the very first. But you see, wherever he went, he was always recognized instantly. Nobody that ever had a glimpse of him ever forgot him. And even his best friends were a little bit afraid of him. Well—you know that it's easy to betray things that you're a bit afraid of!"

"Yes, I know that!"

"And that's exactly what happened to Single Jack. It seems that he was always fairly square with the people around him, and it seems that they have always been double crossing him, and after seeing his face, I can understand why. They were too much afraid of him to be square with him. Isn't that it?"

"I suppose so, of course!" granted Andrew.

"And the man has been going like a shadow through the world, doing impossible things, and playing a single hand because he could never find another living creature in whom he could trust!"

There was a silence, and then Andrew murmured:

"By the way, Dave, the trip to the West—"

"What about it?"

"You remember our wager of a few moments ago—if any-one ever dared to put his hand on the head of the wolf dog—"

David Apperley struck his hands together with an exclamation.

"Confound it," said he. "I'm caught. Well, Andy, we'll start whenever you give the word."

5.   Single Jack Again

A week later, David Apperley had started with his brother for the West. He was to make a six months' stay, and if he did not like the country, in that time, he was to come back and continue his old life among his friends in the East. He did not like the idea of making this trip. If he wanted good hunting, as he repeatedly told his brother, he could go to places where there was something better to be had than wolves and ante-lopes, and only a very occasional bear. This was a sheer waste of time. However, Andrew would never give way, and there-fore the trip had to be made, the trunks packed, the tickets bought, and the long journey overland commenced. In the baggage car went the great wolf dog, Comanche, whirling back to find his own home range, and learn to bay the moon from the hacienda of Andrew Apperley. But even on the train, Comanche was a trouble.

At Buffalo, while two of the well-tipped porters were tak-ing the big, muzzled brute for a walk, a man dashed at them, knocked one down, and tore the leash from the hand of the second. But at that very moment, by great luck, a mob of section hands answered the yells of the Negroes. They swept over the would-be dog thief, and he had to abandon Comanche in order to take care of himself. With a revolver which flashed and threatened many times, he slid through the crowd without firing a shot and escaped.

The Apperleys talked the matter over with a great deal of astonishment, but they finally decided that it must have been some circus agent, for both agreed that Comanche would make a magnificent show attraction if he were once well-lodged behind bars!

They dismissed that matter from their minds, therefore, except that there were extra large tips for the men in the baggage car, and extra guarding of the big dog day and night. And so the miles spun away behind them, while Andrew Apperley showed his younger brother why it was that he looked upon the West, not as a strange land, but as a region in which he himself already possessed almost imperial rights. He showed his brother the nature of his empire.

Great changes were passing over the West. For many and many a generation that land had been covered with cattle which were of little importance to the rest of the world. Their hoofs and hides and horns could be used, to be sure. But meat and bones were wasted. Men only killed a steer for the sake of a single steak, and passed on. There was no sinful waste, if only the hide were saved.

By tens of thousands, the gaunt-ribbed longhorns wandered across the plains and filled the valleys. The summer burned them thin. The winter drifted them before the snow and killed them like flies. But still they increased in numbers.

Yet all this beef was useless until the engineers and the wealth of the nation had blasted a way across the continent, and the railroad began to tap the vast food resources of the West. That beef was not so good as that of the corn-fed cattle in the East. But it was good enough to fill the poor man's pot. And beef is beef, even though it may be tough! So those thousands of cattle, wandering across the plains, acquired a sudden value, and Andrew Apperley, out West on a camping and hunting trip, had seen the possibilities which were opening here. He had plenty of money, and a venturesome spirit. He did not know the cattle business, but he could find hired men who did. So he went at the thing in the most whole-souled manner. He came on the heels of days when cows in Texas could be bought for a dollar a head. Immediately values changed. He saw steers sold for thirty-five and forty dollars a head. The Indians had been fenced away on reservations where they were supposed to remain, and those Indians had to be fed. The railroad was rushing tens of thousands of cattle toward the East. Vacuums began to appear on the crowded ranges. The market was buying a little faster than the source could supply the want; therefore the prices remained good.

Buying foundation cattle for his herds, here and there, Andrew Apperley soon spotted the country with great droves of his cows. He would buy twenty-dollar beef in the south and herd it north where it sold for forty dollars. Every year made him richer as his capital doubled. He grew so great in wealth that he himself was beginning to lose track of the details and of the total mass. All that he could do was to evolve new combinations; open new markets and flood them with cows; arrange sweeping drives over vast distances—and buy off and fight off the Indians, the petty white thieves, and the organized rustlers.

For such a great and rapid growth was not unaccompanied by envy, and there were men who would harm him if they could. The markets were open for any man's cattle. Foolish questions were not asked concerning brands and bills of sale. The East wanted cattle; the railroads were eager to have their string of cars filled; and the buyers simply raked in the beef by the herd, not lingering too scrupulously over details such as brands.

In such a time, the temptation was great. One needed only run one's horse around a neat little group of beeves, and head them through a cut among the hills. A few days later, one's cows were in the hands of the shippers, and a few solid thousands had sunk into one's wallet.

That was not all. On the great range, the squatters dropped down, here and there, and quietly they set to work, at odd moments, with their ropes and running irons. They devised brands which were merely mild alterations of those of the nearest cattle king. From season to season, the home herd of the squatter grew with a strange speed. Finally he was strong enough and rich enough to be honest. His fortune was established. He stepped into the ranks of law and order and began to oil up his gun to get the "confounded rustlers!"

Now such a colossus as Andrew Apperley was sure to attract the attention of all of these thieves. He lost cows and calves by ones and twos every hour of the day, and now and then little rustlers clipped off a dozen, or fifty head. Then there were bolder bands who slashed away cattle from his herds a hundred at a time. Worst of all, there were the well-organized, highly paid, professional, and thorough-going bands of rustlers who took five hundred head at a time, and thought that year lost in which they did not manage to make one great drive of two or three thousand head in a single haul!

David Apperley heard these tales with increasing excitement.

"But, Andy," he would cry, "there's a law in the land! We pay taxes to our government. It must protect us. You're being bled to the extent of half your profits, almost."

"Don't blame the government, Dave. It does what it can. But it can't keep pace with the growth of our country in square miles of cattle and cattle interests. Law is working its way toward us, but it will be some years before it arrives, and in the meantime, Alec Shodress grows fat on me!"

"Who is this Shodress?"

"The smoothest, cleverest, deepest scoundrel that ever smiled in your face while he sent a man to stab you in the back! He has my section of the country by the throat, and he's bleeding it white!"

"I'm growing hot under the collar. Tell me about Shodress!"

"It's no use, Dave. I've brought you out West to have a good time and to see the country. I don't want you to pitch in and fight my battles for me. I'll try to handle them for myself! Besides, the Shodress story is too long!"

But David insisted, and so the story was forthcoming. Alexander Shodress, of a dim or unknown past, had dropped into

24

the West and suddenly found himself at home in the region of cattle and cattle thieves. But he believed that there was nothing like a life of security; therefore he started to make himself secure. He arranged matters so that he could steal with a perfect security to himself.

"How can he do that?" asked David, hot with interest.

"It sounds odd. The point is that Shodress himself remains in the background and sends out his thugs and his crooks to do the active riding themselves. He supplies the money and the rewards. If any of them are caught and jailed, he hires good lawyers to defend them and almost always brings them off. Or, if peaceful means don't work, he can bribe the jail keeper to allow an escape, and in a pinch, he has sent along his entire little army to get one of his adherents out of jail. So he's surrounded by men who believe in him. He runs the biggest store, the biggest hotel, the biggest saloon in the town of Yeoville. He's the informal banker of the place. In fact, Shodress is Yeoville. Everyone knows that he is crooked, but no one wants to talk about it. He's polite, good-natured on the surface, and very much given to acts of charity. There's not a poor family within a hundred miles that can't tell you how Shodress has helped them out time and again. They never stop to ask where the money came from, and they are just a bit amused if they guess that the money which comes to them has been dipped out of my pocket by their Alec Shodress. And so they continue to vote for his men for sheriff; he practically appoints the judges; he runs the county, and the county, on the whole, is glad to be run. I own the major portion of the property of the countryside. Shodress makes it a rule to be scrupulously just to everyone except to me, so that he has a thousand men praising him, and only one man to damn him. Well, Dave, in a country like ours, a thousand votes always weighs down one, and while he can do what he likes, there's no way in which I can lift a hand against him. I couldn't possibly find a jury that would vote in any way against the desires of big Shodress."

David listened to this tale in an impatient agony of indignation.

"There has to be a way out!" he exclaimed. "My word, Andy, you forget that I'm a lawyer. I haven't been a very active one, but maybe this is my chance to hang out my shingle!"

"Where?" said Andrew, smiling.

"In Yeoville!" exclaimed David.

"Hello!"

"I mean it. By the powers, Andy, I've always liked a little spice of danger, and instead of hunting wild beasts, let me have a fair chance to hunt what trouble I can find in Yeoville!"

"I'd never consent. They'd kill you in five minutes!"

"They wouldn't. I'll show them one decent man willing to stand up against crooked Shodress. And in the long run, even crooks prefer honest people. I'll meet Shodress on his own ground. I'll open a store, and a saloon, and a hotel—and I'll use my lawyer's training to fight every case against him through the courts. At first I'll lose everything. But after a while, I'll begin to get my hands on a little of the estimation of the county—"

Andrew Apperley leaned forward and looked deeply and earnestly into the face of his younger brother.

"You would be taking your life in your hands," he said gravely.

"The game would be worth it."

"It will kill you or make you. Are you really willing to take the chance?"

"Hot to do it!"

The train was rolling southwest from St. Louis as this conversation progressed, and the black of the night turned the faces of the windows into deep and polished pools of ebony in which the lighted interior of the car was reflected.

David, shaking out his newspaper, his thoughts far away on the new life which he was even now planning, suddenly exclaimed: "Hello! Here's what you've done, Andy! This fine hero of yours, this Single Jack, is raising the very devil in Boston! Look!"

The headline spread halfway across the front page. In a Boston bank robbery, three men had been shot down in cold blood, and the deed was attributed to Single Jack Deems. The police were sure that his was the cruel heart and the sure hand which had done that black deed.

The train slowed, grinding into a small siding beyond the city.

"He may have done it," admitted Andrew. "I played long chances that he might be worth saving, and perhaps I was wrong. And if—good heavens!"

He sat rigid.

"Look!" he whispered.

"Where?"

"Beyond that lamp beside the station building. There, now, just pressing past two of those expressmen—"

"Ah, you mean the slender fellow with the broad-brimmed hat?"

"Yes. Ever see him before?"

"I don't think so. He looks very much like anyone!"

"Does he? Not at all! Watch his step!"

"What of it? Like the step of anyone, isn't it?"

"Man, man, after you've been in this country a while, you'll learn to use your eyes better. Like a cat's step, I'd say! But wait—what the devil is he doing? He's going straight toward that pair of porters who are with Comanche. Look, Dave, he's offering them money—"

The stranger in question had turned a little, at this moment. Now it was David's turn to exclaim. "It's Single Jack!"

"It's Single Jack," Andrew nodded. "He's trying to bribe those Negroes. He's got a handful of money, there—and look at Comanche!"

The great wolf dog was going into the maddest ecstasies, flinging himself out furiously, again and again, in an effort to get at Single Jack. But those were not ecstasies of fury; even at that distance, they could see that the big brute was vibrating with joy.

Andrew and his brother were already on the way to stop the criminal, whatever his purpose. But when they reached the place, they found the famous thug gone, and the two porters

27

were going up and down to exercise the dog. The faces of both seemed to Andrew Apperley a little drawn.

"What's happened to you lately?" asked Andrew Apperley.

"Mister Apperley," said the bigger of the two Negroes, "I dunno what sort of a lining this here dog has got inside of him, silver or gold, but there was a gen'man here, just now, that would have given us anything we asked for, if we'd only let him have that lead rope for half a minute, so that the dog could get to him—"

"Don't worry about that," said Andrew. "I'll see that you get just as much as he offered you. Besides that, I'll see that you have a recommendation for honesty to the president of the road. Beyond that, keep your eyes sharp, and never take Comanche out for exercise unless you have a crowd around to help you."

They went back to their seats in the car, Andrew with an anxious face.

"You see the story?" he asked.

"I see that the Boston police have lied. Single Jack could never have committed that Boston crime in time to get here to St. Louis."

"That's one thing. But the most important thing is that Single Jack is following us trying to get Comanche away from us. And I suppose that it would be a little more comfortable if we had the devil himself at our heels!"

"Following us, for the sake of a dog?"

"You saw for yourself."

"What on earth could that hunted thug do with a dog?"

"I don't know. I don't explain, but I tell you that we haven't seen the last of Mr. Deems!"

6. Casa Apperley

They turned the question seriously back and forth in their minds. It was Andrew who proposed what seemed nearest to a solution of the mystery.

"This fellow Deems is a city rat. Never been out of the shadow of the city alleys in his life, but when he saw Comanche, he lost his head about the big dog. He had never seen anything like Comanche before. He owed his life in the river to that brute. And after he got away from the boat and thought the thing over, he couldn't root Comanche out of his memory. He simply wanted that dog and had to have it. Like a child rather than a grown man. You know, Dave, that most criminals are children in intelligence. He couldn't be happy without Comanche—though he probably hasn't the slightest idea what he'll do with the dog after he gets it. So he crept out from the shadow of the city, and he's dogged this train across the continent. The first time, he tried to get the dog by force, and he would have succeeded, except that luck was against him. The second time, he tried bribery, but he failed that time, also. What will he do next?"

David shrugged his shoulders.

"Do you remember," he asked, "how he headed for that big passenger ship as it came down the East River?"

"Of course I remember."

"Well, I've an idea that he'll get Comanche before he's through with the game. But what a rat he is, Andy! We fish him out of the river and save his hide. Then he turns around and tries to steal from you!"

They talked no more of Single Jack Deems, but they let the word go forth that the man who was attempting to get the wolf dog was the famous outlaw. And that was sufficient to surround Comanche with trebled attention.

In the meantime, the train was streaking steadily west and south. Finally they drew up at their last stop. The Apperleys no longer were looking through the window of the train at the brown desert, partially obscured by swirls of dust. They were standing under the same hot sky, pale and blue-white above them. Into the waiting buckboard they climbed. Their luggage was piled into another and larger wagon, and with Comanche secured behind the seat, they started the drive toward the Apperley ranch.

A bronzed cowpuncher cantered his pinto alongside.

"Is there any news worth telling, Joe?" asked Andrew Apperley.

"It depends," said the puncher. "What kind of thing makes news?"

"Bad news first. What about Shodress?"

"Shodress? He's been pretty quiet, except about three weeks ago. His boys lifted eleven hundred head off the Dingle place."

"Eleven hundred head!"

"Sure. They came down in a mob. They killed Christy Barr and old Lewes. They shot up Lefty and Smith. And after that there was nobody even to trail 'em. They got clean away. A lot of us tried to pick up their trail. But they were gone. We couldn't locate a hoof of the whole bunch except one old cow that had been cut off by lobos and part of her ate. Shodress is still riding high and pretty."

The rancher listened to this story with an emotionless face. But his brother inquired anxiously: "Wait a moment, Andrew. Eleven hundred head at twenty dollars a head—"

"At thirty-five dollars a head, if you please."

"Why, Andy, that's close to forty thousand dollars snapped away—"

"Gone right up in smoke, of course!"

"And nothing done about it?"

"What can be done?"

"Why, you know that Shodress did it?"

"Don't we! But how can we prove it? And if we bring the case to trial, it will have to be before Shodress' pet judge. And it will be a jury of his hired men who listen to the case. We tried once or twice before. But the law has only one leg, out in this direction, and Shodress possesses the only crutch that enables it to walk!"

He spoke with a good humor and self-control that amazed his younger brother.

"How have you learned to stand this stuff?" asked David.

"Poker, Dave," said the other, good-naturedly. "Poker taught me how to keep my face—and how to wait for my turn at the cards. One of these days I'll run up a stacked deck and hand the Shodress gang a deal that will finish them off, I hope."

"Comanche don't look no thinner," sang the puncher, pointing to the big hound and muzzled brute.

"He's found a friend," said Andrew Apperley.

"Hold on! You mean that?"

"Yes. Ever hear of Single Jack Deems?"

"No hombre by that name ever been heard of around here," said the puncher.

"Well, you may hear of him before long," said Andrew Apperley, and he added to his brother: "That's fame for you, Dave! There's the most spectacular criminal in the country, and he isn't known. I tell you, there's a border line between the East and the West, and no news comes across it that's of any importance out here!"

"Then what is of importance?"

"Why—how much water is in the tanks, in the summer. How much snow there is in the winter. What diseases are bothering the cows. Whether the screw worm is bad. Who have been shooting up any of the towns, recently. What is the name of the buckaroo from Montana that rode the outlaw horse in the Jennings outfit, and are they giving a dance tomorrow night at the crossroads. That's the sort of thing that makes up the news out here."

"No papers? No magazines?"

"Oh, a few. But we don't believe what we read in them. They're all fiction to us. If we believed them, we might grow lonely, and it's better not to do that! Look ahead, Dave!"

"Well?"

"As we go over the top of that hill, sight down the valley."

They swayed up the hill, and as they lurched into a trot at the crest, David had a glimpse far off of a great green blur of ground, at the head of the valley, and in the middle of that rolling greenery, fenced in with lines of splendid young trees, there was a wide-armed house, sprawling wide across the ground.

"That's the Casa Apperley, Dave!"

7. Comanche Barks!

The dining room opened on the patio at one end, and at the other on the front garden.

"So that the guests will never be hurt in a stampede," Andrew Apperley explained with a smile.

There was almost room to believe in such an explanation, for that night, on each side of that long table fifteen men sat down to eat, and one man sat at each end. David, Andrew, and the foreman were the only members of that party who could be said to belong to the "family." The rest were strangers. They spoke a cheerful word of greeting to Andrew, and they acknowledged the introduction to David with a silent glance of interest and criticism. But after the small ceremony, matters went ahead quite as though each man were sitting at his own board.

In the middle of the meal, while roast pork and fried potatoes and cabbage and flapjacks and hominy and buttermilk and coffee flowed by the hundredweight and the gallon, a thirty-third guest entered that room, a slow-moving, dark-faced man who hung a saddle and a bridle on one of the many pegs at the farther end of the room and then advanced with long strides.

He stood with his back against the wall, his hands dropped on his hips.

"I was sort of pressed for time. I thought you wouldn't mind if I dropped in?"

"Certainly not, Whaley. Did you put up your horse?"

"I left her at the rack."

"I've finished my supper. Take my place, because the rest of the table is filled. I'll see that your mare is fed and grained."

"I think this kind of you, Apperley."

David withdrew with his brother.

"Some old friend of yours?" he asked, amazed at the nonchalant manner in which the stranger had taken the place of the host at the table.

"That's Whaley, the murderer. He killed four men in Tucson, not long ago. I didn't know that he was in this part of the country."

"Good heavens, Andy! Killed four! Are you afraid to tackle him?"

"Afraid? I have enough men on this place to blow twenty Whaleys to the devil and back again. But this man came in and hung his bridle and his saddle on the peg in my house. He asked for shelter and hospitality, Dave. And that request is irresistible in this part of the world. When he leaves the house, the moment he's off my land I can follow him and stop him, if I wish to. And I can shoot him to death if I'm clever enough and fast enough. But once he passes my threshold, he has a claim on me to do everything that I can to make him comfortable—except that it's not considered good form for an outlaw to ask for ammunition or a change of horses."

David, fresh from the law courts of the East, turned and looked back at the noisy table, for the conversation had not been in the least depressed by the arrival of this famous criminal. Instead, the merriment seemed to have increased. Hard cider was going the rounds, borne in enormous pitchers by the busy waiters. And the joy at the board of Apperley increased every moment—with a murderer sitting at the head of the table!

So David went outdoors with his brother, with many of his former ideas of men and events in this world spinning around in his brain.

He watched Andrew while the latter, with the greatest care, took from the hitching-rack the sweating, trembling down-headed mare from which the outlaw had just dismounted. Her flanks, David saw, were reddened by frequent visitations of the spur. Andrew conducted her to the stable, threw in a pitch-fork full of choice hay, and placed grain in her manger. Then he called a stable boy and bade him rub down the mare while she ate.

He returned to the open air with his brother.

"What do you gain by it?" asked David.

"I don't know. Nothing, perhaps. Or again, if I'm ever an outlaw myself, I think that people will be kind to me. Or if that never happens, at least, I sleep sound at night."

"You've been doing this for years?"

"Yes, ever since I made my big stake and built this place."

"And yet with all your liberality, you can't win a chance at even-handed justice? That speaks hard for the men whom you entertain here!"

"Hospitality is one thing, and a law court is another. These men don't like the law. Many of them have good reasons—the very best of reasons—for not liking it. But at the same time, they give me great privileges. Decency is never wasted out here. I can ride through the wildest parts of the range without a gun, and never be in the slightest danger. I like these people, and I think they like me. That mutual liking is a sufficient reward to me for this money I spend in running a sort of free hotel, as you might call it. Shodress and his crew help themselves to my cattle when they can, and they know I am biding my time to get them in trouble for it. Nevertheless, I can ride right into the town of Yeoville, where Shodress is lord and master, and be in no more danger, hardly, than I am at the present moment on my own place. I've worked hard to get a reputation which means as much as this, and it's worth money and effort to maintain the good name. It makes it possible, for instance, for me to trust your own life in Yeoville, if you really are hardy enough to plan on going through with your idea. But if you were not my brother, Dave, you wouldn't last five minutes in the place after the first time that you showed them your hand!"

To this speech, David listened with the greatest attention! It was still another proof that he was in a world which was entirely new.

"Now tell me frankly," said he, "what I should do if I want to get on in this part of the States?"

"I can tell you in a nutshell. Forget manners; remember to be simple and honest. I don't mean that you're affected or conceited now. But in our own part of the world, perhaps, it amounts to a little something to be an Apperley. We're fairly rich; our family is rather old; we move among the best sort of people. All those things make most people we meet take us for granted. But out here you'll find affairs are different. A man is exactly what he proves himself to be. To be rich and of an old family is rather against him, than otherwise. They will take nothing for granted. The first touch of conceit and manners makes their lips curl. Do you understand me? Be simple, straightforward, direct. Talk to every man as though he were your brother—but a brother without the slightest interest in your past greatness or your future success. If you can say something important or entertaining, then talk. Otherwise, shut up and stay silent until you can think of something that's worth listening to. And remember that the fellow you're talking to didn't know your name five minutes before, and that he'll forget it five minutes hence. The greatest thing that can be said about any man in the cattle country is that he's square. That means honest, but it means more than honest. A great many 'square' men, I have no doubt, may sometimes have played rather a shady game at poker, and may occasionally lift a cow or two for amusement or for beef. But they're fellows who are known to stick by their friends in a pinch; they're men who don't gossip about men who can't defend their own good names; they're fellows who give you half of their last dollar and half of their last drink of whiskey not because you're a friend to them, but because you're in need. Now, Dave, I hope and pray that I've been able to make myself known in this section of the world as a square man, and before you leave me, I want them to call you by the same name. And when one of these cowpunchers who work for me says that my brother is 'Sure a square-shooter,' then I'll know that you've passed muster and received the accolade!"

"I'll remember all this carefully," said David quietly. "Why, Andy, this game is going to be harder than any tiger hunting, and just about as dangerous!"

He added: "There's Comanche yelling at the moon again; or is he calling for his pack?"

"He never had a pack. He's always been a lone wolf."

"Too infernally mean to get on with even a mate, I suppose?"

"He's one of those queer mixtures that can't find a place," said the elder brother thoughtfully. "He's too much of a wolf to get on with dogs, and too much of a dog to get on with wolves. He's too wild to be tamed, and, perhaps, for all we know, he may be too tame to be thoroughly at home in the wilderness."

"You're making a problem out of him," David said with a smile.

"Why not? I'll tell you, Dave, that I never see a strong man gone wrong that I don't feel what a cracking good man has gone to waste in the rub of things."

"Tush!" said David, who was far the more hard-headed of the two. "There's nothing to that. No matter what's in a man, life brings it out, either good or bad, and so there's no use in shedding tears over a wolf dog! A savage brute, mark you my words, that'll never have anything to do with any man except to put teeth in him—"

"And yet, Dave, you yourself saw him act to Single Jack Deems like a mother to a child!"

David fell silent, but still he smiled, and then went off to the room that had been assigned to him. He completed his unpacking, while the rancher went to his office which stood with a door open upon a little private veranda. That open door was a sign that all the world could come freely in to talk business with Mr. Andrew Apperley.

He was no sooner seated at his desk than a flood of work poured in upon him. He forgot time. The afternoon slipped into the evening. Coffee and sandwiches were brought to him at supper time, which was always the rule unless he came out for the meal, and still into the night he went on with his work and picking up the many reins which had been dropped even by his efficient foreman. From the outside he heard a noise that made him lift his head from his work and listen in amazement, for it was the voice of the wolf, Comanche, not baying at the moon with the melancholy wolf yell, but first howling, then growling, and then breaking into a harsh barking!

If Andrew needed any positive proof as to the dog blood in this animal, that sound of barking was enough!

8. A Price for Comanche

All the noises that a wolf makes are businesslike and have a meaning. His growl, his snarl, his whimper, his howl, and all the ringing cries of the chase, have definite meanings, and any wise old trapper can tell you exactly what words stand for most of them. But barking is usually a mere noise. It may have fury in it; it may have happiness; it may be mere noise for the sake of noise. Comanche never before had been guilty of such a folly.

Instantly, other dogs around the place took up the chorus, far and near. They had been silent in awe while the terrible wolf voice rang through the air and shrilled at the moon. But now they took sudden heart. They barked savagely. The rancher could not help smiling as he listened.

He looked out the open doorway, and after his head had been turned from his lamp, for a moment, he could see the dim stars sprinkled low along the edge of the sky, like gold dust sprinkling velvet of the darkest blue. The sharp taste of alkali was in the wind that puffed lazily through the entrance, and he closed his eyes and smiled again. For it was a good world, in the eyes of Andrew Apperley. He only hoped that his idle younger brother might find in this new region some sort of challenge which would make a man of him.

Then he turned back to his work and kept busily at it until he felt that the distant eyes of the stars, behind him, were replaced by others, watching him coldly, and closer at hand.

He raised his head and waited, and felt his blood turn cold. Then, whirling about in a sudden panic, he saw, just on the verge of the shadows at his door, where the weak lamplight met the black heart of the night, two eyes filled with green, terrible fire, watching him intently. After that, he distinguished the whole mighty form of Comanche!

He laid his hand upon the revolver in his holster, but he hesitated to draw it, for the instant that he made such a movement, he knew that the monster would fly at him. And though his bullet might plow straight through the body of the wolf dog, still, unless it reached the heart, Comanche would be at him for a few dying slashes. Andrew Apperley knew beforehand what even one of those white sword strokes could mean.

He grew tenser. He thought of calling out. But he felt that a call, or anything more than a move of the hand, would bring terrible danger flying at his throat.

So he endured through a few terrible seconds until a man's voice said gently from the black of the night:

"I came down to get Comanche. But I thought that perhaps I'd better see you first, about the price!"

Into the glimmering verge of the circle of light, stepped the form of "Single" Jack.

"Deems! Deems!" exclaimed the rancher. "Come in, man!"

The criminal stepped into the doorway and out of it, with a movement swift as a boxer's. Having removed himself from the glow which framed him in the doorway as an excellent target for any marksman, he took up his position against the wall, at an angle from which he could watch both the rancher and the open door, with all of the perils which might lurk beyond it.

Comanche, still snarling silently, with a lifted lip, slunk in with his master and planted himself in front of him, his mane bristling as he faced Apperley.

"Sit down," said the rancher, "and tell me how in the name of all that is wonderful, you managed to get across the open range to this place! Didn't you know that they were looking for you all up and down the line of the railroad?"

The other nodded gravely.

"They were looking for me," he admitted, "but I was looking for them, too, and so I drifted along until I heard Comanche calling."

There were many, many things that Apperley would have been glad to know, but he felt that it was useless to ask. What would be the sense in addressing questions to the wolf dog which crouched at the foot of this strange youth? And in the dark face and the black eyes of Single Jack, he saw, or thought he saw, the same wolfish spirit which caused Comanche to bare his fangs. How had he eluded the searchers? How had he journeyed across the range? Whom had he dared to ask questions of? But there was no way of drawing out the answer.

"After I got Comanche," went on the other, "I couldn't help remembering that you helped him fish me out of the river when I was spent. I owe you something for that, and I owe you something for Comanche. About what does the bill come to?"

"I've never put a price on such things," said the rancher, drawing him out.

"You never have?"

"Never," said Andrew Apperley, finding it a little hard to meet those dark, fathomless eyes. For there was no human kindness in them. There was nothing but the dark watchfulness of a panther. Neither kind nor unkind, but ceaselessly alert, and always with a haunting fire ready to appear in them.

What were those eyes when the fire burned brightly, Apperley wondered.

"You can make a guess. There's a price for everything," said Single Jack.

"For everything?"

"Why, yes. You're a business man!"

"But for fishing a man out of the river?"

"Well, there's ways of guessing at a price on me," said the youth as gravely as ever. "The government has staked eleven thousand dollars on me—dead or alive."

"Dead or alive!" murmured the rancher.

"Yes."

"Any man who dares to fight you and can down you gets that much?"

"Yes."

"And any sneak who can worm his way up to you in the dark and put a bullet through your head gets that much, too?"

"Yes."

"It's hard!" said Apperley. "It's hard practice!"

The other shook his head.

"I don't ask anything better," he said. "I don't ask them if they mind when I blow a safe, do I? There's a lot of good men that have been ruined because I've cracked a safe or lifted some bonds, here and there. So why shouldn't the government put a price on my head?"

It was not the logic of this so much as the calm conviction with which it was stated that amazed Apperley.

"In one way," he consented, "it makes a business out of it."

"Or a good gambling deal, at least," said Single Jack. "With the cards crooked on both sides!"

"Crooked?"

"Is there anything that they haven't tried, to get me? Even bribing people that might have been my friends. Even poison—"

"Hello! Not poison!"

"Let someone put eleven thousand on your head, Apperley, and see how long it will be that they hunt you fair and square! However, I don't mind. I crook the cards on them, too. I bribe cashiers, now and then. I stack the deck whenever I can. And so we're all square. I've given them as much as they've given me. The rope that's to hang me is still on the stretch. And I hold no grudges against them, or anybody. I hold no kind feelings, either, except—"

He paused, and the dangerous glimmer that had come into his eyes faded and was lost in a shadow of perplexity.

"Except with you, Apperley!" he said. "You could have had that eleven thousand dollars, if you wanted it. Just by speaking my name—and you didn't. Why not?"

His amazement stared blankly at the face of the rancher.

"Why, man, being on my boat, you were a guest, weren't you?"

"Eleven thousand dollars' worth of guest?" sneered the criminal, his eyes flashing into the very soul of the other.

"Or eleven million dollars' worth of guest," said Apperley firmly.

"I see," said the other, as cold as ice. "Your honor got mixed into it. Your honor wouldn't let you. Was that it?"

"Perhaps you can call it that!"

"We'll let that slide, for a minute," said Single Jack Deems very crisply, as though he were filled with doubts concerning the current value of honor in his host or in any other man in the world. "We'll let that slide, and I'll simply ask you please to explain what is the price that you want for Comanche?"

"Is there a price on everything?"

41

"You're a business man," said the other for the second time. "I don't have to talk nonsense to you."

"You'd have to pay me," said Apperley, "for the pride I have in owning Comanche."

"That's one item."

"Then for the long hunt I followed on his trail."

"Very well."

"My time has a value. I spent twenty or thirty full working days trailing him."

"Yes."

"I thought, planned, dreamed how to get him. I imported a pack of dogs and watched them slaughtered. I carted him all the way East with me, and there I spent more time and money over him."

"It's a bill. Add it up."

"Still, more than all the rest, I am fond of the great brute, Deems!"

"I'll admit that, too!"

"Now on the other hand, I consider it shameful to sell a dog for money—shameful for a rich man like myself."

"I'll pay you for your shame, too," said Single Jack.

"How much money have you then, to invest? I don't mean to ask that, but what would you do if I asked you several thousand?"

"Five thousand, say?"

"Yes, let's say five thousand."

The left hand of Mr. Deems slipped into his pocket and suddenly five one-thousand-dollar bills lay on the table before the rancher.

"And that settles the ownership of Comanche, I hope?" asked Single Jack.

9. The Wolf Dog's Answer

It should be borne in mind that Andrew Apperley was not only a man of money, but he was one who was accustomed to taking what pleased him, regardless of the price. But in those days money meant more than it does today. One paid five dollars, perhaps for an Indian pony which was good enough for most of the uses of the range, and one paid thirty dollars for a very well-broken saddle horse, whereas a hundred would buy one with at least a liberal strain of Kentucky in it. And a thousand dollars brought home a fine thoroughbred racer. And here was a fellow whose fortune was his wits calmly laying down five thousand dollars on the table for the sake of a wild dog!

It was more than a mere shock to the rancher. It slipped back the doors of his mind and allowed an entire new vision to enter—a vision of a Deems quite other than the man he had been picturing before. It was plain to him, at a glance, that money was a mere nothing in the life of this fellow. He could not help saying gravely: "Tell me, Deems, what does money mean to you?"

A touch of blankness appeared in the eyes of the youngster, and then he replied with an equal gravity. "Why, everybody else is out for it. I suppose that it's worth the game!"

"Very well," said the rancher, "no matter what money is worth to you, your money is worth nothing to me. I can't take the five thousand dollars."

Single Jack Deems regarded him with a keen scrutiny, not as one admires largeness of soul, but as one who searches for a hidden and unworthy motive.

He pocketed the money slowly.

"Still," said the rancher, "I don't give you the dog for nothing."

Jack Deems smiled a little, as though at the idea of charity even for a moment's consideration.

"All right," he said. "I guess what you want, but I'll tell you in the beginning that I'm not the kind."

"Not what kind, Deems?"

"You've got a grudge and you want me to wipe it out for you, eh? Is that it?"

"Man, man, I handle my own enemies! No, it's not that!"

The other waited.

"It's a job, Deems, that would keep you in this part of the country. Could you stand that?"

"Where else can I go with the dog?" asked Single Jack gloomily. He cast a glance toward the door.

"But if I stay here with him," he said, "I'll be hounded across the mountains—and it's easier to hide in alleys that you know than in mountains that you don't!"

The rancher shook his head and explained: "You're in no danger out here except the danger that you make for yourself."

"I'm not known, then?" asked Single Jack, smiling a little, with an odd mixture of vanity and gloom.

"Not a whit known," replied the rancher.

Single Jack waited, his face as enigmatic as usual, and it was plain that he placed not the slightest credence in what he heard. Apperley went on to explain.

"News comes slowly out this way," he said. "Papers may be half a year old before they fall into your hands. They're almost sure to be a month old, and so you form the habit of reading newspapers as though they were ancient history. In that way, you pay attention to the stories, but not to the names. Half the men out here could hardly tell you the name of the President of these United States, because that doesn't matter. What matters in the cattle country is the name of your boss and the names of the horses in your string. Other things are decorations. You understand? And Single Jack Deems, with a list of dead men as long as his arm, is no more out here than John Deems, cowpuncher, if he cares to start that way. And after that, men will take you just as they find you!"

Perhaps the rancher was enlarging upon the truth a little, but at least he had painted a picture which attracted the elusive attention of the younger man, and that was what Apperley wanted.

"It's a queer idea," said Single Jack. He looked far away, as though at a vision. "A very queer idea," he repeated. "Do you half mean it?"

"I mean it altogether."

"You mean, Apperley, that I could actually walk down the street of a cow town and let men look in my face, just as it is, just the way God made me?"

"I mean exactly that!"

Deems frowned at the floor.

"Why man," went on the rancher, "literally thousands of men have come West because their crimes made it hot for them in the East. But out here, they're lost. I think that half of them turn into decent fellows. A quarter of them are half good and half bad, and it depends on how you take them. The rest of them are born bad, and they stay bad. They wind up with their boots on, and lead in their bodies, most of that lot."

The other nodded.

"I see that you mean what you say," he murmured. "And it would be odd to do that—to walk down a street with your hands in your pockets—not caring—to sit in a room without your back to the wall—"

He broke off, and a violent shudder passed through him. For an instant, he looked a very facsimile of the wolf at his feet, and as though he sensed something wrong, Comanche turned his head and looked up into the face of his master, with a snarl lifting his upper lip and exposing his gleaming teeth.

"Well," sighed Deems, "how many days would it be before someone recognized my face and used eleven thousand dollars' worth of memory?"

"He wouldn't shoot you from behind," said the rancher, "because if he did, he would be strung up as high as a kite in less than two minutes by the other men in the room. And he probably wouldn't be able to shoot you from in front. At least, I suppose that that's a danger that you don't often worry about."

"Do you mean one man?"

"Yes. We never allow two men to pick on one—not out here!"

"Why"—Single Jack smiled, with a sudden and strange illumination of face—"if what you say is true, I might live another five years as safe as could be!"

"Five years, man? Yes, or fifty!"

"I'm not a fool," said Single Jack quietly.

"How long did you have back East?"

"They were dodging me pretty closely. Perhaps five days. Perhaps five weeks. With good luck, I might have lasted a whole year. But that was hardly likely. They had me in their hands twice in the last nine months."

"You were going to die, then?"

"Not that. I was going back to play another hand at the game. You don't like to quit while you're winning, you know!"

The rancher stared. In the presence of this boy, he repeatedly had a feeling of complete helplessness. He could reach far, but never quite far enough to comprehend the depths of this nature.

"Let me tell you," said Mr. Apperley, "that if you act like a decent man out here, you can live as long as the end of your century. I mean that. And yet you'll have plenty of action, of any kind that you want! But I should say that the chief thing for you to do, just now, is to take up with the suggestion that I make to you."

"I'm listening."

"I have on my hands, just now, my younger brother. He's a boy perfectly honest, straightforward, frank, open. He's strong in his hands, a good shot, a straight eye, a clear head. He's educated to be a lawyer, and he has the making of a

46

good one in him. But the only thing that he's ever been able to take an interest in is the hunting of big game. Now, finally, he's grown heated about a great idea of his, which is to go up into the town of the cattle rustler, Shodress, and there open up his lawyer's office, and make it his business to fight out the cases which I—and other cattlemen—wish to push through against some of the crooked cattlemen. He has been appointed special prosecuting attorney. Now, once he gets there, his life will be worth about a damaged nickel. He is perfectly willing to fight any man in the world, especially with guns. But he doesn't understand the Western system of fanning a gun. And he hasn't spent a lifetime of practice at hitting the mark, as most of these gun fighters have done. Before he is a day in Yeoville, one of them will pick a fight with him and shoot him six times through the heart before he can strike the ground. You understand?"

"Yes," said the other calmly. "I've seen it done."

Mr. Apperley did not ask him to enlarge the thought. But he could not help wondering whether, at the time he had seen it done, Single Jack had been on the stage or in the audience.

"Now," said Apperley, "the price that I want you to pay me, the price I ask for Comanche, and for your own life, when we fished you out of the river, is to take my brother to Yeoville and there try to nurse him through about the first ten days. After that time, he'll be on his feet. He'll know those men, and those men will know him, and I don't think that either side will be apt to take liberties with the other. But the first days are the fatal ones to be passed. And I tell you, Deems, that if you can see my brother through that critical period, you may be giving the world a useful citizen in the place of a useless waster!"

"Ten days?" asked the criminal.

"About that."

"It's a long time—for me!"

"Yes—I know it."

"For Comanche? After that, I'd own him by rights?"

"Exactly."

47

"Whist!" said the criminal. "Comanche, shall I go?"

The monster turned, and flattening his ears, he whined.

"Listen! Listen!" breathed Single Jack. "He tells me to take you up, and I shall. But look at him now. Do you think that he really cares for me, Apperley?"

10. Caught Red-Handed

It was necessary for Andrew Apperley to use a good deal of diplomacy with his brother. For when he suggested that Single Jack accompany him as a bodyguard to secure him from the possible attacks of Shodress and the hired murderers in the employ of that scoundrel, young David curled a lip of scorn.

"I'll take care of myself in every company of men," said he. "I've always been able to stand on my feet before this, and I don't expect suddenly to stop, now. As for their guns, I have a pair of Colts, and I've been practicing with them, between you and me, very steadily for the last three days."

Andrew Apperley said no more in the way of argument upon this point. He did not even try to describe the painful years of effort by which one of these same Westerners attempted to tame a Colt before he felt, as the saying went, that he could ride it.

He shifted his grounds abruptly.

"Naturally, Dave, I wanted to use an argument which I thought might convince you of the actual utility of Deems. But between you and me, I'm sure that he'll be nothing but a terrible handicap."

"He would be that—if I let him," assented David with much surety.

"But I think, Dave, that if you were to take him along with you, it might prove the actual making of the fellow. It might be what he needs to jerk him out of the Slough of Despond, you know! You might be the actual making of him, Dave!"

"Nothing will make him," said David, with his usual cocksureness. "He was born bad, he's grown bad, and he can't help dying bad."

"It's rather un-Christian to cut a man off and damn him before he's had even a first chance!"

"I'd rather be a bit un-Christian than totally illogical. I really would, old fellow. This Single Jack Deems is a man-murdering scoundrel, and he deserves to hang. I don't want him under my wing."

"But I tell you, Dave, that unless a strong and resolute fellow like yourself takes him in hand, he's utterly damned."

The exquisite poisoned point of flattery touched David to the heart. He wavered in his resolution.

"He'd have to take strict orders from me!" he exclaimed.

"That could be arranged," said Andrew, though he felt the ground slip rapidly from beneath his feet.

"Then I'll take him along with me and give him his chance!"

Quite hopeless, Andrew Apperley went to Single Jack and found the criminal lying under a fig tree, with his hands clasped beneath his head. Over him rose the ominous form of Comanche, teeth bared and mane bristling.

"Whist, boy!" said the youth.

The mighty Comanche retreated and lay down, his head on his paws, his reddened eyes constantly on the alert to follow the rancher. Mr. Andrew Apperley was filled with deep wonder to see how quickly and how perfectly this slender young man had reduced Comanche to perfect obedience.

The thief and gunman rolled upon one elbow—upon his left elbow, leaving, as always, the snaky strength and speed of his right hand unimpeded.

As Apperley looked into the dull black eyes of the other, he felt suddenly how useless any attempt at subtlety on his part would be, so he simply said:

"My brother is playing a very bad part. He doesn't want

you along with him as a guard, he says. He says that he won't have you at all, except with the feeling that he's giving you a chance to reform. And you'll have to take strict orders from him on your behavior!"

He waited. Not a single alteration appeared in the deep, black eyes of Single Jack.

"You understand me, Deems. I realize how absurd it all is. I simply want you to know the truth."

"What do you expect me to do?"

"What I expect you to do is to throw over the job, of course. But what I hope that you'll do, is to swallow your pride and go along with David and even let him talk down to you a little."

Beyond all the expectations of Apperley, the gunman answered softly, for his voice was hardly raised: "I'll go along with him and do as you say."

"Do you actually mean it?"

"I do."

"I tell you what, Deems, it means the saving of his life, in spite of himself. Then if that's arranged, you'd better let me have you and David meet for a talk."

"Of course."

The attitude of David was particularly difficult, on this morning.

"When you touch a nettle, grasp it hard," said David to his brother—and he straightway assumed the most overbearing attitude. It was plain that he wished to establish instantly and once for all that he was to be the master during the days that followed.

"During the time that you're with me, Deems," said David, "you'll take my orders about everything, you understand?"

It was a volley between wind and water, to be sure. Andrew Apperley turned a little pale. Such a speech to a real Westerner would have been a tolerable excuse for a gun play on the spot. But to Apperley's amazement, Single Jack's expression did not alter. He merely nodded.

"And you'll keep yourself out of the way of trouble. That's the main thing."

"Very well," said Single Jack, as meekly as could be.

"In that case," said David Apperley, allowing himself a smile of triumph in the direction of his brother, "we may get on together."

That day they departed for Yeoville, and the stronghold of the king of the rustlers, Shodress.

They traveled in a buckboard, which was swept along by a span of fine horses. They had three saddle horses tethered behind, and their luggage was piled into the back of the wagon. Half a dozen law books were included. With such a meager preparation, young David was prepared to storm the bulwarks of the enemy!

After he was gone, many doubts possessed the mind of Andrew Apperley. For the last bit of the picture that remained to him was not of his brother and the departing wagon, but of the monster wolf dog which slunk along with them, fifty yards away in the brush. It seemed to him that there was danger, danger, danger lying before the face of his only brother.

He was not reassured by a note that came back to him two days later.

Dear Andy: I'm here in Yeoville, in the Shodress Hotel. I could have gone to the other hotel, of course, but I thought that by coming directly here, I'd show them that I'm not afraid. Shodress is not in the town. The moment that he arrives, I'm going to see him and lay my cards on the table, face up.

At least, they'll have no chance to call me a sneak, in this part of the world. When the first man comes in, accused of rustling, I'm going to push the case through as hard as I can. On the first case of all, depends a good deal. I hope you'll see to it that the man who is first sent is somebody with a very black case against him. It will be necessary to have the thing very plain before I can get any favorable verdict out of a jury here. You are entirely right. They are all Shodress men, and they hate the very name of Apperley. When I signed on the hotel register, the clerk turned pale.

In the meantime, I'm in higher spirits than I've been for years. This will be a great game.   As ever,
                                                              DAVE

There followed, as though entirely by afterthought:

About young Deems. It seems I was right in taking up a firm line with him. No matter what a dare-devil he may be considered in the East, in this new environment he does not seem at all sure of himself. He seems rather timid, even shrinking. But he does all that I tell him to do. He asks no questions, and he never answers back. I think I can assure you that the cure is going to work with him. But he seems to me rather a sneaking fellow, and when he's saved, I wonder if the job will have been worth while.

Over that letter, Andrew Apperley pored with perspiration starting out on his face. It did not seem to him possible that, knowing what was in the past of Deems, his brother could be so extremely obtuse in his treatment of the man. But here were the facts, set down in black and white!

Everything else in the letter seemed to him in the highest degree foolish and dangerous. To place himself in the Shodress Hotel was literally to abandon all defense. Andrew knew that there was little or no honor in Shodress and many of his men.

He was on the verge of sending off a hard-riding messenger to call back his brother at once, but this he decided not to do. In the first place, David would probably not answer such a peremptory summons. In the second place, perhaps it was better for the young man to work out his own salvation, and that could not be done without some considerable risk.

So Andrew set his teeth and resigned himself to waiting.

Every moment of the day he was filled with worry for his inexperienced brother, and for the high explosive in the form of Deems which David was handling with such mad carelessness.

How long would it be before Single Jack Deems burst out in fire?

He thought of these things ceaselessly. They wakened him in the middle of the night and fixed his eyes upon the swirling darkness above him. But he had no obvious answers for these riddles, and so he waited.

In the meantime, he prepared to send up the first rustler so that David could have an opportunity to show his wares as a lawyer in the town of Yeoville, and so score his first defeat. But that first rustler must be one caught absolutely in the act. The word went out from the home ranch of Andrew Apperley to all his men. It was no longer necessary to let the rustlers go. There was now a lawyer to fight the cases through in Yeoville. And he wanted one caught red-handed in the act.

In twenty-four hours he had exactly what he wanted.

11.   David's First Case

Two hours after Alec Shodress arrived in Yeoville, David was sitting before him. He introduced himself gravely and stated the purpose of his coming with a becoming modesty and terseness.

"I'm up here, Shodress, to represent the cattlemen. They've found it hard to get a lawyer who'll honestly push through the cases which they have to present, and I'm here to play that part of the game. I know that you and my brother have been at outs for a long time, and I want to say in the first place that I'm not here as his hired man. I'm on my own responsibility. I don't intend to try to buy up juries to get convictions. I want to let every case rest on its own merits. I know that you practically own this town and every man in it. And I have to ask you if you're going to let me have a halfway fair chance, or are you going to begin to block me from the start?"

Now, that was a speech which David had conned over and over, and before he spoke it, he felt that it was about all that any man could say, with perfect frankness, under the conditions.

However, he was not prepared for the reply which he received from Shodress.

That gentleman reached out a broad and powerful hand and placed it on the shoulder of his caller.

"Apperley," said he, "I'm glad to have you here! There's been a long and bad understanding between your brother and me, but there's no real reason for it. As a matter of fact, there have been a lot of low hounds that've gone about to make trouble between us. Why? I'll tell you in a word! In this part of the range, to be frank, there are two big men—Andrew Apperley in the lowlands, and Alec Shodress in the mountains. The little skunks that lie in between us, jealous of both of us, have been carrying tales. They tell me all sorts of yarns about how Apperley has it in for me, and how he's trying to get me. They go back to Apperley and tell him stories about how I'm the head of the rustlers that are working the herds and cutting off thousands of them every year.

"Well, sir, I'm an old hand in this country. I know the people, and so I don't listen to their talk. But Apperley is a newcomer. He doesn't understand, and he takes the yarns too seriously. He doesn't stop to think that among other things, I've got a cracking big herd of cows, myself, and I've got too much property here and there for me to be on any side except the side of law and order. We've needed an up-and-coming lawyer for a long time. Perhaps you're the very fellow for us! Block your game! No, sir, I wish you all the luck that I can give you, and when you're in doubt about anything, you come to me and talk things over. I might be able to give you some good advice!"

Now, as he said this, there was such a kindly light in his little gray eyes, set close under the shadow of his big nose, and such a smile wrinkled the beard which covered his fat cheeks, that David felt half of his suspicions drop away from him on the instant.

"Well, Mr. Shodress," said he, "I've an idea that everything you tell me may be entirely true. At the least, I'm willing to go on that basis!"

He gripped the hand of the other with all the force in his arm. It was like seizing a rock—such was the power in the hand of Alec Shodress.

"And as for advice," said David mildly, "I'm always open to it."

"Do you mean that, young man?"

"I do."

"Then let me start off with something that may do you a lot of good. The boys round this neck of the woods are a queer lot, and they don't like folks that ain't open and aboveboard. They have a particular dislike to that slim gent that you got along with you."

"You mean Deems?"

"That's what I mean. They say that he goes soft-footing around the town like he was a cat, or a spy, or something. And yet he don't seem a very nervy fellow, either. No, sir, he's got a big dog along with him to protect him if he was to get into trouble. But let me tell you, Apperley, that when trouble starts in this part of the world, it strikes like a thunderclap, and dogs ain't much use, no matter how loud they might bark!"

David smiled.

"Deems is not a bad fellow," he said patronizingly. "As a matter of fact, I have him here trying to make a man of him. And I think that I may succeed. But I can tell you right away that he's no spy of mine!"

A little later, very well pleased with this interview, he went back to his office, for which he had rented a little shack, on the door of which there now appeared the pleasant legend:

"David Apperley, Attorney at Law."

He had never had an office before. He had never unsheathed his knowledge of law and used it as an actual tool for the business of life. Now he regretted that he had not begun the work long before. For he could feel new mental muscles coming into play. His heart was lighter than it had ever been, even in the midst of a lion hunt.

First of all, he felt that he should send an immediate letter to his brother, advising him that Mr. Shodress was rather a rough diamond, but that in his heart of hearts he was really a very good chap, and that the mischief between the two of them had apparently been entirely caused by tale carriers. But upon second thought, he assured himself that it would be foolish to send such a letter. Not mere words were to be used upon stubborn Andrew, only the irresistible logic of facts!

So he was sunning himself in the thoughts of the future, when business suddenly came to the door of his office and stopped there.

Business came up in the form of seven galloping horses, upon whose backs were seven cowboys. One of those men had his arms tied together and secured to the pommel of his saddle. The others had their hands free and looked as though they were very capable of using the big-handled Colts which projected from holsters at saddle and hip.

One of these sun-bronzed fellows strode up to the door and stood in the opening.

"You're David Apperley?"

"Yes."

"I got something for you. Boys, bring him in."

They brought in the man whose hands were tied together.

"This is Bill Whaley. Got him redhanded stealing cows."

"Whaley? Is that the name?"

"Look here, Apperley," said the prisoner. "This here has gone far enough for a joke. I warn you about that. Just because I was trying out a brand-new cutting hoss, that I got,

56

these here boys thought that I was running a bunch of cows—"

"Whaley!" snapped the leader of the band.

"Well?" snarled Whaley, who was a big man, with a large, crooked mouth that now pursed and puckered up on one side of his face.

"Whaley, tell Apperley that you're a liar, but that he ain't a fool!"

"I'm going to get you for this, Briggs!" declared Whaley savagely.

"You crooked hound," said Briggs with enthusiasm and force, "wasn't it poison to me to have to bring you up here where the law will find a chance of getting you free? But if there was fight in you, why didn't you offer to have it out with me when I first met up with you? You was afraid, Whaley. You showed yellow. And you'll show yellow again, if you ever get out of jail. I could eat a salad made out of a dozen swine like you!"

So said Mr. Briggs.

"One moment," put in Mr. Apperley. "I think that this man should be brought to the jail and taken care of there. You will swear out the warrant and everything in due form—and which of you can stay here as witnesses?"

"I got to stay," said the leader, "and Johnson ought to stay, too, because he was the first one to sight that gent. He seen all of the early workings. Two eyewitnesses ought to be enough."

"I think so. Just start him for the jail."

"But after he's in the jail, who'll keep him in there?"

"The bars, I suppose."

"The bars, while the keys are in the hands of old Shodress' gang?"

"If that's the case," said Apperley, "then we'll watch the jail, and the man that's in it. Now take him over, if you please!"

He sat down to smoke a cigarette and think things over. But before five minutes was out, a large form bulked in his doorway. It was Shodress, shouting: "Look here, young feller. There's been a terrible mistake!"

57

"Hello! What mistake?"

"Why, man, they've arrested one of the best men on the range. Known him for years. Clean as a whistle and honest as steel. Bill Whaley. They've trumped up a charge against him, and they say that you're behind the charge, Apperley. I only have to say that I hope that you're not mixed up in any such business as that!"

David was rather glad, suddenly, that he had not hurried to send to his brother the letter in praise of Mr. Shodress. For the man was swelling with violence.

"What can I do?" he asked.

"Do? Why, you're your brother's representative. And you can have those fellows withdraw the charges!"

"As soon as the case comes into court I'll—"

"Hey, Apperley, are you one of those that always wants to go by every legal form? Don't you stand for any shortcuts?"

"None," said David quietly.

"Then, young man, you're going to get yourself into a great deal of trouble! You're not going to last long in Yeoville, I can tell you!"

"Then I'll finish soon." David smiled. "But my present conviction is that Whaley is guilty."

"Is that final?"

"It is."

"Then get yourself ready to leave this town—or you'll have your grip packed for you!"

12. Agents of Murder

It will be observed that the good nature of Mr. Shodress had disappeared completely and one could see nothing except the snarling of the wolf nature which lurked just behind the front door of his fat smiles. He was shaking with rage, and he fairly filled the door with his bulk.

"I've made men like you and smashed 'em!" he told David. "I've offered to give you a square deal and a fine start in this town. And you turn around and cut my throat!"

"I turn around," said David Apperley, "and ask you to remember that I never begged for your help. As for this fellow Whaley, I'm simply going to use the strictness of the law on him, and nothing else!"

"Law?" shouted Mr. Shodress. "The law of this town I've got in my pocket, and I'll show you that I mean what I say, before I'm through. Apperley, do you really think that you can stay here in Yeoville and stand up to me?"

It was very patent that young Apperley did think so and with a vengeance. He merely smiled in the face of the big man.

"To begin with, to show you what I'm made of, I'm going to snuff out this young sneak that you got around the town, snooping into affairs that ain't got anything to do with him!"

He turned in the street and shook his fist back at David.

"The jail won't hold Whaley for a single day!" he yelled.

To this, David made no reply. He knew that this was a serious matter, and yet he could not help smiling. For Alexander Shodress was behaving like a child, and a spoiled child, at that. He had flown into a tantrum, and revealed his plans. What could be more foolish than that? Moreover, he had made the greatest mistake of all in threatening David. Because, in spite of numerous faults, David was neither a fool nor a craven. And all that was best and strongest in him rose up to meet this situation. Yes, he would prosecute Whaley, and he would do it with the last ounce of power in his very soul.

In the meantime, they planned to show their power by stamping out Single Jack Deems.

Perhaps it should have made the young lawyer smile, to think of their being so full of folly as to attack that poisonous fighter, Deems. But David did not smile. He was very, very far from smiling. No matter how formidable Single Jack might be considered in the cities of the East, David was convinced that here, in Yeoville, he was a fish out of water. He looked upon Single Jack with nothing but apprehension, as a burden to his progress, and a helpless weight, which must be cared for. So, every morning, when Deems came to report and asked: "What are the orders for today, Apperley?" David would simply answer: "Just keep yourself out of harm's way, that's all!"

So far, it seemed as though Deems had done it, but perhaps he had overdone that quiet part, and had been so very stealthy that he had given the impression of being a cowardly spy sneaking about the town.

So David locked his office and started out in haste to find his ward.

He was much, much too late. Indeed, had he known how swiftly events transpired in that town, and with what snake-like speed the hand of big Shodress could strike, he would have mounted his horse and started at a frantic gallop, shouting the name of Deems. Even then he might have been too late.

For as Shodress went raging up the street from the office of the newly arrived attorney, he saw two men ride by on cow ponies—two men who waved their hands to him in a sort of informal salute. Shodress ran into the street and called them.

"Hey, Sam and Lew, come here!"

They reined swiftly to him. They were two sun-thinned fellows, who shaved once a week, and that present week was approaching an end.

Mr. Shodress could not have stumbled upon two more likely instruments of his vengeance. Both Sam and Lew were graced with prison records, and though those records were long, they were not so long as they might have been. Twice, at least, the strong hand of Alec Shodress had intervened to rescue them from the grip of the law, and therefore he was a part owner of their very souls.

"Boys," he said, "I'm bothered with a little, sneaking rat that's spying into my affairs here in Yeoville and making life dangerous for all of us. Name of Deems."

"We know him!"

"D'you know any good of him?"

"Not a thing!"

"Boys, I wish he was dead!"

"All right, chief, we'll see that he is."

"Do you know where he is?"

"We seen him not five minutes ago back at the store."

"I hope you make it hard for me to find him. So long!"

"So long, Alec!"

They swung their horses around and cantered blithely up the street, and Shodress watched them go with a smile of gratified vanity. It pleased him to the core of his soul to have such winged messengers in his service. Men strong as thunderbolts, willing to fly to the ends of the earth in his service. Strong, keen-edged tools which he knew how to use so that they were not blunted, but ever rendered sharper for his work!

It did not occur to him that there was something brutal in ordering the murder of a man in this casual manner. It was necessary to strike a sharp blow in the face of Apperley, and the slaughter of this adherent would be enough to drive him out of town, even though the nerves of an Apperley were apt to be most steady. To have Apperley himself killed—why, that was a different matter, and the sort of a thing that might cause a government investigation, with all of its attending evils. But for the murder of such a cringing fellow as young Deems— that could not be an affair of much importance!

In the meantime, the two brothers, Sam and Lew Tucker, swung down the street at a round gallop. It was long since they had been seriously employed, and not having been employed, they had begun to feel that they were forgotten. Their funds had been eaten very low. Their spirits had become depressed.

But now all was altered. To them, the killing of a man was hardly more than routine labor.

"You see," said Sam Tucker, "the old man was just saving us for something important."

"You were right," admitted the other brother. "I thought that the old fathead had plumb forgot us. But I never done nothing that pleased me more than wiping this sneaking coward of a Deems out of the way!"

"Nor me neither. I never liked his looks! A sneak and a rat! There he is! Lew, you edge up to him and begin it."

"Leave that to me!"

There were several verandas in the town of Yeoville, but none in more demand than the long stretch of shadow which ran up and down past the front windows of the general merchandise store. That was owned by Mr. Shodress, just as everything that was really worth while in Yeoville was owned by the same gentleman. There could hardly have been a better place to meet and idle. For, whereas, on the hotel veranda important matters and people often got together, still in front of the store something was constantly happening. People came in for supplies, and as they went out again, they lingered for a while in the shade to hear the latest news—not cold news read out of a paper, but rich and spicy news, flavored by all the tongues over which it had passed. News which could be heard and re-heard. News which, in the second or third telling, could be re-enforced a little by one's own repeating. Each arrival from a different part of the range was sure to carry his own bit of treasure to the general feast of knowledge.

For other reasons, the front of the store was a favored place for congregation. On that deep and wide veranda, one could turn one's head and grace the eye with the prospect of good saddles, richly carved, and giving forth the fragrance of tanned leather; then there were chaps of all kinds; boots decorated with graceful, spoon-handled spurs; sombreros and felt hats; guns; fishing rods; cutlery; hardware such as gladdens the heart of the camper, and clothes worthy of any man's wearing. From the interior deeps of the store, moreover, one could enjoy the smell of roasted coffee, richest of perfumes, and the mingled spicery of dried apples, sides of bacon, and a hundred other necessaries which were luxuries also, on a range where pork and beans made up so great a portion of the regular ration of every cowpuncher.

It was in a corner of this porch that Single Jack now sat, between a great pair of saddles.

"Look at the sneak!" said Lew with a virtuous wrath. "Where he can hear everything, and where he ain't goin' to be noticed, much! Why it's a real pleasure to have to finish him off!"

"I'll do the job myself, without no help from you," said Sam.

"And get the price from the old man, all by yourself, too? No, I'll just take a little hand at the deal, old-timer, and split the reward with you."

They journeyed up the veranda, leaving their horses by the watering trough.

They lingered along the way, speaking here and there to an acquaintance—because friends the Tuckers had none—and so they came at last to the vicinity of the chair in which Single Jack Deems was sitting, with his hands clasped in his lap— what long and slender fingers!—and with his head tilted back a little, and a faint, Oriental smile in his eyes and on his lips, as though he were brooding over distant things too terrible, or too trivial, to take the attention of other men.

Lew Tucker began it.

He made a blundering step and stumbled straight over the big dog which lay at the feet of Mr. Deems.

13.   His Back Against the Wall

Now the side rip of the white fangs of Comanche cut just as deep as a heavy bowie knife, wielded by the hand of an expert, and the movement of his head was just as inescapable as the dart of a snake when it strikes without warning. So that one of the brothers Tucker was apt to be put out of action before the battle began had it not been that there was something else present which was just a shade faster than the light-ning snap of the wolf dog. It was the hand of Single Jack.

It darted out and checked the danger. There was only a formidable clash of teeth as Mr. Tucker stumbled past, but that sound made him whirl about in real apprehension. He marked the snarl on the lips of the great brute, and he saw the green fire in its eyes, and the hand which was wound into its mane, restraining it.

"Curses on you and your dog!" exclaimed Mr. Tucker. "Why are you always in the way?"

Mr. Deems was never in a hurry in his speech. Usually he spoke just loud enough for people to hear, by straining their ears a little. You would have said that there was something wrong with the organs of his throat, that he was not able to raise a sufficient volume of sound. But on the other hand, he enunciated with such peculiar distinctness that even his whisper would carry a surprising distance. But like everything else about him, his voice was oddly relaxed. When he lifted his hand, it was as though a weight were attached to it, and when he raised his eyes, it was as though he were rousing himself from sleep.

Said he in his very gentle way: "I have been sitting here because I was sure that I would be in no one's way."

"You were sure, were you?" snarled Lew Tucker. "You were sure that you could set around and spy on everybody else in the town, hiding in the dark corners, like this. Do you think that the rest of us are fools?"

"Oh, no," said Single Jack gently. "I didn't think that, of course."

"By Jupiter!" cried Lew Tucker, "you admit that you have been spying, here!"

Now the noise of the raised voice of Mr. Tucker had rung up and down the veranda, and there was a sudden murmur of assent and sympathy.

"That sneak of a tenderfoot is going to get his!"

No one liked Mr. Deems in this new part of the world. His strange, dark, watchful eyes troubled them, and the odd silence of his step disturbed them, for they would find him among them without knowing exactly how he had approached them.

Now they were very glad, when they felt that punishment was about to descend upon the head of Deems. Not that they had anything concrete against him, but we always hate most that which is least known to us—unless we have picked it out for worship! Strange people are ridiculous and disgusting; so are strange gods. And never had the blunt and free-swinging West seen a man less like itself than was Single Jack Deems!

The two brothers could see at a glance that they had the matter entirely in their own hands. There would not be the slightest interruption from this obliging crowd. They would stand by and see summary execution done upon the stranger without so much as lifting a hand in his defense, and therefore Sam Tucker roared: "I'm going to have it out of him with my own hands. I'm going to tear it out of him. I'm going to make him tell who it was that hired him to do his dirty work in Yeoville!"

He reached out a strong right hand and fastened his grip upon the neck of Deems.

I mean to say that he reached out, intending to fasten his grip upon the neck of Single Jack, but somehow he missed, as Mr. Deems glided from his chair and said mildly:

"I hope that there will be no trouble, sir. I don't want to make any trouble for anybody!"

"It ain't a trouble. It's a pleasure," snarled Lew Tucker, closing in from the other side.

There was a sudden, throat-rending snarl from the wolf dog, who plainly apprehended what these maneuvers on the part of the two men might mean. He rose, bristling, his reddened eyes turning up to his master for the slightest signal.

"Kill the brute!" cried Lew Tucker, springing back from the danger. "Shoot that wolf dog. It'll have its teeth in one or both of us, in another minute!"

"I'll finish it!" said Mr. Sam Tucker, and laid his hand upon the butt of his Colt.

But now we must go slowly, because we have arrived at the

moment when Mr. Deems first dawned like a new star upon the mind and the heart of the free West. It must be noted that here was Deems with his back against the wall, and the wolf dog crowded against his legs, and twenty pairs of eyes not far away to note everything that he did, or tried to do. Every man in the crowd waited confidently, knowing that both of the Tuckers were tried and proved gunmen, who lived by their craft, and whose weapons, Colts and rifles, were in their hands for practice every day of their lives.

They heard young Deems saying in his gentle voice: "Please don't hurt my dog."

"Please don't hurt his dog! The rat won't even fight for his dog. D'you see that?"

Then came the roar of Sam Tucker: "Get back from that wolf, or I'll miss him, maybe, and sink a shot in you!"

"Please don't shoot!" said Mr. Deems. "Please don't shoot! Won't some of you other men give me a little help to keep them from murdering my dog?"

He looked vaguely around him at the semicircle of faces of the spectators who were observing all of these actions. But there was a brutal contempt in every eye. Not a one but was pleased to witness this little sample of harshness. Justice, they called it. It had the making of a story that would be worth repeating.

"Stand back, you fool!" shouted Sam Tucker. "I warn you for the last time!"

His fingers tightened on the butt of his Colt.

"I've asked you fellows to help me," sighed Single Jack. "But you don't seem to want to!"

A roar of brutal laughter answered that almost feminine appeal.

"And so," they heard the soft voice of Single Jack continue, "I'm afraid that I shall have to shoot them both! But you be my witnesses that I have tried to avoid all trouble!"

They gaped at him in a sort of horror. There was no sign of any gun carried by this stranger. Could it be that the poor fellow was a half-wit? No, his face seemed intelligent enough.

If one looked a little more closely at it, one could see that it had lost a bit of its usual pallor, and there was almost a smile upon the lips, and in the dark, dead eyes, a spark had at last been blown up.

So he meant what he said!

"Look out, Lew!" called Sam Tucker in mockery. "You'll be getting yourself killed, in a minute. This here rat is going to show his teeth. All right! Here goes the dog—you watch the man!"

He snatched out his Colt to fan it from the hip, intending to send a liberal spray of lead in the direction of his opponents— the first bullet at the dog, and then if his next shots flew a little wild, flew heart-high, say, and reached the man, why who could really blame him? And would it not appear in any court before which he might appear, that he had merely defended himself when attacked by a wild brute of a wolf dog? And that an accidental shot which he greatly regretted—

So flew the thoughts of Mr. Sam Tucker, a little faster than his gun, but not much. But just as his thumb pressed the hammer of his gun, a miracle happened.

For Mr. Deems had made a sudden gesture toward the left armpit of his coat, and when his right hand came away there was a gleam of steel, something to be guessed at rather than seen, until it blossomed into a flash of fire, a spout of smoke, and the plainly heard impact of a large caliber bullet as it struck the body of Sam Tucker and knocked him down.

Lew Tucker had not waited to see more than the first flash of steel in the hand of the stranger before he himself made his draw, and he was admittedly a better and a faster fighter than his brother, and yet Lew Tucker did not seem to be moving rapidly. It seemed that he was reaching most leisurely for his weapon. It seemed that he was drawing and holding it at the hip with the deliberation of a madman. Or was it only because the hand of Mr. Deems was no longer moving as though weighted, but traveling with electric surety and speed?

As the Colt came to the level at the hip of Lew Tucker, a second shot from the gun in the hand of Deems struck Lew on the left thigh and ripped its way through both his legs, so that he pitched forward upon his face and discharged his weapon into the boards of the veranda floor as he fell.

Then over the two writhing, groaning, stricken men leaned Single Jack, saying in a voice of pleading eagerness: "I hope that you gentlemen will all be witnesses for me, that I didn't want to do it! And you'll agree with me that I didn't hunt for the trouble. And won't you please notice, also, that I haven't killed either of them? The first one is just through the center of the right shoulder, so that he wouldn't have the use of his gun hand, you see, and the second one through the upper legs, just in front of the thigh bones—I do hope that the bones were not broken."

He fell to work with a singular dexterity, using a knife to open the clothes above the wounds of the two fallen men, and examining their hurts.

The doctor came at that moment, and Single Jack said to him gently:

"There's no need for you to worry. They'll both just need a cleansing of the wounds with a good antiseptic. And then a little rest. I'm so sorry that it happened!"

The doctor did not answer, because he thought the man was jesting. And no one else answered him, as they saw him retreat, solemnly, from the veranda, with the slinking wolf dog at his heels. They had no breath, indeed, for speech!

14. Too Much Confidence

Straight down the street went Single Jack Deems and found David coming hastily up toward him.

"I thought I heard guns. Was someone practicing?" asked David.

Mr. Deems seemed very much perturbed, and he answered gravely that he trusted that he had not made any undue trouble for David Apperley.

"Trouble? Trouble?" asked David. "What do you mean?"

"Two of them backed me into a corner," said Deems, "and they were going to shoot Comanche. I had to do something!"

"And you ran away, I suppose?" suggested David.

Which shows how far Single Jack had fallen in the esteem of the young lawyer.

"I came away as soon as I could," said Single Jack seriously. "But before I could leave, I had to shoot them both."

He added, while David stared: "Not fatally. But just one through the shoulder and the other through the legs. It was that or have bullets in Comanche and me!"

He remained looking earnestly into the face of David, and then said: "You'll tell your brother that I didn't hunt for the trouble?"

"Yes," said David, "I'll tell him that."

But he could not find any word of comment. He chiefly wondered, now that he had time to think of it, that the town should have remained so quiet, immediately following the double shooting.

He could see, now, that he had most arrogantly and stupidly misjudged this slayer of men. The dark-eyed, slender youth continued:

"You'll be leaving town, now, I suppose, Apperley?"

"Leaving town? Why?"

"Because now it'll be war to the finish. They'll never stop until they've had a chance to sink some bullets into me—and you! And they're more apt to shoot you than to shoot me!"

"Leave town? Let myself be bluffed out just after I've opened my office! No, I'm going to stay here and prosecute the case against Whaley."

It seemed to young David Apperley that his companion had a hundred words hanging upon the tip of his tongue, but he crowded them all back as though seeing that they would be of no use. And, in fact, if there had been an attempt to persuade David to leave Yeoville, it would have been totally futile.

David went on through the town to get to the little court-house and open the proceedings against Whaley formally. And before he had finished, he had fresh business on his hands, for the men of his brother, combing the range carefully to fill the hands of the lawyer in Yeoville, had found another rustler caught red-handed in the act. They carried him to the town among the hills. It was Steve Grange, still in his teens, lean and strong as a young lion, with a bandage tied around his head. A glancing shot had knocked him out of his saddle. Otherwise, everyone said, he would never have been taken alive.

David Apperley saw the new prisoner and rubbed his hands. Then, going down the street, he encountered Charley Johnson and Les Briggs.

"I'm going to make cattle rustling the most unpopular sport on this range!" said he.

"Go to it!" said they. "We're behind you. Though I don't suppose we count much, now."

"Why not?"

"Now that you got a gent like that Deems around you! You've kept him under cover pretty well, though, we got to admit!"

"He seems to have made a great impression even on the ruffians in this town," said David, who was not quite sure.

Les Briggs turned his quid of chewing tobacco in his mouth and then spat accurately at a nearby stump of a tree.

"I talked to old Porky Smith. Porky has seen pretty near everything in the way of fighting that is worth seeing, and he says that there was never nothing like it. Not for speed and for accuracy and for style, y'understand? You could imagine a gent with speed and luck, and everything, able to drop even two gun fighters like the Tucker boys. But you couldn't imagine placing the shots, and being able to call them, both before and afterwards! You got something valuable in Deems. Do they call him Single Jack because he just uses one gun at a time?"

To these remarks David could not return any answer, but that night he had occasion to write to his brother:

Single Jack has been cornered by two of the bullies of Shodress, who is trying to drive us out of town. I think that he wanted to kill Deems, so that the example would frighten me away from Yeoville. But Deems shot down both the would-be assassins, and, in so doing, it seems that he has stunned even a place as rough as this Yeoville. The people look upon him as a prodigy. They have no word or way for explaining his speed and his skill. In this single fracas, he has made Single Jack a byword.

The fellow is not the least changed. He goes about as softly, and as much like a cat as ever. But I have changed my mind about him. It seems, Andy, that he's quite devoted to me. At least, now that the shooting has brought a good deal of active peril about the heads of both of us, Single Jack is never far from me. If I walk down the street, I can be sure that he is an unobtrusive shadow, lingering behind me. A dozen times I have seen these gun fighters finger their guns greedily as I go by. But they dare not draw, because they know that Single Jack is near me. So that the man you sent to have me save, Andy, is really saving me ten times a day. I have no doubt that Shodress has placed a very high price upon my head. His men are anxious to claim the reward, but at the same time they don't want to walk into the very intelligent gun of Mr. Deems—and I don't blame them. In the cool of every morning, for one hour, Single Jack does his practicing in the back yard behind my office, and I've sneaked out and watched him at his work twice. It isn't like marksmanship. It's like an uncanny will power at work. As though he were simply wishing things to happen—and they occur. I can't tell you things that he does in much detail. He always works in the dimness of the dawn, as though he wants to test his skill to the utmost by giving himself difficult light. But I can give you a sample of the things he accomplishes. I have seen him throw small pebbles into the air with one hand and shoot them to pieces as they fly. And he has a little game of jack-stones, as you might call it. He takes a rubber ball in his left hand and starts it bouncing. On the ground before him lies a set of six small stones, and a Colt. He bounces the ball. While it is in the air and on the recoil, he snatches up a pebble and flicks it into the air and flips up the revolver's muzzle and fires. By this time the ball has struck the earth again, and it seems that he must have finished the tossing of the pebble and the shooting as the ball recoils the second time, or else it is a point against him. If all goes well, he continues this queer game, bouncing the ball, from hand to hand, and firing with alternate hands, until he has struck the six pebbles with the six bullets. You can see that this is a fiendishly difficult task. I have only seen him work out the whole affair twice, I think. Usually something goes wrong. He fails to catch the ball, or else he misses one of the pebbles. And instead of being elated by the wonderful skill which he shows, he always appears downcast. But having seen what his practice is like, I tell you, Andy, that I would freely back him against any three men in a stand-up gun fight. He is extremely modest, and never refers to what he has done in the past or what he expects to do in the future. I have repeatedly begged him to do some target shooting that I could watch in open daylight, but he always finds some excuse.

I have just had a singular example of his devotion. I had to leave my room, where I had been sitting up, writing this letter quite late at night, and, as I opened the door, I saw a shadow stretched across the hall. The green-eyed devil Comanche stood up and glared at me, and there was his master just sitting up and throwing off the blanket which had covered him. He told me it had been too hot to sleep in a stuffy bedroom on a bed. I said nothing, but I understood. He was guarding me through the middle of the night by lying across the hall in front of my door, his devil dog beside him!

This touches me a great deal, and I think it will touch you more, because from the first you saw something in this fellow, and I was so stupid as to think him a thoroughly bad case!

He has overwhelmed the whole town and all of its ruffians with his bravery and his peculiar gentler, unassuming, but thoroughly terrible manner. There is a sort of inhuman, feline dreadfulness about his step, his eyes, and his soft, drawling, purring voice.

In the meantime, the case gets on against Whaley. I have the jury selected, and I don't think, though most of them are confessed Shodress men, that they can possibly turn in any but a verdict of guilty. The case is as plain as can be, and I intend to drive it home as hard as I can.

At the same time, I am working matters up against young Steve Grange. He is younger than Whaley, but I think that he is infinitely the more important prize. The people in this town appear to respect him as though he were a much older and wiser man. He is an absolute daredevil. His record is a very wild one, and I think that I shall be able to lodge him in the penitentiary for a number of years.

You will see that there is plenty of excitement up here. I like it. Without young Single Jack, I could not live for a single hour, I presume. With him, I think that I can get through any difficulty.

So wrote David Apperley in the small hours of the morning, and then went to the window to watch the waning of the stars. He was very contented with himself and with all that had passed in the last few days. He was beginning to lead a real life.

Of course he had no prescience which enabled him to see that he was momentarily rushing into more and more terrible dangers. He was building up a fatal self-confidence. Well would it have been for him if he had scrupulously trusted to the guardianship of Single Jack. But his self-confidence was his undoing—that and a girl!

15. Enter the Girl

She was the lovely, red-haired sister of Steven Grange.

But before we go back to her, we have to push ahead with other events, though they seem of no importance compared with Hester Grange.

She would never have been called into the affair, perhaps, had it not been for the fine work which David performed against Whaley. That gentleman was defended by a capable lawyer hired by the money of Shodress. And Alexander Shodress and his cigars were always in the courtroom, giving countenance to the defendant, and scowling bitterly at the prosecuting attorney. But even such influence could not absolutely down the facts in the case. Those facts were attested by competent eyewitnesses, and the final speech of David was really a little masterpiece, as he sketched in the evils of cattle rustling, and the future desolation of the range if the practice continued, pointing out that already even great owners of many herds of thousands could barely stand the yearly losses, whereas the small owners were wiped out root and branch by a single raid!

At any rate, the verdict was guilty, and the judge, scowling at the floor, gave the minimum sentence of three years. He was a perfectly good Shodress man, that judge, and he had made his final summing up as partial as any summing up could be. But he had to pronounce the sentence, and Whaley was packed away to serve a three-years' sentence.

It was the first great victory for young David. He had worked for it like a beaver and a hero, and he smiled with a calm triumph that promised more trouble for evildoers in that part of the world.

It was not the rule for that court to turn in convictions. It was distinctly not the rule. It appeared that even fellows as corrupt as those jurors had a certain honor, and they were heard to say with many oaths, as they left the courtroom: "Facts is facts, and they got to be listened to! What is the world coming to, otherwise?"

What, indeed?

Shodress, sitting by the window, allowed the cigar to droop down from his soft-lipped, pursy mouth, while his fat face sagged, and a grayness overspread it. He was seeing signs of the coming of the end. His empire of graft and treachery and crookedness, supported by brutality and money, was threatened with its end and he turned blazing eyes toward the young lawyer who was striking so valiantly for the right.

Other eyes marked that glance, and they understood it. Twenty guns were ready, but in the shadows of a corner, behind the lawyer, there was always seated a slender, boyish figure who watched all that happened with singular, dark, lackluster, feline eyes. And as they looked at Single Jack, and at his slender, bony hands, always moving slowly, as though bearing a weight of drowsiness, their own guns were forgotten, and they looked suddenly down to the floor again.

So the crowd left the courtroom, and in the ears of many the words of Whaley were ringing, the words which he had uttered when the judge asked him if he had anything to say before sentence was pronounced.

"I got this to say: There's some think that money will buy anything. But what's the price of living behind bars?"

He had turned and glared openly at Shodress.

Yes, it might be the beginning of the end. Everyone felt it. They had felt that Shodress was a sort of invincible archangel—an archangel of darkness, if you will, but a superhuman power, at the least! And now that power seemed to be falling. He had lost his first case. How many other cases would follow? It seemed a prophecy of the end of a great reign, and men

75

looked soberly, one to the other, wondering what would happen next.

All of this is directly important not so much because it shows the ability mingled with courage which David Apperley had exhibited, or because it was the first trenchant blow delivered at the great Shodress, or because it sent a rascal to the penitentiary for three years, but really because it had a vital bearing upon the next case which was coming up.

That was the case of Steve Grange. If Whaley was manifestly guilty, was not Steve doubly so? And if the lawyer had spoken eloquently in the case of Whaley, what could he do about the man who had resisted arrest, gun in hand, until a chance bullet happened to knock him off his horse? And what light would he throw upon the wild career of this youth?

No, Steve Grange was undoubtedly doomed before the trial, and there was all likelihood that the sentence would be nearer the maximum than the minimum, because there were open rumors of a breach between the judge and Shodress. The judge had said that his conscience had already been passed through enough fire. He was beginning to want to breathe a fresher air!

All of this portended much. Men walked scowling through the streets of Yeoville, uncertain what to do next.

Then the Grange-Shodress forces struck an unexpected blow, in the following manner.

Other business than that of the rustlers was beginning to flow into the hands of David. Men saw ability in him, and ability is always used in the West. There were men on the range about Yeoville who were, in fact, only waiting for some vital sign that law was in force before they rallied against Shodress. These men had grievances of many kinds which they wanted to have represented in the court, and they rallied to David with much enthusiasm. So work flowed steadily into his hands, and he began to go down to his office early in the mornings.

So it happened that, on this morning, he had barely opened his office and taken his place behind his desk, when he was called upon by what seemed to him the loveliest woman in the entire world. She was dressed most unpretentiously, like any girl from the range, but she was one who needed no adornment. When she stood before David, he found himself setting his teeth to keep his heart from fluttering, and all the time that she was talking, the beauty of the coiled masses of that red hair, and the wonderful blue of her eyes unsettled poor David and made him much at outs with himself.

She said: "I am the sister of Steven Grange. Will you let me talk to you about him?"

"Of course!" said David. He looked at her with a sinking heart. She was the sister of Steve Grange!

But Heaven alone could tell wherein the relationship appeared. For Steve was like a young lion, and this girl with her alluring rather crooked smile, and the dimple that appeared and disappeared in one cheek was a delicate creature. Besides, Steve Grange was a youth of an iron nerve, and this girl was very badly frightened. See, where her soft hands were clasped together, how the flesh whitened with the pressure as she strove to keep up her courage!

Only one thing reminded him of Steve. Steve always looked one directly in the eye with an unwavering glance, and so did this girl. Her eyes clung to his, but not with challenge or force —with a sort of clinging, pathetic, frightened appeal.

The pulse rate of David mounted by tens at a time.

"I want you to say whatever you wish," he told her. "Will you sit down here?"

"Perhaps I had better not sit down. I know you are very busy. I only want to take one minute of your time. I only want to beg you to have mercy on poor Steve, because—"

Tears flooded into her eyes. Still she did not look down to the floor, but studied him, as though she feared lest at any moment a flash of pity might appear in his eyes and she remain in ignorance of it.

"My dear Miss Grange," said he. "My dear Miss Grange, suppose that we look at it in this manner—that I am committed by my honor to work in the cause of justice—"

Her lips trembled, but she did not speak, she only waited.

77

He felt that he was striking a helpless creature, and the flesh of David crawled with horror and strong self-contempt.

"And then again, suppose you admit that Steve is a misguided fellow. Will you admit that?" he asked her.

"We know that poor, dear Steve has done wrong—very great wrong. There isn't any excuse!"

"Very well, with a strong nature like Steve's, the best cure is a strong hand, usually. He's offended the law. Let him learn that no matter how strong he may be, the law is a great deal stronger. That lesson of respect may make the rest of his life a useful one, and while the years in prison may seem long to one who looks forward to them, they are sure to appear short, when he looks back."

She caught her breath. She said faintly: "Then I cannot do anything at all?"

She drew back toward the door, but still with those tearful eyes fixed upon him.

The very heart of David was smitten within him, and he hurried across to her and took her hands in his. A fatal error, David, to touch those hands, so soft, though not half so soft as they look. And to come within range of the fragrance which hangs in her hair. Ah, foolish, foolish David! It mounts through your brain faster than incense ever wafted from this earth of sorrow to the blessed abodes of the gods.

"What can I do?" said he.

"I don't know! I don't know!" she said, and, though she stood so close, her glance never once wavered from his; he could see the open, tear-brightened blueness of her eyes, so like the eyes of a child. "Only, it's my fault, you see," she added.

"Come, come! Your fault?"

"When father died, he left Steve to Mother, and when Mother died, she left him to me, because we all knew that he needed to be taken care of. If I'd made the home brighter and gayer, then he wouldn't have been tempted to go out hunting such terrible adventures—"

"But why in the name of Heaven should he have been left in your care?"

"Of, of course that was right, because I'm his older sister, you know! Oh, there was nothing else for Mother to do!"

Older sister? Older baby.

"I'll tell you this," said David. "I'll—I'll see what I can do —and let you know-er—"

"If you will let me dare to hope—oh, God bless you! Because if Steve were put in prison, he would rage like a wild creature. He would break out. Then even murder would be nothing to him. Oh, I know him so well! He is so terribly strong, and so young—"

She to talk of youth with pity! She!

"Poor child! Poor child!" murmured David, a lump in his throat.

Suddenly she was smiling at him sympathetically through her tears.

"Yes, that is all he is, isn't it? Oh, thank you for understanding!"

16. A Golden Rooster

About every truly beautiful woman all things are beautiful; even her slightest and most mundane actions have their charm. Tears, for instance, which make another swollen and red of face, make her only flushed and more humanly delightful.

Now David Apperley was a great distance from a fool, neither was he a novice who had had nothing to do with women in his life. But to most of us the feminine world is a humdrum affair, very wearisome and silly, and hardly to be borne with; only once in our lives, perhaps, we find her who possesses the key of mystery which unlocks the heart and lets the wind of an unknown country pass through all the chambers. David Apperley had met her on this day, and his heart expanded immensely; he was filled with strength; he wanted to cherish this fragile and gentle creature, and with a moist eye he followed her to the door of his office.

"If I had known that Steve Grange was your brother," said he, "I should have dropped the prosecution before it was started. But now that it is under way, it has to be pushed ahead a certain distance, at least. However, I think that I can find a manner of keeping him from harm! I'll do my best for you!"

She looked up at him with a new hope, half smiling and half wondering, and surveyed his face as though it were a strange country in which infinite good might be found.

"I've never met anyone like you before," said Hester Grange.

"Tush!" said David.

"No," said she gravely, "no one so stern and strong—but so good."

Somehow he got her onto the street.

"You'll be much too busy with important affairs to see me again," said Hester.

"Not a bit," said David. For it seemed to him that only the moment before had anything of a definite importance really entered his life. "I think that I should see you again, soon, so that we can talk the case of your brother over in detail."

Her joy and gratitude dawned in her face with a childlike suddenness.

"Do you really mean that?"

"Of course."

"Thank you, thank you! Then when will you let me come?"

He looked down to her and set his teeth a little, for otherwise a veritable flood of tenderness and joy and love would have rushed up into his eyes and made his lips tremble with words which he must not speak—as yet. He wondered out of what nest this bird had come; he must see her among her people, no matter how savage and crude they might be.

"It would be more proper for me to come to you, if you will tell me when."

"Would you come? No, that would be a trouble!"

"Not in the least—if I may make it after office hours, I have to work rather late, just now."

"Then will you come to dinner?"

"May I do that?"

"I'm not a very good cook, I'm afraid, but I shall do my best."

A little ecstasy of foolish delight made him tremble at the thought of sitting at a table served by her hands, and eating food which she had cooked for him. With a sudden touch of prophecy, he felt that he could see a long prospect of years before him during which, God willing, she should minister to him, while he protected her, and surrounded her with such love as a woman had never known before.

So it was arranged, and he went back to his office, walking lightly. There he encountered an impatient cattleman, chewing the end of a cigar which had long ago gone out. He was filled with troubles. He had made a loan to a certain one of the men of Alec Shodress, and now that the loan was due, the fellow refused repayment, and snapped his fingers in the face of the cattleman. Let the latter try to foreclose! Only let him try! If he had a single footed beast on his entire ranch within a week after the foreclosure, it would be very odd!

That threat was not without a very great deal of point, as the cattleman knew, and therefore he had decided that he would fly to seek the new power which had raised its head so suddenly on the range; a power which had been long a stranger and which was therefore all the more welcome—the law!

But as he stormed forth his case, that veteran of the cow country could not help thinking that this was a strange young fellow to be the brother of Andrew Apperley and the brilliant and courageous antagonist of Alec Shodress himself! For poor David was sunk in a dream from which it would never be in his power to recover altogether.

In the meantime, so deep was he in his thoughts, that he did not notice that his constant shadow, Single Jack Deems, no longer kept post near his door. Single Jack was gone, for the first time in all of these days.

He had started down the street following Hester Grange, and he went after her until she came to a little cottage on the outer edge of town, all embowered among orchard trees, and with a tangled hedge of greenery and flowers rising above the pickets of the front-yard fence.

Through the gate went the girl, calling out blithely: "Oliver! Oliver! Hello, Noll!"

A deep young voice answered her, and through the front door of the house bounded a big youngster of seventeen or eighteen years. It seemed to the startled Single Jack that this must be Steve Grange himself, escaped from the jail, but at a second glance, he was sure that this fellow was a little younger, a little gentler, not yet of a steel so heat-tempered as that of Steve. But it was exactly the same material, and eventually it would be coming to the same end.

"What luck, old girl?"

"Why, Oliver, he's the softest thing I ever met in my life. I left him. If I'd stayed another five minutes, he would have been kissing my hand. I was ashamed, Oliver, to see any man act like such a fool. And he's going to come down tonight and have dinner with us."

"The deuce he is!"

"The deuce he isn't! He wants to talk more about the case of my brother in jail. So he says. He wants to hold my hand and have a chance to be sentimental, really. Oh, Oliver, I wish I were a man, once in a while, so that I could do and say what I really feel, instead of having to wear this baby face!"

"It's the best and the prettiest face in the world," said Oliver Grange.

"Well, I'm tired of it!" said Hester with emphasis. "I'm tired of being fussed over and having every man I meet want to paw me about and treat me like a doll that likes to be petted."

"If they dare, I'll cut their throats!" said young Oliver with a sudden savagery.

"You wildcat," said the girl, glancing at him with a spark of fierce admiration. "But I don't need your help to take care of myself! Oliver, how I wish to Heaven that I could meet some man that I didn't despise."

"I know," Oliver nodded. "You'll never be happy until you've met up with some brute that'll beat you a couple of times a day, make you cook for a whole gang, and raise a flock of children while you keep house for him. Some time you'll meet a man like that, that'll take a whip to you—and you'll follow him home!"

"Oliver," said the girl savagely, "do you really think that I'm made of such stuff?"

"You wait and see," said he with the infinite assurance of youth. "But in the first place, what about dinner tonight? Are you going to give him a spread?"

"I am. I'm going to have your golden rooster, Noll."

"Hello, is that a joke?"

"Not a bit."

"Look here, honey, not the one that I raised since it was a sick little chicken that couldn't—"

"It's not sick any longer!"

"But, sis—the one that comes when I whistle to it? Why, it knows as much as I do?"

"Are you going to be soft-headed about a chicken?" asked the girl sternly. "When it may help your brother to come off with his life?"

He winced a little.

"But there are lots of others."

"You know that there's nothing in the yard as big and fat and fine as your golden rooster. And I can see him now, all crusted with brown, when I take him out of the oven and offer him up to this lawyer. I'm going to break up that David Apperley like little kindling, Noll, dear. I'm going to make him get down on his knees and beg me to be his wife, before he leaves this house tonight. And"—she broke out of her fierceness with gay laughter—"it may be that a good roast chicken will be just the thing to turn the trick!"

Oliver looked down to the ground, sorrowfully, but he gave way to the superior strength of her nature.

"Only, is it right to treat him like that—if he really falls in love with you?"

"I can't help it if a man's a fool," said the girl. "And I'm fighting for Steve's life, as Mamma told me that I'd have to do! You go get that rooster, and get it quick!"

Poor Oliver turned away with trailing feet and a downcast head. Single Jack Deems watched him go into the yard behind the house and whistle, whereat a magnificent golden-plumed rooster came running, heavy and waddling with fat, and rushed with beating wings in haste to get to its master. The boy took it up, caressed it, and put it down again in haste.

He turned into a shed and came out again with a .32-caliber rifle, which he poised. He looked sternly at the rooster, but that gayly colored bird was picking in the dust at his feet, all unsuspicious. Oliver shook his head. He could not commit this murder!

17.   The Smile of the Wolf

So beautiful Hester Grange ran up steps into the house, with a song trailing behind her as she went. She hurried to her room to take off her hat, and presently she swept into the parlor to begin the house cleaning at that point, for the place must be well furbished before the evening came.

She stopped in the doorway, for she saw seated in the arm-chair at the farther end of the room a slender young man with a darkly handsome face, and graceful hands folded in his lap. Single Jack Deems!

"You sit down over there!" said he and pointed to a chair.

She hesitated. It was the rule with Hester to gain a certain supremacy over men at her first meeting with them. But she felt that it might be very unwise to challenge this masterful young man at once.

With her heart beating fast, she crossed to the designated chair and rested her hands on the back of it.

"You're talking very strangely," said Hester. "I don't know what is wrong. I do hope that you're not bringing me any bad news from poor Steve!"

And she let her big blue eyes fill with tears as they looked softly toward him. For that was perhaps her mightiest weapon. Men melted at once before those blue eyes.

However, in this case, the slender young man merely smiled in turn, but it was not exactly a pleasant smile. It touched the corners of his lips, but his eyes remained as dull and deep a black as ever.

"I'm bringing you bad news," he agreed, "about Steve, and about other things, maybe."

She stared intently at him, trying to guess. But there was no hope of finding out his hidden meanings. He was as obscure as the grave itself.

"In the first place," said he, "you can make up your mind that Steve is going to the penitentiary. That's the first point to rest on."

She gasped a little.

"Did your employer tell you to talk like that?"

"I have no employer," said he. "If you mean Apperley—no. He's still dazed and half sick. It will be a long time before he gets over what you've done to him."

He leaned forward and the faintest of lights glistened in his eyes.

"You work fast," said he. "I've known some nifty ones, but never any like you. All that I don't see is—what are you doing in the bushes?"

"Bushes?" she answered vaguely, for she was stunned by the manner and the voice of this cold youth.

"Yes, why in the sticks? You should be on the soft end of a

confidence job, my dear. There are some mighty clever men in the country who'd be glad to use you. Inside of six months, you could be taking down thirty or forty thousand a year for your share of the loot. So why waste yourself out here?"

Now she fired.

"Do you think that I'm dishonest?" she asked him fiercely.

The answer was a slightly curling sneer.

"Will you listen to me?" he said. "I'm not a baby, like the rest of 'em. I know you, Hester. I know you like a book. Because I've read your kind before!"

It was the ultimate insult. For whatever else a woman may be, she is always sure that she is unique, and to be placed in a category is more terrible for her than for a man to be placed in a prison.

"I've heard you long enough," she said angrily. "I don't think that there's any reason I should stay here longer. I'm very busy, Mr. Deems."

She turned toward the door.

"Don't lose your temper," said this smooth youth. "It never works with me. I don't want you to try the baby stuff with me, but the haughty air won't work, either. You sit down here and stay till I've finished with you."

A little laugh came from her throat, a bubbling little laugh, but her eyes were as bright and as hard as steel.

"How can you compel me to?" she said.

"That's only one of the things I'm going to compel you to do," said Single Jack. "After I've made you stay here, what really counts are the other things I'll lay out for you to do."

"You're a little mad," said the girl. "You can't force me to do anything. Do you know that window is open? And do you hear those men singing. Those are the three Gresham brothers. I only need to call, and they'd be here at once."

As though to punctuate and underline this remark, there was the sound of a rifle exploding. The girl started a little.

"It's all right," said Deems. "It's only Oliver shooting at a mark and trying to work up his courage to murder the rooster."

"Do you know about that?" she asked him, rather shocked.

"It's simple. I followed you down from the office and heard what you had to say to Oliver. I wish that David Apperley had been handy to hear, also."

"You crooked, clever—yegg!" she burst out at him in a passion.

"Names are no weapons," said Single Jack with a smile. "Are you ready to do what I want?"

"Why under heaven should I? Go back to David Apperley, if you wish, and tell him whatever you please, but you can't keep him away."

She breathed hard and fast with her savage triumph.

"He'll come whenever I call him!" she said.

"Yes," agreed Single Jack, "but he'll also stay away, if you tell him to."

"If! But do you think that I'll be so foolish as to send him away?"

He nodded at her in perfect sympathy and understanding.

"I know," said Single Jack. "It's hard to do. When you've planted a good job, and all that you have to do is just to collect, it's bitter hard to give up the profits!"

"You see," said she, "it's no good trying to bluff me."

"Bluff you, my dear?" murmured Single Jack. "I never dreamed of bluffing you. I have never bluffed in my life."

"Then you will tell me what earthly power you have over me?"

"I don't have to tell you. Look out the window into the back yard and you'll see for yourself."

She looked out obediently, for she was as interested as she was appalled and baffled by this conversation.

"There's no one but Oliver and the chickens out there."

"Oliver?"

"Yes."

"You love Oliver, don't you?"

"Dear, silly old Noll! What have you to say about him?"

"I mean that you're an odd one. Hard as nails. But you're fond of your family. You remember your father and mother.

87

And you really love your brothers. But Oliver you love more than Steve. Steve is a bit hard and cold even for you!"

"I'm not interested," said the girl sharply. "Not a bit interested in all of this nonsense!"

"Oh, but you will be! Suppose that you insist on having David Apperley down here—"

"I shall insist."

"Very well. The day following that, I'll contrive to meet your brother Oliver, put a fight on his hands, and lay him dead in the street!"

She started to laugh in fierce mockery, but no sound came from her lips.

"There is no one in the world wicked enough to do such a thing!" she declared.

"Do you think that I wouldn't? Look at me again. You don't know me, yet. But look at me again. I always do exactly what I promise. Exactly. My word is a one-hundred per-cent gold bond!"

He leaned forward a little in his chair, as though when he brought himself that vital bit closer, she could see him more distinctly.

She did see him more distinctly, but she cried with a trembling voice: "I'll send Noll out of harm's way. I'll send him out of the town!"

Single Jack shook his head and smiled.

"He's not that sort of a boy. You try to persuade him to run away. Do you think that he would? Not for a minute, while there's a man's work to do. He seems to be softer and simpler than you and your brother. But when the pinch comes, you'll find that he has a strain of hero in him. He may hesitate about slaughtering his pet rooster. But he'll never hesitate in a fight with other men where there are bullets flying!"

She gazed rapt and amazed at this calm speaker. For he spoke with an absolute knowledge which she could not question, and try as she would to deny it, she had to admit that there was a proper substance of right in what he said. This was exactly the proud, tender, gentle, and strong nature of young Oliver. She could push him along in any direction with a feather, if she chose. But when a certain point came and he felt that such a thing as his manhood was appealed to, then a thousand wild horses could not budge him.

"They would tear you to pieces! They would burn you alive if you dared to murder Noll!" she cried to him.

"I've been threatened with those things before," said the other. "But then, your brother is man sized. And everyone knows that he's very excited because his brother is in jail—and I belong to the crew that's trying to put Steve in the penitentiary. So, of course, in meeting me—alone—if he were to lose his temper and try to murder me—and if I shot in self-defense why—"

He made a little explanatory gesture and smiled into her eyes. And suddenly—she had not seen the creature before—from the dark shadow of a corner behind his master, forth stepped Comanche and regarded the girl with a curling lip and glittering green eyes, and somehow it seemed to her that there was a relation between these two destroying creatures, and the smile of the wolf was no more deadly than the smile of the man.

18. Hester's Bargain

"I think that you mean it," said Hester Grange suddenly.

"I mean it."

"Why do they let a man like you continue to live?" she cried. "If they're so brave and so wild, why don't they crush you—"

"Oh, some day they will. But that mustn't spoil my fun, now. Tomorrow will take care of itself."

She watched him with her graceful head inclined a little to the side. Then she nodded.

"You're different," she said, more to herself than to him.

"I can manage the others. But not you. Did anybody ever make you change your mind?"

"Yes."

"Who?"

"Comanche."

The wolf dog, hearing its name, suddenly depressed its ears and turned its head for a glance back and up to its master. The girl saw a flash of love soften those cold green eyes. She could not help a shudder.

"Then what is it that you want me to do?"

"Keep David Apperley away from you."

"How can I do that?"

"That's simple. Just by sending him a note and saying that you've changed your mind, and that you can't see him."

"He'll be insulted."

"Perhaps he will be."

"And also—it may make him want to come all the more."

Single Jack Deems smiled at her.

"I don't know exactly how you can manage it," he confessed. "I'm not a woman, and therefore I don't know all the ways in which a woman can work. But what I do know is that I want you to keep Apperley away from you, and if you don't I've told you what will happen!"

A flush of anger rose in her face. But she bit her lips and nodded.

"Only," she said, "it's hard for me to believe that I'm being so bullied! But I'll manage it."

"Then good-by."

He went toward the door, and the great wolf dog slouched after him, turning its head to watch the girl as though he feared danger from her.

So Single Jack went from the porch, and down the little path, and through the gate, and she watched his smooth, gliding step take him up the street. He seemed to her, as she stood at the window, like the shadow of a man rather than an actual human being, and he left a coldness of dread with her all the while that she stared after him.

Then another thought came to her. She went to the back door, and in the yard she saw her brother Oliver in the very act of drawing a bead upon the golden rooster.

"Oliver! Oliver!" she called.

Oliver turned a tense face toward her. She could see by his expression how terribly hard was the sacrifice which she had demanded of him. Her conscience reproved her roughly.

"Oliver, I don't think that we'll need the chicken, after all. I want you to take a note for me to David Apperley, instead."

He came gladly and waited in patience for her to write the note, which she scratched off swiftly in a bold, sprawling hand, very like the writing of a man:

Dear Mr. Apperley: I am sorry to say that something has happened which makes it impossible for me to see you tonight. Will you forgive me for making the change?

She considered the note for a moment. What would he make of it? Would his curiosity be intrigued? Would he simply be furious with her? At any rate, it was better to make the note simple and brief.

So she signed her name without delay and dispatched her brother with word not to linger in the office of the lawyer.

"Why should I stay there?" asked Oliver sternly. "Unless I wanted to lose my head and sink a bullet through that hound."

"Why do you call him a hound, Oliver?"

"Why, dear, isn't he trying to polish off poor Steve?"

"That's his business as a lawyer—to make trouble for other people. But don't you wait there. That Single Jack Deems is around the office all the while. And if you should get into trouble with him—" She made a significant pause.

"Deems? Single Jack?" repeated her young brother hotly. "And what's he? He's a man, like the rest of us—and bullets will down him just the same!"

"Oliver!" she cried.

He retreated a little before her outburst of fear.

"I'm going to be good," said Oliver sullenly. "I won't hunt

any trouble, but it makes me sick to see the whole town stand-
ing around on one foot because of a tenderfoot out of the
East that doesn't know one end of a horse from the other.
A sneaking, spying, crooked—"

"Oliver!"

"Well, all right, all right!"

He took the note and strode off with it up the street while
she remained in the door looking earnestly and anxiously after
him. She loved him as a sister and somewhat of a mother, also.
For, though she was a scant twenty herself, yet for five years
she had been the head of this odd little household. And she
had managed affairs for her two brothers and for herself.
She had kept them under her thumb. If she had grown a bit
hard and too short-sighted, perhaps, it could be charged to all
the anxieties with which her young shoulders had been loaded.
Steve had escaped from her influence to a large degree. And
the result was that Steve had been arrested for a serious crime,
and now he was threatened with a prison sentence, which fact,
she well knew, would make him desperate. If any prison walls
were able to hold him, he would come forth from the time of
his sentence a thoroughly terrible criminal. Oliver, she now
felt, was perilously near to following in the same pathway. And
standing in the doorway, watching him disappear, she made up
her mind that she would gather all of her strength, and she
would keep Oliver safe. And if there were any choice to be
made between Steve and Oliver, she knew that her younger
brother was the better and the stronger man. Him she must
save. Even if it meant the necessity of throwing poor Steve
away!

But, ah, how savagely she wished, now, that one of the
Tucker brothers had been able to shoot a little quicker and
straighter and so have put an end to the formidable youth
who had just crossed her path like a shadow!

But if she thought that her note would definitely turn back
David Apperley, she was greatly mistaken.

He read the little letter and blood rushed hotly into his
head, and he could feel an aching pulse in his throat.

Then he sat down by the window where the wind could get to his face and cool him a little. There he strove to think the matter out. And yet the more he thought of it, the more tangled it seemed to become. For there was no doubt that she had intended to use him as the instrument which might soften the fate of her brother. Certainly that was a thing which he might have accomplished as no other man could have done. Beyond that, what motive could have influenced her to change her mind? Did she think that Steve was about to be freed?

The young lawyer looked across the street at the squat, impressive lines of the little jail, with the heavy bars and crossbars which closed in its windows.

Finally he said to himself that it was very doubtful if she believed in a jail break for the sake of Steve. Then what remained that could have made her change her plans? What was there in the world that she held more dear than her brother's safety?

"Something very strange has happened!" said he to himself.

Straightway he went across to the court to open the proceedings against Steve Grange.

For this was the scheduled first day of the trial, and it was to be spent in selecting the jurymen. Against him, there was a stout, florid-faced attorney with a windy eloquence and patently a very small knowledge of the law. He was apt to spring to his feet and bawl out a loud objection at the slightest provocation. He seemed more bent upon impressing the courtroom and his client with his talent and his strength of throat than upon directing his energies at the judge.

David, quietly taking the measure of the other, felt that he was definitely the master. His own voice grew quieter and quieter; his own objections and remarks became fewer and fewer. Presently he had created the atmosphere that he really cared not at all what jurymen were selected for this case—so long as the jury was selected quickly. It made an impression on the judge, on the jurymen as they were gathered, and, above all, it made an impression upon the spectators. And behind David Apperley, ever obscurely to be seen among the shadows of a corner, was young Single Jack Deems with the wolf dog crouched at his feet.

So, that day, the jury was selected, and nearly every man on it, David felt, was willing to listen to him ten times as readily as to the other attorney. He almost felt a twinge of remorse to think that poor Hester Grange was spending her money on such a fellow! However, he had a grim satisfaction in showing her that he was the master of the situation! Now let her regret that she had changed that evening's appointment!

So thought David Apperley, in the brightness of the day, and he reached the evening with a sense of strength and of triumph. But the moment that the shadows gathered, there was a change, and he told himself that it would have been better if he had made more inquiries. He hardly knew what could have caused Hester to change her mind, but as the evening gathered there was a melting of his heart, and the coming of the stars made him remember with a sweet and ghostly clearness the smile and the beauty of Hester Grange.

Suppose that he were to saunter down past her house—there would be nothing wrong in that—and if he should see her on the lawn and enter into a bit of a conversation with her—

As he turned the corner of the street, full of this musing, he heard a light, quick step before him—and there he stood face to face with Hester herself.

19.   Deserted!

You may be sure that he colored; you may be sure that she herself turned a little pale, but she would have gone on with a smile and a nod, had he not turned suddenly upon her and said:

"You mustn't go by like this!"

94

She lingered. He could see that she did not wish to remain near him, the knowledge irritated and bewildered him. She who had been so clinging, so helpless, so full of faith in him that morning!

"You'll have to tell me what's happened!" said he. "You've had trouble of some kind—and you changed your mind about talking over your affairs with me this evening?"

"I—" she began. And then she said: "I can't explain. I'm sorry, but I can't explain!" and she could not help rushing on to say: "But oh, believe me! I never needed to talk to you more than I do now!"

"Then talk, child, talk!" said he.

"I cannot! I've talked too much, already!"

"You? In the name of Heaven, what have you said?"

"He doesn't want me to talk to you at all!" she breathed, and hurried off.

He turned about and stared after her in utter bewilderment.

Who dared to forbid her to talk with him? Who made it perilous for her to have any conversation with him?

He followed the direction in which her glance had traveled when she said that she dared not stay to talk any longer, and at first he could see nothing except the shadows beneath a long sweep of cottonwood trees down the street. But then, among the shadows, he saw something else—the barely perceptible forms of the wolf dog, and of young Single Jack Deems.

Rage and astonishment stormed wildly into his brain. Could Single Jack have dared to speak to this girl? Dared to forbid her to talk with him—with David Apperley?

He almost ran to the spot where the pair were loitering.

"Deems!"

"Yes?" said the mild voice.

"Deems, have you been talking with Miss Grange?"

There was a bit of hesitation, and then: "Did she say so?"

"Not directly. No! But I was given to understand that it was not pleasing to you if I talked with her. I was given to

95

understand that you yourself let her draw that deduction! Deems, is there anything in it?"

There was no answer.

"I say, man!" exclaimed the lawyer. "Is there anything in it?"

Still there was no response.

Suddenly the beautiful face of Hester, flushed and sad and appealing as it had been that same morning, crossed the vision of David Apperley, and fury rushed from his brain to his heart. This was the fellow who dared to stand between him and that dearest of women.

"Deems," said he, "I'm a calm man. I'm a very calm man. But I have never heard of such intolerable insolence—"

"Wait a moment," broke in the quiet voice of Single Jack. "I don't want to hear any more of this."

"You don't want to hear? Confound you, Deems, are you drunk?"

He became aware that Single Jack had drawn a little closer to him, and the ghostly wolf dog strode closer also, and its eyes were eyes of fire.

"I'll let you alone. I'll let you die. I'll let you rot, you fool!" said Single Jack. "Good-by!"

Suddenly he was drifting away from the shadows again, with Comanche skulking at his heels. Then the dog bounded shoulder high beside his master, as though he had been touched by the electric spark of happiness to see Single Jack freed from his service work.

The lawyer watched them departing with a good deal of awe, and now that the back of Deems was turned upon him, he felt a sudden sense of naked weakness. How greatly Deems had supported him through the first days in Yeoville, David himself had never guessed before. But he could see now what it had meant to have behind him always the formidable skill of this strange gun fighter, this crafty destroyer of men. A hundred weapons had been paralyzed because Single Jack lurked in the background!

Now that shield was about to be withdrawn from David Apperley!

It sobered him so completely that he forgot for the moment about Hester Grange, except to remember an old maxim, which declares that women are the root of all evil.

He sat for a time in his office, scowling at the heap of papers before him. That office was in a changed atmosphere, now. Before, it had been simply a place of work. But now it was like a trap. He had had enemies from the first in this town. But if they came here, they would know that they came not only where he was, but where Single Jack was also—and that was a distinction which made a great difference. A very great difference indeed!

Suddenly he felt that he had made such a mistake that he must take direct steps to undo it. He hurried out into the night air, intending to seek Deems. The first place to look was in the hotel.

There he went and asked of the clerk if Single Jack were then in his room.

"Deems just went off with his blanket roll," said the clerk. "I thought that maybe you had sent him away. No?"

The clerk's eyes narrowed, and a glimmer of evil light came into them—he who had always been so fawningly polite! No, even the hotel clerk no longer feared, in fact, hardly respected this lawyer from whom the shield of Achilles had been withdrawn.

Surely never did a man so quickly and so thoroughly repent a hot-headed action as did David Apperley on this occasion. And, as he remembered the almost doglike fidelity with which the other had watched over and guarded him, a qualm touched his heart in another manner—a new kind of pain!

He went slowly back into the street.

But all the while he was steeling himself and squaring his shoulders. After all, he had done very well when he did not know how invaluable was the guardianship of young Deems. He had got on well enough depending upon himself and looking upon Single Jack simply as a vast encumbrance. He must return to that state again! He must see through the battle to the end, because, since he was an Apperley, it must be impossible for him to retreat.

So decided David Apperley, and his strength was renewed by his own courage. And yet—if he had only thought to use a little more patience with Single Jack, to inquire into his motives—

Even that regret grew dim, a moment later. Somewhere a door opened in a nearby house, and a drift of girlish laughter floated out through the still heart of the night. It left a tingle of pain and pleasure in the breast of Mr. Apperley and suddenly the picture of Hester Grange leaped into brightness before his mind's eye once more.

After all, had not that other decision to which he had come been a fair one? It would do no harm to saunter down toward the cottage where Hester Grange lived, and if he found her on the lawn in the cool of the evening, a few words with her—

He turned his face that way. His heart was lighter than ever. He was swinging along with a confident step when a man driving past in a buckboard called out: "Hello! Apperley?"

"Yes, this is Apperley."

"I'm Dunstan."

"Hello, Dunstan!"

He turned into the street and shook the iron hand of the old cattleman.

"Look here, Apperley, what's the great trouble?"

"Trouble?"

"Yes. You and Deems."

"Ah? Nothing to talk about."

"You even sent him away from you, I understand!"

"I had to let him go."

There was a moment of silence, and then the rancher went on:

"I wonder if you'd like to spend a few days out at my ranch? Or stay as long as you like! When you have to come to town, I could send in some of my punchers to take care of you."

"Confound it, Dunstan, I'm not a baby. I can take care of myself! I've spent a good many years hunting. I know a rifle. I can handle a revolver, too, and if any of the men in this town think that I'm afraid to show my face without a gun fighter behind me, they're mistaken, and I'll prove it to them with bullets, if I have to!"

"There, there!" murmured Dunstan. "No one doubts your nerve. They all know that you're an Apperley. And they all know the stuff that your brother is made of. Only—don't you want to think over what I say?"

"I can't do it. I'd be ashamed—"

"Better be a little bit ashamed than a great deal dead, Apperley!"

"Perhaps, but not for me. Besides, I'm not afraid! I'm ready for them."

"Ah, man—well, you're your own best judge. But I want you to keep up your good work in this town. Good night, then."

"Thank you for your kindness, Dunstan. Good night!"

The buckboard rolled off through the night.

Mr. Apperley looked after it for a moment, frowning in the greatest indecision. He glanced over his shoulder. He never had looked back in the other days, for he could always make sure that his back would be guarded. Now he was defenseless from the rear.

20.   Shodress Talks to His Henchmen

In the meantime, the news flew by magic to the ears of the fat boss of Yeoville. And big Shodress could hardly believe in tidings so pleasant. But he wasted no time. In the back rooms of his hotel, busy with cards and bad whiskey, there were sure to be a few rough fellows at all hours of the day and most of the hours of the night. He went into that section of his domain, now, and glanced over the wreckage of the gambling room. Wreckage was the only word for it. Once a month, if not oftener, that room was the scene of a free-for-all fight in which chairs were tossed about promiscuously and guns blazed. This occurred when some member of the party had been caught in a manipulation of the cards, not altogether unquestionable. For some time Shodress had attempted to maintain the good condition of his game room in spite of these domestic wars, but the cost was too great. He started to repair the damage with bailing wire and rope. So the place was filled now with tied-together chairs and tables which leaned on rickety legs as though anxious to fall for the hundredth time to the floor.

There were half a dozen men now in the room, three of them playing penny-ante poker, and three sitting gloomily looking on. The professional eye of Mr. Shodress told him instantly that the three who looked on were inactive merely because they were broke. He scanned them with inquiring eyes.

He never forgot faces, and these were well known to him. They were three weather-beaten wild ones who had made various parts of the globe too hot to hold them, so that at last, like wasps driven by hot smoke, they were forced into the one remaining haven of quiet where their virtues would be appreciated more than anywhere else and where their vices would be instantly forgiven.

In a word, they had come to Yeoville, and there instantly they had come into the service of its lord, the fat, and clever, and monstrously rich Alexander Shodress. And, since the work that was to be done for him was almost infinitely great, so also was his need of men.

He employed them at once, in various ways. Dan McGruder, with his red face covered with blond bristles of unshaven beard, his blue eyes popping out, and with his buck teeth pushing back his lips in a continual unconscious smile, had been dispatched forthwith upon the trail of a pair of Mexican ruffians who, a day or so before, had raided the place of a shepherd in the employ of the great Shodress. The dark, greasy fellow, Lefty Mandell, had the simpler task of hunting down a card sharper who had just passed through Yeoville, collected some money by nefarious tricks, and ridden hastily out again. The third man was Hank Westover, a very long, thin man, with great joints and thin shanks. He had been added to a posse of cow hunters which was about to voyage away through the hills in search of cattle, preferably the cows of Andrew Apperley.

All three had acquitted themselves admirably at the very first essay. When the posse of rustlers was surprised in the midst of its work by a yelling, charging, raging band of Apperley's indignant cowpunchers, Hank Westover had dropped to the rear, seeking orders from no one but his own intelligence. Taking shelter behind some rocks which crowned the ragged top of a hill, he had sent a bullet through the shoulder of the leader of the cowpunchers, and thereafter he fought with such a clever and fast-shooting rear-guard action that the punchers were foiled and beaten off with the cost of another wounded man, while Westover leisurely rode away through the hills and rejoined his comrades.

Lefty Mandell followed a twisting trail for five days and found the gambler at work in a valley town. Lefty watched the fellow clean the pockets of the crowd around his crooked faro layout. Then Lefty stuck him up in the quiet of a back alley and took away from him all his money, his guns, and his faro layout. Then, taking the crooked gambler's horse for a full measure of revenge, he galloped away and carried his spoil to his new master, without attempting to steal a single penny of the sum which was in his possession.

To Dan McGruder had been assigned the most terrible task of all. He went after the Mexicans, found a hot trail, and at the end of the second day, he rushed down and collared them both. But they showed fight. He killed one, but was himself twice wounded.

He crawled away into the hills, nursed his own wounds back to health, and once more dauntlessly took up the long-cold trail. But he knew that he had crippled the Mexican almost as badly as he himself had been done for. For a month he wandered south, following idle hints in the place of real, tangible clues, until at length, following his own nose, he rode straight up to the man he wanted. The Mexican was seated in the door of a house, in the Mexican half of a little cow town. The guns spoke one word on either side. The Mexican leaned out from the doorsill and dropped full length and face down in the thick, velvety dust, and Mr. McGruder, having watched the smoke float off up to the heavens, turned back on the home trail, very worthily pleased with himself.

These were the three chosen spirits who were watching the progress of the game of penny-ante when Mr. Shodress entered the game room. He called them away and talked to them in an empty corner of the barroom, over glasses of red, evil whiskey.

"Boys," he said, "I've got on hand an easy job. Single Jack has quit his job. You know that?"

They nodded.

"Then the track is cleared. You go and get that puppy, David Apperley."

Westover and Lefty Mandell pushed back their chairs with grunts, tossed off the rest of their whiskey, and stood up at once. But Dan McGruder, his buck teeth bared and his lips grinning even a little more than usual, shook his head with vigor.

"What's the matter, Dan?" asked Westover. "You ain't afraid of that tenderfoot, are you?"

Dan had established his own repute for valor so very clearly that he did not even choose to deny this suggestion. But he said with emphasis:

"Most jobs, I don't mind, but I don't want no newspaper work in mine!"

"What do you mean by newspaper work?" asked Shodress.

"I mean the sort of stuff that gets a man into the headlines. I don't mind going after the scalp of a greaser or an Indian. You know that. And I'll take any card crook or gun fighter that has a white skin, too! But to hit the trail after a decent gent, and a fellow that stands for law and order, and that ain't done nothing low-down and mean—why that's different. I may be a gun fighter, but I'm not any murderer!"

This speech was made with such violent earnestness that the two companions of the gun fighter stared widely and admiringly at him. Then Hank Westover's Adam's apple rose and fell in much agitation while a thought worked into his bullet head.

"Now blame me if you ain't right," declaimed Hank. "When a gent gets mixed up with a killing that brings out the reporters as thick as bees after honey, then it's about time for him to wear a loose collar, because it ain't gonna be long before his neck will be stretched!"

Mr. Shodress listened to this talk with a great deal more emotion than he cared to show, and his bright, ratty eyes flicked back and forth from face to face. They were his superiors in downright honesty, but he felt that he would enslave them still by his superior cunning. He said: "Boys, you think that this David Apperley is a square shooter?"

"He is," answered Dan McGruder without hesitation. "I've seen that gent. He's got a clean eye. He looks right down to your backbone, and no mistake. He's kind of up and lofty, but he means well. And he's got a square shooter for a brother, too!"

If Andrew Apperley had been there to hear this tribute to his brother, he would have been a glad man, indeed.

"I'll ask you this," snapped Shodress. "Do you know Steve Grange?"

"Sure, I know Steve. Him and me have rode a good many trails together. He's a fine lad, that Steve. Wild as a tiger, though."

"Yes," said Shodress, "wild and mean and ornery and low-down is what they say Steve is!"

"Do they?" exclaimed Dan McGruder, his dangerous smile increasing in width, while his prominent teeth glistened. "I'd like to catch hold of the rat that dared to pass remarks like that about my bunkie. There ain't no more poison in Steve than there is in mush and milk. He'd give you the shirt off his back, and he'd fight till he died for any man that he liked."

"Wait a minute," interrupted Shodress. "You can't mean what you say. You're wrong about one of the two things. Because you say that both Apperley and Steve Grange is fine fellows. But they can't be, because Apperley is trying to put your bunkie in prison. That ain't all. In prison, Steve Grange is gonna go crazy. It's all that they can do now to keep him from tearing his way through the walls of the jail, he hates being locked up so bad. And when they try to take him to a penitentiary, there'll be the devil to pay. Is that right?"

Mr. McGruder was silenced by this crossfire, whereat Shodress cleverly took him in reverse with the following remark: "And will Apperley ever rest until he's put his man behind the bars? No, you don't know him if you think that he will! He's like a bulldog, when it comes to freezing to his hold, and he's never going to stop until he's got poor Steve in stripes. And that's the same as shooting Steve through the head. You know that. He'll fight his way clear, or he'll die trying!"

Dan McGruder acknowledged the truth of this by saying, as he rose to his feet, "Shodress, I never seen the truth of this until you explained it to us so clear, just now. And I'm obliged to you. I'll go find Apperley myself!"

"Boys," cried Alec Shodress, delighted, "you ain't going to be forgotten for this job. And if it makes talk, I'll see that you're taken care of! At least, there won't be any Apperley to prosecute you in the court and buffalo that fool of a judge! I've got five hundred dollars ready for each of you the minute that you come back and tell me that the work is done!"

Five hundred dollars—more than a year's wages, for the sake of a moment's exercise of the trigger finger? Lefty Mandell and Westover grinned with pleasure, but Dan McGruder answered almost sadly: "I dunno that I'm in this game until I've talked with young Apperley. And if I'm in it, it's not for coin. If I took a penny, I'd be a murderer. But if I shoot Apperley, it'll be because I'm the friend of Steve Grange!"

"I'll remember that," said Shodress, with respect in his manner. "And I'll see that Steve hears what you've said!"

21.   Death's Messengers

No man can tell what would have happened had not the three been led by the singularly unerring instinct of Mr. Dan McGruder. It carried him straight across from the front of the hotel, and down the main street, and then dipped him through a narrow alley and so onto the crooked, winding lane which skirted the edge of Yeoville. And coming down that winding way, now a hundred feet from the edge of the Grange garden, the three suddenly encountered Mr. David Apperley.

"It's him!" croaked Hank Westover. "I've got him, boys!"

But the lightning hand of Mr. Dan McGruder reached out and beat down the gun hand of his companion.

"We're gonna talk to him first," said he. "This ain't no murder party, Hank."

Hank Westover snarled. "There was never any good in talking first and shooting afterwards!" he said.

Perhaps there was a profound truth buried behind the words of Hank Westover, but McGruder did not pause to consider. David Apperley, having seen a flash of steel through the evening light—a flash which he rightly guessed to have been a drawn gun—had paused in his walk, and now he awaited developments, his right hand resting significantly upon his hip. To him went McGruder.

"Apperley," said he, "my name is Dan McGruder. I want to talk to you a minute about a bunkie of mine. I mean about Steve Grange."

"What have you to say," asked David Apperley, casting a

keen glance in the direction of the two who remained in the background.

"Don't you bother about them," said Dan. "They ain't gonna do you no harm. I'm here to talk things over with you peaceable, first!"

There might have been a good deal of gloomy meaning attributed to this speech, and David felt that he saw through it at a glance. He also felt that his time to die had probably come to him. But though he turned very white, and though life at that moment—particularly so near to the fragrance of the Grange garden—seemed peculiarly sweet to him, still he never thought of retreating, or of changing his attitude to one of conciliation.

"I can listen to you for a moment, McGruder," said he. "I suppose that Shodress sent you?"

"I'm talking for myself, and for nobody else."

"I'll give you this warning, McGruder. I know that you've come after me because Single Jack is no longer with me. You fellows think that I'm helpless with a gun. Well, I'm not. So much for that. Now what have you to say?"

You will see that the speeches of David were far from gentle, but McGruder did not take them amiss. He knew that this was a very brave man whose back was against a wall, and for his part, he was filled with nothing but admiration for the lawyer.

He could not help saying: "This is a tight squeeze for you, old-timer. I like the way that you're sassing us back. But I want to tell you that I ain't thinking about Single Jack. If he was with you, it'd make no difference; I'd say exactly what I'm gonna say now. I like you, Apperley. I'm for you. You got nerve, and that's what counts in this chunk of the country. But you're hounding a bunkie of mine to death. I mean Steve Grange!"

"Steve Grange!" echoed Mr. Apperley, and could not help glancing to the cottage. "Did she send you after me, too?"

"You mean Hester?" asked the other, with instant apprehension. "No. I ain't any messenger for a girl. I'm telling you that I've rode trail and rode range with Steve Grange, and that he's all right. I'm giving you that testimony outside of the court."

The mind of the lawyer could not help sifting this evidence and trying to find out what it was worth.

"You tell me what you know about Grange. I tell you what I know: which is simply that a herd of cattle belonging to Andrew Apperley were cut out and driven away by this man when he was surprised by five men and surrounded. Even against odds like that, he started to fight back—"

"Aye," said the other in a ringing voice, "there ain't any yellow in old Steve!"

"Like a desperado, he fought with perfect recklessness, regardless of his own life and the lives of the other men. One of his bullets went through the hat of a puncher; another clipped a hole through the side of a man's coat, and no doubt the third bullet would have brought down a victim. But just then his shooting was interrupted by a slug that struck him a glancing blow on the head and knocked him to the ground. That is the only reason we have Steve Grange before he had committed a murder or two! For all of these reasons, and partly, also, because we know that he's always been a proud, careless, free-swinging, gun-fighting cowboy, ready for a fight, and never very ready for work—"

"That's wrong," said the other, breaking in at once. "I've worked side by side with Steve. Nobody at a camp could ever call him lazy. He'll do his share of range riding in February, through the snow, and he never quit in August because it was hot. He ain't a welsher, any way that you look at it! I've bunked beside him. I've rode trail beside him. There was never a squarer shooter in the world."

"In a way," said David, "I think that you may be right. Heaven knows that I haven't the slightest feeling of malice against him. He's a brave fellow, and, in his own way, honest. But—he steals cattle, and he tries to kill people who want to stop the stealing. There's only one answer to that—the penitentiary!"

There was a little pause. The wind, stealing softly up the

street, rolled a small column of dust by, barely seen in the mingled starlight and dusk. It was like the form and the whisper of a passing ghost, and David knew that he was near to the end of his days!

"I got this to say," responded Mr. McGruder. "I ain't a head for fancy arguing and thinking things over. But I got to say that a friend is a friend, and I wouldn't give anything for a friend that wasn't ready to stand by me forever. Take you, Apperley. I like you. You're straight. You're a man. Gimme half a chance, and I'd be willing to talk for you just the way that I'd talk for Steve. But I say: Steve is my friend. I ask you will you please let him off of this bad job that he's got into? Because if you herd him into prison, he'll go mad!"

There was a great deal of moving emotion behind the voice of Dan McGruder, and his buck teeth glistened as his lips grinned back from them. So vast was his earnestness!

"There's nothing that I can do," said David Apperley. "He deserves the bars, and he's going behind them!"

"Apperley, you must change your mind!"

"I can't, McGruder. That's final."

A strong, full, high-pitched woman's voice broke into song that swelled up through the dusk from the Grange cottage. It was Hester singing in her garden, and it struck David Apperley as a most strange thing that the woman he loved should be singing so gayly and so near to him when he was about to die.

For in the grim face of the man before him, and in the sudden edging closer of the other two, he saw that the last moment was at hand. He wondered at himself, for feeling no more fear than he did. His brain was clear, crystal clear, and he felt that he could look deep, deep in the secrets of himself and of others.

He saw himself and the rigidity of his ideas, and how much of life he had missed, having failed to know that there is nothing really worth while except the work which a man can do. How shallow had been his insight into other men, especially into that grave, kind brother of his, whom he had treated so lightly. There was another man about whom he had made a mistake, and that was Single Jack. Just how great the mistake was, he did not know. Just what sort of a man Deems might be, he could not guess. But the sudden peril in which the flight of Deems had placed him, made him realize how vast a power had been in his employ when Deems was with him.

There was only a second for such thoughts.

Then a horseman turned sharply into the winding street and swung toward them at a full gallop.

"Dan!" sang out Hank Westover.

"Well?"

"There's someone coming."

"Let him come. I'm busy."

"Dan, I think it's—I think that it's Single Jack!"

"What?"

Dan McGruder cast a hasty and frightened glance over his shoulder in the direction of the approaching horseman.

The road was too shadowy for them to make him out clearly. It could only be seen that he was riding in great haste.

"Westover! Mandell! Who is it?"

"Aw, I dunno, but it might be him. Finish off, McGruder!"

"Apperley," said McGruder, savage with haste, "here's your last chance to change your mind!"

"I'll never do that!"

"It's Single Jack!" chimed in Westover. "I can see the wolf dog! He's coming fast!"

For answer, a revolver glittered in the hand of Dan McGruder. David Apperley whipped out his own gun with such an explosion of nervous energy that he actually got off the first shot. However, it flew wild, and before he could shoot again, he felt a shock and a sense of numbness in his breast. His balance grew unsteady. Then two weapons boomed in the hands of the pair at his side, and David Apperley was struck to the earth.

Hoofs rushed up and seemed about to trample him. But they

were checked just short of the spot where he lay, and the clear, cutting voice of Single Jack was in his ear.

"Who did it? Apperley! It's Deems! Who did it?"

"McGruder, Westover, Mandell," answered the young lawyer slowly. "I heard all their names distinctly."

"McGruder, Westover, Mandell. I'll remember. Where's the pain?"

"They've finished me, as they said they would. They've shot me three times through the body, Single Jack, and any one of the bullets would account for me! I need a minister rather than a doctor. Get me one!"

"We'll see about a minister afterwards. We want light for you, the first thing!"

He was a slender fellow, this Single Jack, and yet he was able to stoop and lift the body of the lawyer lightly in his arms; and he half ran with his wounded man down the street and into the nearest house—which was the house of Hester Grange. She came running into the hall.

"I've brought you your murdered man," said Single Jack.

22.   Deems and the Law

They laid him on Hester's own bed, and while her shrill voice sent young Oliver racing away for the doctor, Single Jack ripped away the clothes from the upper part of David's body and laid bare three wounds.

Trembling, Hester came in with hot water in a basin. Deems raised his dark face and looked across the body of the wounded man with a meaning glance. The girl grew from a red to sudden white.

"Do you think that I planned this terrible thing?" she asked him.

"I don't think," said the other. "But he's a dying man. And he was mobbed by three of Shodress' crooks right under the shadow of your house. And as soon as he's dead, I start out to collect payment for him. And I begin with the men of the house!"

He was busily washing the wounds as he spoke; then the doctor entered and took the case into his professional hands. They assisted him, moving hastily as he barked rough orders. He was probing the wounds.

"Two clean through him—two clean through!" said the doctor. "And here is—"

He turned the body of the senseless lawyer on its face, made a shallow incision in the back, and removed a big, misshapen slug of lead.

Then the bandaging of those wounds commenced with a swift, rough hand.

"He will live? He will live?" breathed Hester Grange.

"Is he a friend of yours?"

"No."

"Well, then, it won't make so much difference to you. He'll die along about three or four in the morning, most likely. That's the time when the endurance sags. He's maybe got one chance in a hundred to last till the sun comes up— Hello! Are you off?"

Single Jack paused in the doorway.

"I have business," said he. Then to Hester, "I want to speak to you before I go."

Hester Grange came hastily up to him.

"I know what you want to say," said she, trembling violently. "But I didn't have a thing to do with it! Never! Never! Do you think that I would stand by and see them make a trap for a man—three against one?"

The lips of Mr. Deems twisted suddenly and violently.

"How you lie!" said he. "So easily! You could murder a man one minute and smile at his mother the next. I tell you, I'm cold-blooded, and I've known some of the worst of the world in that way, but you go in a class by yourself, with your baby face and your wickedness all locked up behind your pretty eyes. You baby, blue-eyed devil! What a good thing it would be for the world if I sent a slug through your brain and stopped it ticking out trouble for more men!"

He spoke these things with deliberate coolness, but she could see that he was shaken with a terrible passion. A sort of white insanity lived in his face, and made his eyes seem darker and bigger than ever. But they had at last become lighted, and with such a fire as she hoped never to see again.

She could not speak to him. She could only watch, completely enchanted by terror.

"I've stood up to some clever ones, but it took you to beat me, tie my hands, make a fool of me," said Single Jack. "I'm going out now to get the three dogs that pulled him down. But after I get 'em, I'm going to come back to this town and find your brother Oliver. Maybe Steve will be out of jail, too, now that you've got Apperley off the job of prosecuting the case. In that case, I'll have both of 'em before me. I'm telling you beforehand. I want you to have something to look forward to. And every day you can pray that there'll be an end to me. But there won't be an end. I'm coming back here like poison to finish my job!"

He turned on his heel and hurried from the place, but not straight from the town.

He went first to the hotel. As he came through the doorway, a whisper went far and wide on the veranda, and sped through the building. Single Jack had returned, and Single Jack in a most singular mood. There was not a vestige of color in his face. Looking at it, you would have thought that all of the blood had been drained from his body.

He went straight across the lobby and sat down at the table where some cheap stationery was always available.

Just over the table, against the wall, there was a long, narrow mirror. From one corner, through which a rifle bullet had clipped long ago, a number of cracks spread across the face of the glass. But nevertheless there was a wide reflection which was capable of showing most of what happened in the room behind him. Besides, the wolf dog stood guard at the back of his master, and watched all that passed with a restless eye.

So though many men passed back and forth across the room, and though perhaps all of them were greatly tempted to try for name and fame by taking a shot at the slender youth whose back was turned, yet no one had quite sufficient daring to make the attempt.

Single Jack was writing.

Dear Mr. Apperley: Your brother David has just been shot down by three of Shodress' men. The doctor says that he cannot live till the morning. He would never have been touched if I could have stayed with him. It was my fault that he went down.

Shodress, like a cur, when he found that he couldn't beat us with men, got a woman. He had Hester Grange work on your brother until he lost his wits about her. I threatened her and made her promise to see him no more. But when he got wind of the fact that I was behind the thing, he was very angry with me. We had some words, and I left him.

When I got out on the road a mile from Yeoville, I remembered that I had given you a promise, and that I'd taken Comanche as advance payment for my contract, and that I'd quit my job without any notice to you!

I turned around and rode back into town as fast as I could come, and just in time to see three men shoot down a fourth. The fourth was David.

I took him into the Grange house—you see, he had started back toward it as soon as I left, and he had walked into a trap which that fiend of a girl had laid for him.

Of all the devils in the world, man or woman, she's the most complete!

McGruder, Westover, and Mandell are the names of the three who killed David. I'm off on their trail, now. I'm only going to wait to take a shot at Shodress. Then I'm away. I've tried to go straight, out here. I've walked a line, and now I see that it's no good. The thing for me to do is to play my own hand, and I am going to plant at least one row in the cemetery to make them pay for your brother's death.

There's nothing more for me to say. I admit that I was to blame. But I'll give you so much revenge that you won't know what to do with it.   Deems.

He signed and sealed and stamped that letter and was passing out across the lobby when he saw the fat bulk of Shodress in a doorway not far off. Just in the act of finishing a talk with Mr. Shodress was a short, stocky man wearing a derby hat which seemed out of place in Yeoville. The rest of his attire was instantly printed in detail upon the mind of Single Jack. There was a pair of broad-toed shoes, designed specially for a man who has to be much upon his feet. There was a neat blue suit. There was a turned-over collar and a narrow, four-in-hand tie.

This fellow advanced across the floor and nodded to Single Jack.

"Deems," he said, "I've come for you!"

And he added: "Don't move! This hand in my coat pocket has a little cannon trained on your heart, my boy, and I'd a sight rather handle you dead than living!"

"You've got me," assented Single Jack without emotion. And he added: "I suppose that Shodress called you out onto my trail, didn't he?"

"The big boy has a pair of eyes in his head. And he seems to be the only man in this part of the world that has enough sense to read the papers and put two and two together. I'll have to split twenty thousand with him, on this job!"

"Have they put my price up there?"

"Get your hands up, you sap! Do you think I'm kidding you?"

Slowly the hands of Mr. Deems rose along his sides and crept higher and higher up his body toward his head. The detective watched him like a hawk.

"You're Cranston of Newark," said Single Jack.

"Hello! What do you know about me?"

"I keep my eyes on the wise ones," said Single Jack. "And I've been hoping for a long time that they wouldn't have sense enough to put you on my trail."

"You have! Hey, keep those hands well away from your shoulders, kid, and get them up fast! Fast!"

So snapped the detective, Cranston, watching all the time with an eye that missed not a quiver of the fingers of Single Jack.

Other men were watching with equal interest. And the loud voice of the great Shodress was heard in the background saying: "When I sent for that dick, I didn't dream that he could nab the great Single Jack without firing a shot. But you see yourselves! We've been buffaloed by a bluffer. The Tuckers must have been drunk the day that he dropped them!"

Other men stared, with popping eyes, incredulous of what they saw, not trusting their own powers of vision.

"All right, Cranston," said Single Jack. "You win!"

For, though he had been fighting himself for seconds, he had now pushed his hands well up above the line of his shoulders, so that he was in the most awkward possible position for snatching a gun from that most favorite hiding place—the armpit. As the detective noted this fact, his keen vigilance relaxed a little, and he nodded with satisfaction. That instant the right thumb of Deems hooked in under his collar and caught the line of a very thin strip of braided horsehair. A twist of the hand whipped up from his shirt what hung at the end of the tiny lariat, and that was a two-barreled, old-fashioned derringer which snapped into his hand.

Too late the detective saw the move and leaped to one side with a shout, pulling the trigger of his pocket gun blindly. The unerring hand of Single Jack, firing even shoulder high, sent a raking shot plunging down into the body of Cranston, and the hand of the law had failed again! Single Jack was triumphant.

23. Comanche Takes the Trail

That Cranston was a brave and a clever man, let no one deny, for even as he sprawled on the floor, gasping and groaning, he snatched the short-nosed revolver from the pocket where he had already fired it once in vain, and strove to plant a better-aimed bullet in the heart of his arch-enemy. The toe of the boot of Single Jack anticipated him and knocked the weapon from his fingers.

More than that bullet and kick Mr. Deems did not bestow upon the detective, except to say calmly to the other man:

"You lucky rat! If I'd fired a half inch lower, you'd be a dead man by this time, Cranston!"

Then he leaped across the lobby with a wonderful speed, and raced straight through the doorway where the fat form of Alec Shodress had been leaning only the moment before.

The great Alec was not down that hallway, however. But the wolf dog, fleeing ahead, scratched frantically at a door half a dozen paces away.

Single Jack needed no other hint. He smashed the lock of that door with a heavy bullet, while a hoarse shout of fear from stentorian lungs within the chamber told him that he was on the right track.

He kicked open the door, and Comanche bounded ahead of him. He had only an instant's vision of the flying coat tails of Mr. Shodress as the boss of Yeoville dropped through the window down the wall of his hotel, while the white, swordlike teeth of the wolf slashed just near enough to rip away half the back of his coat.

Single Jack, rushing with gleaming eyes to that window,

leaned out, his revolver balanced for the finishing shot with which he would break the back of Yeoville's master.

Bad luck was with him! Just beneath that window there was a door, and through that door the great Alexander was crawling. Deems had sight only of the last foot being hastily drawn into cover. Even at that small target he tried a quick shot.

There was a wild screech from beneath him, and then he saw on the ground the heel and sole of a shoe, badly mangled by the force of the bullet which had just torn them off. However, there was no blood, and so he knew that Shodress had escaped unscathed from that shot.

There was still a chance, however, that he could catch the big man. Through the window went Single Jack, and, leaping to the ground, he sprang at a heavy door just as it was being swung shut. His shoulder struck it an instant after the latch had clicked, and as he recoiled and flung himself at it once more, he heard a ponderous bolt cast home.

Once, twice, and again he fanned rapid bullets into the lock of the door, but the lock was as formidable as the door to a jail. It was of solid steel, and broad and thick, and all his bullets accomplished was to wedge in and lodge firmly in the interior mechanism of the lock.

He drew back a little, and as he did so, the long, shining barrel of a rifle was thrust through a barred lower window. He leaped back into the shelter of the wall just in time to escape a whistling slug. More voices constantly sounded, and from within the hotel there was the thundering shout of Mr. Shodress, as he marshaled his men in his defense against his enemy.

Perhaps you will say that people should have stood back, in Yeoville, and allowed this single-handed fighter a chance to work out his own destiny without being checked by numbers. As a matter of fact, such was usually Yeoville's policy. But Single Jack was different, and the cruel efficiency with which he handled his weapons had convinced all men that he should be regarded as though he were a whole company of warriors. Verily, a host in himself.

At any rate, here was a score or more of excited, heavily armed men on the alert to kill young Mr. Deems at that moment, and he saw that his fate was not to take him to the death of Shodress on this day, at least.

Straight beside the wall of the hotel he ran, and, darting off into the street, he had half a dozen shots fired at him as he crossed the open space.

But it was thick night, now, and though there was enough mingled star-shine and lamplight to discover him as a target, still he was safe enough so long as he kept moving, and that was exactly what he intended to do.

He had left his horse behind him, but that was a small matter. Yeoville at least owed to him a horse and saddle, according to his determination. So he picked out the likeliest of those which stood tethered before the store, at the hitching rack. In was a clean-limbed bay. Single Jack climbed into the saddle and started on down the street at a raking gallop.

He swung into the open trail beyond the town; behind him, there was an increasing turmoil, voices and lights danced in the heart of Yeoville, and now there was a confused mustering of horses.

He drew rein suddenly, and turning in the saddle, he put up his naked revolver and drew from the saddle holster the rifle which he found there. It was a fifteen-shot Winchester. By the weight of it, he knew that it was loaded to the brim. By the feel of the mechanism, he knew that the working parts were all in order. By the gleam of the barrel, he could tell that the chances were great that this was a new, straight-shooting weapon.

Then let them charge out of the town after him if they dared! The wolf smile was curling on his lips as he waited!

Now there were some wise heads in Yeoville who said that well enough should be let alone, and that enough had been done in driving Single Jack from their midst without the loss of a single life—since Cranston seemed likely to live. They refrained from listening to the great clamor which Mr. Shodress raised, as he urged his followers to take the trail and instantly erase this man-killer from the landscape.

But there were younger and hotter bloods who did listen to Mr. Shodress. They had seen Deems flee, and just as even little house dogs will chase a great, ranging wolf, so these youths tumbled into their saddles and rushed out of Yeoville and down the road along which they had seen him disappear.

Six abreast, whipping up their horses, driving deep their spurs, swinging their hats, filled with joy by the night wind in their faces, and braced by a sense of the power of numbers and the invincibility of their charge, the first of them tore around the bend of the road out of Yeoville, and there they saw a solitary horseman seated with a steady rifle at his shoulder, and a bead of starlight sitting like a dim diamond upon the rifle's upper edge.

Each youngster in that procession could honestly swear that he had seen that deadly rifle aimed straight at his heart. They did not wait for the explosion of the gun. With wild yells, they piled to the right and to the left away from the path of that fatal weapon, and sheltered themselves in a tangled, swarming, cursing, shouting mass among the trees.

Single Jack had not fired, and he did not fire now. Sliding the lucky rifle back into the long holster, he turned the head of the bay and jogged up the road in a leisurely fashion. Much noise still arose behind him, but they did not venture anything further. They let him journey along unmolested, quite unaware that they were making Yeoville a laughing-stock to all the towns in the mountains. For it would be many a day before the rest of the range would forget how Yeoville, so bold and so famous for its hardy badness, had allowed its beard to be not only twitched but literally jerked by a single man—and a tenderfoot, at that!

Single Jack, you may be sure, had no thought of that. All of his heart was now bent before him down the trail, and he rode with his mind filled with doubts.

Had he been in the cities of the East, among the myriads of alleys and by-lanes, he would have known well enough how to conduct himself, and what clues to look for, but here it was all different.

He came to a forking of the road, about three miles out from the edge of the town. There he dismounted, and with a lighted match he examined the hoofprints on the forking, with little hope that he might be able to know the right way.

That which held straight forward, indeed, he discovered to be blurred by the sign of a score or more of horses, but that which turned to the right carried the tracks of only three.

He waited to see no more. His heart told him at once that these were the three men he wanted, and as he swung into the saddle again, the wolf dog darted ahead and began to follow the road, head pitched well forward and a little down, as though he were really reading the news of the trails with his nose.

Here was a matchless leader, to be sure; here was a trailer born and bred in the wilderness, and the heart of the master leaped with satisfaction and with confidence.

Another brace of miles, and they struck across a broad road deeply scored with wheels, and covered with the sign of cattle and horses. The wolf dog did not hesitate, but turned instantly down the road, and in half a mile, darted to the side and leaped through the wires of a fence.

Mr. Deems was no expert horseman, but he did not hesitate to follow such a leader. He gave his fine bay the spurs, and the splendid animal soared suddenly into the air.

Single Jack felt as though his back were jerked in two, and as though a strong hand had caught him by the shoulders and tried to jerk him out of the saddle, but he managed to stick in his place and come down on the farther side of the fence without so much as losing a stirrup. Then he was streaking away across the field with the wolf dog hot at his work in the lead. Clever the quarry that escaped that trailer.

Now and then the big creature would turn and make a little circle back toward the rider, then scurry off again to show the way, as though it were trying with all its might to hurry the avenger along this freshening trail.

Very gladly Mr. Deems rode by that guidance as though following a light from Heaven, and so they worked hard across the country, with the bay horse now laboring and gasping like a dog for breath, but sticking valiantly to its work.

Then, between a dark-headed wood and a curve of gleaming water, where a stream ran around the shoulder of a hill, Single Jack saw first a long ray of light, and next, behind this, the pointed roof of a little shack. To the very door of this shack, the wolf dog slunk, and Single Jack knew, as he saw the monster crouching there, that he had come to the end of his quest.

24. Two Out of Three

He dismounted at the edge of the trees and left the horse there, with the reins hanging, for he knew that a well-trained cow pony would not stir from the spot if the reins were left in this fashion. After that, he paused an instant to pat the sleek, sweat-polished neck of the pony. The little horse tossed its head and pricked its ears under the kind touch. It was a new experience for Deems to find any creature that loved him merely because it had worked for him without hire or reward; and he was looking back over his shoulder with a smile as he left the trees and started toward the house. There was work to be done here.

First, keeping carefully to cover, as though it were broad daylight and faces were watching him from every window of the place, he laid a circle around the house, with Comanche working ahead of him with busy nose, and tail thrust out straight behind. All the ground around the shack was fairly cleared, but to the rear there was a small shed, and at the entrance to it, the wolf dog came to a stand and then sank to a crouching position.

It was a sufficient advertisement to Single Jack that here he must proceed carefully. He slipped up to the open door, and peering into the blackness of the interior, he counted five horses. He could smell the rankness of sweat through the little barn, but to make his assurance doubly sure, he entered and touched the horses one by one. Two were dry and had not worked. Three were dripping. And now he was sure that he had his men.

So he turned back to the shack.

The sky above him was patched with clouds which had recently blown over its face. Only here and there the small rain of stars was sprinkled, and he was not displeased to have little light abroad. He took note of that, and then of all the lay of the land, so that he could tell where the fences stood, and where it would be best to ride in case of any emergency.

After that, he slipped up to the unshuttered window. Merely by rising to his tiptoes he could look through, and he saw within five men seated around a table at the eternal game of poker. Each man of the five, loaded with weapons, looked fit to fight for his life against any champion. He regarded them with an infinite satisfaction. In two minutes he had their names in order. Westover, McGruder and Mandell were the three on the right side of the table, and Pete and Sam Wallis sat on the other side. They were the hosts, and the game flourished until McGruder tossed down his cards exclaiming: "That breaks me the second time today. I'm done!"

He pushed back his chair and rolled a cigarette.

"I've had enough, too," said Pete Wallis, a large and dignified man. "Now, you fellows unbuckle your guns and make yourselves at home."

McGruder and the other pair looked at one another and smiled.

"We ain't parting with our gats," they informed their hosts.

"Look here," said Sam Wallis, younger and more eager than his brother, "what sort of a game is up?"

"Tell 'em, McGruder," said Westover.

"We got Dave Apperley," said McGruder, without triumph —for which the listener outside the window gave him a favorable mark—"and now we're lying low."

"You got Apperley—Andy's brother? Andy'll make the range howl until he's even with you!"

"Even?" said McGruder gloomily. "I dunno that if he killed the whole three of us, he'd have the worth of a fine young gent like David."

"Hello! What the deuce, Dan?"

"Leave me be," growled Dan McGruder.

"This job rides him," explained Westover yawning. "But I'm glad that we done the trick. It means something to the old man, you know. Besides, what a crust for a fool tenderfoot to come to Yeoville to run things!"

"What about Deems? You mean that you got him, too?"

"No, I don't mean that! You would've heard us shout about that first," explained Westover. "Fact is, Deems split with Apperley, and that gave us a clean shot."

"Then what chased you out of town after the job?"

"Not Deems. We seen somebody coming down the street that looked like it might be Deems and his dog, but we didn't wait to see. I wanted to stay in Yeoville. So did old Mandell, here. But McGruder wouldn't listen to us. Suppose that Deems was to change his mind and come gunning for us? That was the way he was always putting it."

"And suppose that he did?" said Sam Wallis. "Can any one get the three of you?"

"No, but he might get two," explained McGruder.

Sam Wallis grunted and scowled at the floor, but his older brother put in: "They're right. You'll understand that when you get older, kid. Trouble with Sam is that he thinks there's nothing worth while except fighting. He'd fight a bull, if it dared to shake its horns at him! But you got to understand, kid, that it ain't right to pick trouble, or even to wait for trouble, with a slick hand like this Single Jack. I hear that he's got a long record behind him that has just showed up."

"The chief got a detective out to look him over," said Mc-Gruder. "I dunno how it turned out. All I know is that Deems is the kind of poison that I keep away from. Hand me that coffeepot!"

He poured out a steaming tin of coffee.

"I'm gonna step out and see how the ponies are cooling out," said Westover. "We certainly burned up the road."

"Why?" asked Sam Wallis, still gloomily doubtful of these three.

"Because we had a chill down our backs in the idea that Deems might've changed his mind about being no friend of young Apperley. We thought that he might possibly be following down our trail."

"How would he follow your trail through a dark night?" asked Sam Wallis, more and more aggressive in his doubt.

"Don't ask how, kid," said his brother. "It ain't what a gent is likely to do that counts, it's what he might do, either by good sense or self, or chance. That's the way that you got to figger. Are you going, Westover?"

"Yes."

"Chuck a forkful of hay to my pinto mare, will you?"

"Sure."

The door was cast open by Mr. Westover, and at the same time the broad, bright hand of the lamplight pushed against the face of Single Jack Deems and glittered in the eyes of the wolf dog beside him.

"How's the night turning outside?" asked Dan McGruder from within.

"Deems!" screamed Westover and tore out his gun.

A slug of lead struck him in the breast and knocked him backward, staggering. The Colt dropped from his extended hand and struck with a crash against the floor. So he reeled, dead on his feet, until he struck the table and sent it down behind him, the lamp toppling with it.

But in the meantime, a shadow crossed the doorway. Four revolvers instantly poured a flood of lead at it, but the shadow had crossed again instantly to the farther side of the door. Only, as the shadow leaped across the opening, a single tongue of flame darted from the mouth of a leveled revolver, and Lefty Mandell curled up on the floor just as the lamp, striking the wall, went out with a tinkling of broken glass.

Blackness had swallowed the interior of the shack, and in that darkness there was groaning.

"Get out of this place!" cried Dan McGruder. "He'll be in here, and I think that he can see in the dark! I know he can!"

Suddenly feet scratched on the floor of the shack.

"The wolf! God, he's got me!" shrieked McGruder.

For a great body had loomed against the shadowy black of the place, and McGruder, throwing up his arm in defense, felt it slashed from wrist to elbow.

At the same time, Sam Wallis, quite forgetting all his desire for battle, had burst open the rear door of the shack and all three of the men leaped into the sheltering open of the night, firing at wild random behind them.

They were not safe. Behind them, lying low in the doorway, was Single Jack, eyes glittering, and revolver ready, but he could not distinguish one from the other, now, and rather than pour his fire into the wrong man, he let them go. They ran wildly for the darkness of the trees, with Comanche bounding behind them.

A call from Single Jack brought the big creature back to him.

Then he let the fugitives go, for he saw that it would be the sheerest folly to follow them into the covert of the trees by night. Instead, he turned back, and with the light of a match he saw Westover lying face up, dead on the floor, while Mandell was curled in a knot, gasping and groaning.

"Are you a goner, man?" asked Single Jack, kneeling without pity at the side of the wounded cowpuncher.

"I'm done," said Mandell.

"Let me see!"

He ripped the shirt away. One glance at the wound sufficed.

"You could get up and ride a horse now," said Single Jack

coldly. "That slug just glanced around your ribs instead of ripping through your heart, the way that I intended. Keep your head level. Tie a bandage around your body after you wash the cut. You'll come through all right, and when you're back on your feet, I'll come and call on you again. So long!"

He was gone through the door, and Mandell pushed himself up on his hands and looked after the victor, bewildered. Beyond the door, he could see the faroff glimmer of the stars close to the horizon. A sudden thankfulness that life was still permitted to be with him surged through the heart of the wounded man.

Then, far off, he heard a faint sound of hoofs, and after that the wild, long-drawn howl of a wolf on the trail—a dismal sound.

"Is he after the rest of 'em?" gasped Mandell. "Then Heaven help 'em!"

He waited and listened again, but there was no sound.

Then he fumbled for matches, found them, and lighted some dry tinder on the hearth of the open fireplace. By that light he set about following the instructions of Deems to clean and bandage his hurt, and with shaking hands he completed that business. Still, from without, there was no sign of the routed three returning and Mandell did not wonder.

Utter silence now. Then, from the far edge of the world, again the smooth, melancholy howl of a wolf, sounding through the night.

25. Action on All Fronts

After this, things began to happen so rapidly that Yeoville must be looked upon as a sort of storm center rather than as a mere focus for attention. In the first place, there was

Andrew Apperley. He heard first a sharp-edged rumor that David was dead. Then he received a letter from David that caused him serious apprehension, and immediately after that there arrived the note which Single Jack had written from the hotel in Yeoville and in which he announced the shooting down of David.

Then Andrew Apperley prepared for action.

First of all, he sent out a call through his foreman to all of his lieutenants. He gathered in his cowpunchers, all except a skeleton force who were to remain on the range and take care of the cows that were there. These were the least sure shots, the least dashing riders.

At the same time, a hurried call was sent around among the neighboring ranchers and the small squatters who had everywhere experienced his kindness and generosity to a greater or lesser degree.

There was a general response. While this work of half a day was in progress, a fast rider was cutting south toward the railroad. He carried a very important dispatch to be telegraphed to Washington, asking for protection from one of Apperley's friends there, should the deeds which he hoped to be about to perform call down some sort of government action upon his head. By noon, the force was mustered and swung into the saddles.

There were seventy-five hardy fellows in that band, when Apperley and his foreman, Les Briggs, counted them over. When they themselves were added to the force, it made just over four score, and as Andrew Apperley surveyed the column, each man equipped with at least one pair of Colts, and each and every man armed with a good repeating rifle, usually a Winchester, he was fairly sure that the doomsday of Yeoville had arrived.

So they sat forward, and they rode at a smart pace through the hills, and followed the winding trail toward the distant domains of Alexander Shodress, with Apperley ever in the lead, his face set, and his eyes dull, so great was the misery of his inner spirit.

But in the meantime we must look right and left and high and low to see what was happening in Yeoville with Shodress and the rest.

First we see the great Alec Shodress in person calling upon Doctor Myers. This doctor had the case of young Apperley in hand, and he now was the subject of Shodress' conversation.

"Doc," said the fat man, "does Apperley live or die?"

"A toss-up," said the doctor.

"Now listen to me," said Shodress. "You've been getting on fairly well in this town, ain't you?"

"Gettin' on fine," said the other.

"And my friends have been going to you right along?"

"Sure," said the doctor, "and the men they've been shooting up."

"Right," said Shodress. "You're getting prosperous. I'm glad of that. I like to see a friendly young man getting on in the world. Nothing would please me more than to have you keep right on climbing up in the world. Now tell me, in the first place, how is young Apperley getting on? Tell me really!"

"He's a dead man," said the doctor calmly, for he was not a youth, that doctor, to be moved by the miseries of others. "He's a dead man. He ought to have been worm food days ago. But the reason that he keeps up is because that girl won't let him die. She's laid her hands on his soul, as you might say. I've seen her talk three degrees off his fever in three minutes!"

"You don't say!"

"Yes, I do. But it's not so queer. Maybe he's sweet on her. I've seen such things. Mostly, though, when a mother is fighting for a baby's life. You wouldn't believe what a mother can do by way of cheating death, Alec!"

"Mothers," said Mr. Shodress, "are all right in their own place, but their place ain't in Yeoville. Now I'll tell you what, my young friend, it's awkward as the devil, this boy hanging onto his life, that way. Very awkward! Suppose that he was to come to and recite the names of the gents that plugged him? All friends of mine, as you know. Well, Myers, it wouldn't be so sweet for me, as maybe you can guess!"

"I can guess it, well enough," agreed the doctor. "They might even have you up for assisting at a murder, eh? But what d'you want me to do?"

"Look here. This Apperley is right on the edge of the dropping off place, ain't he?"

"More than that. He's halfway down the edge."

"Doc, suppose that you was just to lay a hand on his shoulder and give a little push—to sort of assist nature along!"

The doctor turned full around and looked Shodress in the face, and then they both nodded, for each understood and appreciated just what sort of a man the other was. Faint smiles appeared upon their lips.

"Well?" said Doctor Myers.

"I don't know," said Shodress. "It ain't the hard cash that counts. It's the good will. There's that other doctor—Goodrich. Suppose that I was to pass a bad word around among the boys about him? They might even escort him out of the town and leave you the field to yourself. And you could double your rates!"

"I wish they'd ride him on a rail!" snarled Yeoville's other doctor. "I hate him. He's called me a quack, and a poisoner. Did you know that? There's only one trouble about this job, though. Can I get back into the house of Grange?"

"Get there? Why not?"

"That girl don't like me. She won't have me around. Partly because she don't think I've treated this Apperley careful enough, and partly, maybe, because I patted her hand, the other day."

He grinned again, and Shodress shook his head.

"You step soft and light in that direction around here, young man," said he, "because if the boys had anything real against you in that line, even me, I couldn't help you much!"

"I'll change all that," said the other calmly. "I'll change all of that. You won't have any fault to find with me. And if I can talk my way into the house—"

"If Goodrich is carted out of town, she'll have to let you in."

"That's true."

"Then Goodrich is gone, right now!"

Turn to the outskirts of the town and see a ragged man on a staggering horse riding in and falling off his horse at the first house and asking for a drink of whiskey, in the name of Heaven.

They looked at him with amazement and with horror.

"Who are you?"

"I'm one of Shodress' special men. I'm Dan McGruder. There's Charley Patrick. Charley! Gimme a hand!"

Charley Patrick came running.

He received his friend and passed an arm beneath his shoulders.

"What in the world has happened to you, Dan?"

"Single Jack happened to me."

"But there was with you old sureshot Westover and there was that devil Mandell, too."

"I can't talk. Gimme whiskey. I been through hell for five days!"

They laid him on the veranda with a coat rolled under his head. They gave him some whiskey, and then he asked for food, and devoured a great chunk of cold boiled ham.

After that, some strength seemed to flow back into his exhausted body, and he braced his shoulders against the wall of the house and cursed feebly. His face was thin; his eyes were bloodshot; his clothes were in tatters, and his nerves were so completely gone that his lips trembled almost too violently to allow him to frame speech.

Finally, his swollen right arm was bound around with a mass of rags by way of bandages.

"I say, there was Westover and there was Mandell with you, old fellow. What's become of them?"

"They've gone to the devil."

A violent fit of shuddering seized upon the body of Mr. McGruder.

"What happened?"

"I can't think about it!"

"It'll do you good to talk it out!"

"Maybe! We three hit for the Wallis shack. And that first night, Single Jack jumped us—"

"Who was with him?"

"Alone. Except that he had the devil along; and he killed Westover the first crack out of the box, and then he dropped Mandell with a slug through the body, as near as I could make out. And then, with the lamp out, him and the wolf tore into us in the dark of the room, and Comanche give me this!"

He pointed to his bandaged arm.

"Then we broke away through the back door and got loose, though I never could understand why that devil didn't chase us into the ground, right then."

"But he came along behind us, soon enough. He run us down into the Big Silver marshes. I lost the Wallis boys there. For three days I lived there with him following—"

He shuddered.

"Gimme another shot at that whiskey!" he said.

They held the whiskey flask to his lips. Then he raised himself to his feet.

"Where's Shodress? One of you show me the way to him. I don't want to be alone. Not even in the streets of this here town. I don't ever want to be alone again, as long as I live!"

26. Two Drops of Colorless Liquid

In the dusk of the day, Doctor Rudolf Myers went toward the Grange cottage. The doctor preferred, as a rule, to make his professional calls before or after daylight, because so long as the sun is shining, there is sure to be a modicum of hope; but in the dark all that is terrible and unknown, including the fear of death, comes more intimately close to us, and the whisper which in the sunshine we know is merely the wind in the leaves, becomes at night a wordless prophecy of evil—a vague forewarning of doom.

Doctor Myers was acutely aware of these things, and so he chose to be idle in the day and busy when the shadows began. For this very reason he approached the Grange cottage in the dusk. He was swinging his stick—because he affected the manners of a gentleman newly out of the East—and whistling now and again to Jerry, the great mastiff which jogged ahead of him, wandering from side to side of the path, sniffing old trails. Doctor Myers was a little afraid to carry a gun, lest he might be called upon to use it, but he had bought a man-killing dog in the belief that this would be a sufficient protection. And he had never had occasion to regret his choice, for though Jerry was a stupid and intractable beast, at least he was a splendid warrior.

The doctor, having come within view of the Grange house, paused to adjust his thoughts to the thing which he was about to do, and to admire the glistening yellow rays of the lamp which shone through the open front window of the cottage. In the past of Doctor Myers there were various unsavory affairs which the world had frowned upon, but there was nothing quite on a par with the deed which he was now prepared to do.

He fingered the little vial in the pocket of his vest. It contained a colorless liquid, nearly odorless, except that it might leave in the air a faint aroma of crushed peach pits. And yet a drop or two in a glass of water would finish the case of young David Apperley, and at a stroke, win Doctor Myers the lasting friendship of Shodress. That accomplished, his fortune was made.

That very afternoon, he had had the pleasure of seeing a riotous crowd of the Shodress cowpunchers whirl down the street, harrying his rival, Goodrich, out of Yeoville. And by the panic-stricken, enraged look on the face of that physician, Myers could guess that he would not soon return.

There followed, in due course, a message from the Grange cottage. Young Oliver had come to him with a word that the other doctor was no longer available, and that they would need the presence of Doctor Myers. Would he come at once?

He was very sorry—pressing work to do—but as soon as he could manage it, he would arrive.

And so he was arriving, several hours late, and now he lighted a cigarette and steadied his nerves by reviewing the facts of the case. There is nothing so soothing to the nerves and so destructive of apprehensions as lifting one's head and examining the actual facts. And what were they?

In yonder cottage lay a young man wounded terribly in three places by bullets which had been fired from expert hands at close range. It was only miraculous that David Apperley had lived so long. And what more natural than that his strength should suddenly fail, that a convulsion should seize upon him, and that his heart should stop its functioning?

If, afterward, there was that faint, faint fragrance of crushed peach pits perceptible about his lips, who was there in Yeoville capable of identifying the odor? Certainly no one except that same Doctor Goodrich who had been escorted out of town in such a providential haste!

This reasoning was flawless, and before the cigarette was half consumed, the doctor knew just what he was to do, and exactly how he would do it. He had faced the consequences, and he was not afraid.

So he started ahead, and as he did so, he suddenly became aware that Jerry had strayed far from him. He whistled anxiously. There was no response. He had last seen the big brute wandering off aimlessly among the trees toward the cottage, and he himself now hurried in that direction.

He had not gone fifty yards before he stumbled over something lying in the path. It was not a fallen log, because it gave a little under the impact of his toe.

He leaned to stare. It was the body of a dead dog—it was the body of Jerry!

The hair bristled upon the head of the doctor. The slayer of the mastiff must be his enemy. The dog had been removed to clear the way for the destruction of the master!

Doctor Myers was on the point of taking to his heels, and bolting from the trees toward the street. But he checked the impulse of panic and delayed his flight to light a match and examine the body.

There was no mystery about the death of Jerry. His throat was torn open horribly wide. The doctor looked closer. The slashing had been done by huge, tearing teeth; such teeth as it was hideous even to think of! It seemed as though this must have been the bite of a tiger.

And were there tigers prowling through the brush near Yeoville?

Doctor Myers, at least, had seen enough to make him scurry back to the street, and when he arrived there, he ran out into the middle of the thoroughfare and paused, his breath gone, and his eyes rolling in his head.

But he made sure that he was not followed. Then he steadied himself and merely stammered through his teeth:

"Twenty-five dollars thrown to the devil!"

For that was the price he had paid for poor Jerry.

Then he went ahead toward the Grange cottage, and now with a heightened resolution, for he felt spitefully that the world owed him a good deal. It had stolen from him the life of a dog. Why should he not make rejoinder by stealing from it the life of a man?

The idea pleased him much.

At the front door, he tapped lightly and waited, summoning his most professional air of gravity.

Lovely Hester Grange let him in, and she exclaimed with impatient relief when she saw him:

"We've waited for hours and hours."

"Unfortunately, my hands were very full," said the doctor. "Now let me see the patient. How is he?"

"The dressing has to be changed. Doctor Goodrich told me that I must never do it alone. And now he's gone! What fools! How could they have driven such a man from Yeoville! Will you come in at once? He's restless and in a good deal of pain."

"We'll soon have him right," said the doctor, and went into the sick room.

It was the best room in the cottage, and the most spacious, but nevertheless it seemed shabby enough and small enough. And in the bed lay young David Apperley, his face white and thin, and his eyes surrounded with great blue circles, like the shadow of coming death.

He opened his eyes and looked at the doctor without speaking; then closed the lids again, and Doctor Myers knew what that meant. This was no nervous and whining invalid. This was a man who was bent upon conserving every atom of his strength of body and mind to regain his health. He was fighting. And the miracle of his continued existence could be attributed to that iron will constantly at work.

The doctor felt the pulse. It was not strong, but it was not blurred or stammering, and when he had counted the breathing and noted the temperature, he was certain that this man was not to die today, in the natural course of events. Nor tomorrow, either. He would live on until he was healed, unless something unforeseen happened. And Doctor Myers nodded his wise, wicked head in satisfaction. It was plain that he would be earning the praise of the great Shodress.

But first he set about changing the dressing, and he managed it with such skill of hand and such tenderness and speed of touch, that Hester Grange, who stood by frowning and ready to criticize—for she did not trust this physician—could not help murmuring in admiration, for it seemed as though Doctor Myers were thrice as skillful as Doctor Goodrich had been.

When the dressing was changed, a faint smile appeared on the lips of the patient.

"I'm going to do well with you," Apperley said softly, and he closed his eyes again.

"You have his confidence!" whispered the girl, and she smiled upon him so brightly and kindly that the doctor looked at her again.

She was much changed from what she had been. Her color

was faded. Her face was thin, and the shadows of watching were beneath her eyes. Men said that day and night she was never for thirty seconds away from the sick bed.

Doctor Myers now held out a glass of water into which, openly, he had dropped two minims of colorless liquid.

"This will give him a good night," said he.

"Shall I give it to him at once?"

"Yes. Or perhaps a little later. When he's ready to sleep."

"I'll let him have it now."

She went to the bed and slipped her arm beneath the patient's head.

"There's only a little, David. Not much to swallow. Are you ready?"

"Yes."

"Not quite ready," said a voice from the doorway of the room. And they turned and saw standing there that much-dreaded and much-hunted criminal, Single Jack himself.

27. What the Doctor Wrote

Then Doctor Myers did what the bravest and most conservative citizen of Yeoville would probably have done under similar circumstances. He threw his arms above his head and backed against the wall.

"Oh," he moaned, "have you come for me?"

"Not at all," said Single Jack. "But I've had to learn a bit about the care of wounds. That drink—I suppose it's a bromide to quiet the nerves of Apperley?"

The doctor could not answer.

"Get a pen and ink and paper," said Single Jack.

The girl hastily and silently obeyed.

"Take the pen, Myers, and begin writing. Shodress offered you money to do this, didn't he?"

Myers moistened his white, dry lips and looked at Deems with a dull eye.

"It's the main fault of Shodress, I know," said Single Jack. "And here's your chance to place the blame where it belongs. Do you understand, Myers?"

Myers looked at him wildly. Then he seized the pen.

"I never would have thought of it!" he almost shouted. "It's that murdering devil of a Shodress that made me do it. He made me do it!"

"Of course he did," said Single Jack more gently than ever. "What have you to gain by poisoning Apperley? But just write down the details, and begin with the price that he was to pay."

Doctor Myers beat his fist against his forehead.

"Not a penny, really. He was just going to run Goodrich out of the town, so that I could get the practice! That was all he was going to do! And for that—"

He made a gesture of despair.

"Write it down," said Single Jack quietly. "That's what we want!"

And the doctor began to write, slowly and haltingly, at first, but then with a gathering impetus, as though he were gradually warming to his work. At length his eager temperament had mastered him altogether, and he was pouring forth in many words every detail of all that had passed between him and Alexander Shodress concerning the convenient removal of Apperley from this vale of tears.

Whether there was anything terrible and shameful in this confession did not seem to occur to the worthy doctor, after he had warmed to his epistle. He was only concerned in making the villain Shodress the root of all evil, in this matter, and as the pages flowed off his active, scratching pen, Single Jack and the girl read them.

They found enough to make their eyes lift, now and then, and meet—the girl's eyes sometimes ablaze with hot indignation and sometimes with cold horror, and the eyes of Deems always inscrutably dark and deep.

The doctor had thrown himself into this work of confession with such violence that twice the nib was broken by his vigorous and sweeping strokes, and twice he had to be refreshed before he could continue.

Single Jack, from a flask in his pocket, poured forth a good stiff dram of the liquor and placed it at the elbow of the man of medicine; and the latter, while he wrote, sipped the brandy with enjoyment. He ceased to be a doctor; he became a literary artist. Tears of self-pity rose to his eyes as he described the manner in which Alexander Shodress had inveigled him into taking a part in this detestable affair.

When, at last, the work was finished, Doctor Myers leaned suddenly back in his chair and pushed away paper and pen, after the manner of one who has completed a hearty and full meal.

"That's done with, and Shodress is done with, also!" he declared.

"Yes," said Single Jack, "if only we're able to bring him to trial for it. But you won't be here to witness against him. We'll have only this paper of yours. By the way, Hester, just sign this as a witness, will you?"

"Not be here? I wouldn't miss that trial for a million dollars!"

"Wouldn't you?" Single Jack grinned. "However, if you stay in this town, you can depend on it that Shodress will have you put away very shortly."

"Shodress? How could he learn about this?"

"He learns everything, sooner or later. He can't help it. Every pair of ears in the town belongs to him. That door onto the garden has been open all the while, and if anyone were out there, every word we've said could have been overheard."

The poor doctor turned from red to white.

"And if I were you, I'd do what the rat does when it smells the cat."

"And what's that?"

"Run away as fast and as far as I could, Myers. And then find a hole, and get down into it as deep as you can go—and lie there trembling!"

28.   Crushed Peach Pits!

The good doctor blinked at the younger man. He glanced at Hester Grange, also, but what he saw in her face was such scorn and horror that he did not wish to look again.

He stood up. Comanche shrank nearer, with a soul-stirring growl.

"The wolf!" gasped Doctor Myers.

"It's all right," said Single Jack. "Here, Comanche."

The great beast leaped back and planted himself at the side of his master.

"Now get out!"

The doctor "got."

"Will you watch him?" breathed the girl. "He may try to sneak back and murder us both."

"Comanche is giving him all the watching that he'll need," said Jack Deems. "Look!"

For as the doctor made for the door, Comanche slipped unbidden at his heels, sniffing at each foot that Myers placed on the floor, and convulsive shudders rippled through the body of that poor victim.

At the door, the nerves of Myers gave way completely, and he leaped across the porch, tripped, and fell headlong into the great climbing rose bush. He arose with a yell of pain, as though a hundred cats had scratched him, and bolted for the street.

The pair in the Grange cottage listened with mirth to the

sound of the flight. Even Comanche, lolling beside the door, and running out his long, red tongue, seemed to be laughing.

"How could you guess what was happening?" asked the girl, forgetting Myers in her outburst of curiosity. "How could you guess? How often do you watch this house?"

"Off and on," said Jack Deems. "I come around now and then in order to see how Apperley is getting on. I have to do that, you know!"

She looked at him in fear and bewilderment.

"And what made you guess, when you saw this glass of water?"

"The face of the doc. He looked sort of smug and happy, as though he was tickled with what he was doing. And that started me guessing. By the make of him, I guessed that he'd be up to almost anything. And he was, you see. It didn't take many questions to get that out of him!"

The wolf dog stalked back from the door and lay down softly across its master's feet.

"Don't do that!" exclaimed Jack Deems sharply.

Comanche twisted his head up and around with flattened ears and eyes that asked what possibly could be wrong.

"Steady!" murmured Deems. "It's all right, then!"

He ran the tips of his fingers across the massive head of Comanche, and that great dog twitched from head to foot with pleasure.

"He'll have me in trouble this way, some time," explained Deems. "This is his favorite place, on my feet. And some day when I need to move fast, why, he may be in the worst possible place!"

She could understand what the other meant. For, hunted day and night by a thousand head hunters, at any moment Jack Deems might need all the strength and skill and agility of which he was capable; and the slightest encumbrance, or possibility of an encumbrance, might be the most deadly handicap to him.

"After all," she said with a laugh, "it's a rather tangled muddle. Shodress has been a friend of ours. You're the enemy of Shodress. And here you are shielding us as though this house were filled with your brothers and sisters."

She leaned forward, her lips parted a little, her eyes shining. "Tell me why you do it!"

"It's my job," he answered her, shrugging his shoulders.

But she shook her head.

"Suppose that I ask you why you take care of Apperley?" said Deems.

"To save his life—poor fellow!"

"You wanted him dead, and then you want him, alive again?"

"Wanted him dead? Who said I wanted him dead?"

"You laid a trap for him, as though he were a bird, and he walked into it, and your fellows shot him down!"

She started up from her chair, savage with indignation, but after a moment, she mastered herself.

"It's no use talking back to you," she said. "There's nothing but such devilish wickedness in you that you can't believe there's goodness in any other person."

Mr. Deems smiled upon her, that odd and impersonal smile which had no mirth in it whatever.

"It's no good," said he. "It's no good at all!" He held to his point.

Comanche rose and stood between his master and the girl, snarling silently at her, with his neck fur bristling.

"It's no good to tell you what I think of you?" she echoed. "No, you don't care. You know yourself, and that's enough. You don't care what the rest of the world thinks of you. Every man and woman detests you, and there's not even a child that doesn't hate you, and tremble at you, and you're so dyed in badness that you think there's no kindness existing!"

"You're cool," he said, canting his handsome head a little to one side and criticizing her without a change in his impersonal manner. "You're cool, and sharp, and clever, and you act well. If you were back East where the big-money crooks are working, you'd soon be teamed up with someone better than this Shodress, this cheap poisoner. But don't throw this bluff at me any longer. I know you. I've always known your kind."

"Know me?" she asked. "How could you?"

"I've seen you fish, and the waters you fish in, and the kind of bait that you use!"

"What do you mean by that?"

"I'll tell you how clever you are, though you know that already. When I first saw you, Hester, I almost believed in you. When I saw your big eyes and your smile and your dimple, I thought that for the first time in my life I was looking at a real woman. When I followed you down the street from the office of Apperley, it wasn't because I had more than a tenth of a doubt about you. It was only that I couldn't keep away. I wanted to see more of you. I wanted like the devil to see you smile again."

He laughed silently, to himself and at himself, as she could see.

"So I got to the cottage and I heard you talk to Oliver. And I had my eyes opened. But for half a minute I confess that I was more than done for. You had me giddy and dizzy. I was weak. I felt foolish for the first time in my life. But then I saw the truth. And I'll go one step farther. I'll admit that there are times when I find myself dreaming about you. Not really about you, but about what I thought you were. Then I open my eyes and see the facts—that you're the coldest-blooded man-trapper and crook that I've ever run across."

She listened to him with a flush burning in her face.

"Suppose that I wanted to have David Apperley dead," she said. "Why shouldn't I simply move the bandages a little, or dress the wounds clumsily? That's all that I would have to do! Or leave him alone during one night! That would finish him! Did you think of that?"

"Because you knew that I'd come back. Because you knew that the moment he dies, your brother Oliver follows him as fast as I can get at him!"

"But with the whole town raised against you, how could I ever expect that you'd dare to come back into Yeoville?"

The wolf dog glided to the door and looked out into the night. Then he turned and whined, but his master paid no heed, for he was thoroughly taken up in the conversation with the girl.

He nodded at her now.

"You're not as simple as that. You knew that I could slip in and out of this town," he told her.

"Nobody else in the world would dare to try it!" she exclaimed. "Nobody but you, for instance, would dare to stay here now, knowing that Doctor Myers may have run straight to Shodress to tell him that you're here—or have been here!"

"He'll never do that. By this time, Myers is riding out of Yeoville as fast as a horse can gallop, and he's only hoping that he can beat the men of Shodress to the railroad running East!"

She marveled at his calm and at his assurance.

The wolf dog slipped back to the side of his master and pulled at his sleeve.

"Coming, Comanche," said Jack Deems. "I only want to make sure of this stuff!"

He raised the glass of water to his nose and inhaled a slow breath. Then a faint glint of light came into his eyes.

"Smell this!" he told the girl.

Her hand was trembling with her anger and her excitement as she took the glass.

She, too, breathed the faint aroma which rose from it.

"What is it?" asked Deems.

"It smells—rather like crushed peach pits, I think. But I'm not sure. There's hardly any odor."

"You've hit it, though. That's exactly what the fragrance is like."

"Then what does it mean?"

"Prussic acid has that smell."

"Prussic acid!"

"And a moment after Apperley had tasted that stuff he would have died, in a good deal of pain. And quickly. Like

143

heart failure! That would have been the end of him. He's calling you, now!"

For a faint, hurried, troubled voice sounded from within the bedroom adjoining. The girl listened to it with a start, and then with a smile and a frown together.

"I'm going," she said. "I only want to ask you one question. How many thousands and thousands of dollars does Andrew Apperley pay to hire you to work so hard for his cause?"

"Dollars?" said the criminal, and then with his usual cold. smile he added: "He pays me with kindness and squareness, the first that I've ever known. I'm coming, Comanche!"

And he turned toward the door, while the girl stared after him, with more bewilderment than ever in her eyes.

29.   Five Hundred Strong!

Turmoil had spread through Yeoville a little earlier on this same day. It was not long before honest Doctor Myers started from his house to stroll toward the Grange cottage that a messenger on a sweating horse arrived at the hotel of Mr. Shodress and demanded admittance.

"Who are you?" asked the scowling hotel keeper.

"I'm Blagden, from up-country. I got some news that'll make the old man's hair stand on end. Where is he?"

"You wait here and take things easy. I'll find out if he wants to see you!"

"Hold on. Is this here Shodress turned into a fool rajah, or something? Can't a gent see him even when he's got big news?"

The hotel keeper regarded the messenger with a doubtful eye. But it seemed that this man was exactly the type of the true adherents to the fortune of Alexander Shodress. Here was the correct wild eye and reckless swing. Here was the squared fighting jaw and the pair of Colts swung low down on the thighs, just in twitching distance from the tips of the hanging fingers.

"I'll tell you the straight of it, partner," said he, in a lowered voice. "The old man don't like to have it talked about, but the fact is that he's nervous."

"Him? There ain't a nerve in his body!"

"Ain't there? Well, maybe there wasn't in the old days!"

"Old days? Man, I was with him a week ago."

"Sure, maybe you was. But since then, that devil Deems has been here and changed things a lot."

"Deems? I've heard about him. He shot up the Tuckers—"

"That? That was nothing. Only showed half the length of his claws, that day. But what we all remember about him now, is the soft-stepping, fire-breathing, straight-shooting devil that come for Alec Shodress right in his own town, and climbed right here into the hotel after him, and pretty near nailed him, too! And ever since that time, the old man has been a bit scary, and Heaven knows that he's had reason to be! And if he wasn't, the yarn that Dan McGruder tells would be enough to raise his hair."

"What yarn is that?"

"Where you been keeping yourself, man? The whole range ain't been talking about nothing else! I mean, how McGruder and Westover and Lefty Mandell—"

"I know 'em. Three mean gents!"

"How those three mean gents and the two Wallis boys— all five—was piled into by this devil, and how they was run ragged—and how—but what's the good? You wait and let poor Dan talk for himself. All I'll say is that the old man has a spot cash offer of ten thousand dollars for the scalp of Mr. Deems! And there's more money back East. He's got a record as long as a book. They say that there's another twenty thousand offered for him back yonder. Anyway—that'll explain the nerves in Alec. Now if you got bad news, you'll see that this is a poor time to break it to him!"

"I understand!" said the messenger. "But you tell the old

man that Blagden is here with word about Andy Apperley. That had ought to raise him, no matter what he's got on his mind. About Apperley and eighty men!"

"Eighty men!"

The proprietor favored his guest with one glance, half wildly startled and half quizzically doubtful. Then he fled to find the fat man.

A moment later he was shouting down the stairs: "Hey, Blagden!"

The latter hurried up and was shown into the private sanctum of the great Shodress, where Alexander himself sat in a pivot chair, with his huge flat feet hung upon the edge of his table, whose edges were deeply scarred by the old marks of burning cigarette butts.

"Blagden, how are you?"

"I'm fair. So's Andy Apperley."

"What's his move—and what's this nonsense about eighty men?"

"I counted 'em," said the other. "I counted 'em myself. I laid up behind the rim of a hill, and I turned my glass on 'em and I picked 'em off one by one. Eighty gents with more gats on 'em than an army would need, and all drifting this way!"

"It's young Dave," said Shodress. "He's heard how Dave got himself shot up brawling in the streets of this town. It's a shame, Blagden, that the Apperleys ain't contented with damning me black and trying to run me off of the range, but they got to come in here and start shooting up Yeoville. I say, it's a shame!"

"Sure it is," said Blagden, with a faint grin, for this was the usual attitude of Shodress. "They ain't got no conscience, particularly when they start in working on three men at a time —three fine, peaceable, quiet, upstanding gents like McGruder and Westover and Mandell."

Shodress sighed.

"And after that, the old hound hired a sort of a magician —a gun juggler—to murder me!"

"You mean Single Jack?"

"Yes! I'll never rest peaceful until I've downed that poison-ous rat! Now tell me about the eighty men—and Apperley! They were headed this way?"

"They were."

"How far off are they now?"

"I killed a hoss getting to you. But they can't be many miles back!"

Mr. Shodress rolled the cigar in his fat mouth and half closed his eyes.

When he opened them again, he was smiling upon both sides of the cigar, and the smile made a bulge of fat appear in either cheek.

"It ain't so bad, Blagden," said he. "It ain't really bad. I got to admit that it sort of sounds queer to me—because, between you and me, he's put himself right into my hands. I never thought that he would be fool enough to start a mob war. But now that he's done it, I'll wipe him right off the face of the earth! I ain't even going to leave the grease spot where he stood!"

He jumped up from the chair, and the floor quaked under his flabby weight.

"Wait a minute, Blagden. I want you. I need you! But first, there's the price of that horse. A good horse, wasn't it?"

Blagden shrugged his shoulders. "Just an Indian pony, Alec."

"No!" exclaimed the other. "Because it couldn't be any-thing worse than a thoroughbred that could bring me in such good news as this. It couldn't be! Here—you take this for the horse, will you?"

He snatched from his pocket a wallet stuffed with bills of large denomination and jerked out a number which he stuffed into the hand of Blagden.

"Well," said Blagden, "this is the best day's work that I've ever done."

"And then go down into my corrals and pick out the best-looking nag in 'em. That hoss belongs to you, kid. And get your saddle onto its back and be ready to ride quick. Y'understand?"

There was a wave of the hand. Blagden, quite overcome with gratitude and excitement at such good fortune, had set his jaw harder than ever, determined to show his gratitude by fighting to the death, if necessary, in this good cause.

He fled down the stairs, and behind him the voice of the fat man was thundering.

"Phil! Harry! Locke! Chalmers! Slim Jim!"

A pounding and rattling of feet answered from all parts of the house as the voice continued to thunder. And at last, as though mere vocal summons were not enough, Shodress jerked out his revolver and began to punch neat holes in the ceiling of the hall.

That roar of the gun brought others scurrying.

In the dimness of the hallway, there gathered around Shodress a dozen of his firmest adherents, his chosen gun fighters.

"Boys," he said to them with a ring in his voice, "you're riding, tonight, and I'm riding with you! I'm gonna show you that I ain't too fat for a saddle, and that I ain't too slow with a gun. And I'm going to wipe Andy Apperley off the range, tonight!"

There was such a joy in his throat that it choked him. And in the brief pause that he made, there was a stern murmur of excitement and content from the others.

Then he went on:

"How many people in Yeoville?"

"Near nine hundred," somebody answered.

"And how many grown-up men?"

"More'n five hundred."

"And how many that'll wear guns and shoot straight and ride hard for me?"

"Every man in Yeoville, chief!"

"Get out and scatter, all of you, and pass the word. Ride through every part of the town, and turn the boys out. It's the battle for all of us. And remember, once we start riding, that we got the clear and clean law on our side. There ain't no doubt about that. We got the law on our side. The fool started it first. The fool!"

Joy choked him again, and then he gasped: "Tell 'em their best horses; and rifles and Colts for every man. And everything in my corrals is free. And—get me young Chance. Tell him that I'm waiting for him in front of the hotel. And Steve Grange— oh, he's in jail. But what's the jail? There ain't any Apperley to stop me from running this town, now. Split the jail open like it was a tomato can and bring me Steve Grange here. And tell him on the way, and let the others know, that after we've smashed Apperley, we're gonna have some sweet picking on everything that used to be his on the range! Now get out, boys, and get fast! Every man for himself and me!"

They answered with a joyous shout, and in an instant they were swarming out upon their errand.

Who could have been more cheerful than they, at this moment? For they knew that they were riding out upon a trail on which they would have overwhelming odds in their favor, and three men to one, at the least, would be striking beside them against the doomed band of Andrew Apperley.

30.   Comanche Strikes!

Through Yeoville went a cyclone of confusion and noise. It reached the jail and put forth an eddying current which, like the arm of a tornado, smashed in the door and bowled over the frightened jailer.

There were two men in that jail as prisoners. One was a tattered, dirty tramp, jailed because he had made himself a public nuisance by asking through the streets for alms. After he was liberated, he had cringed in a corner until these bold, shouting men were gone. The other prisoner was Steve Grange, and he was hailed with enthusiastic voices, and a rifle and a pair of revolvers were thrust into his hands.

In another moment he was out on the street and mounted on the back of a good horse, capable of bearing his sturdy weight along.

A few seconds more, and that winged cavalcade was streaking out of Yeoville, and as they galloped, a kind moon rose in the east and showed them their way.

There had been no delay in gathering every possible recruit for the campaign. Now several hundred rough riders rushed from Yeoville with Alexander Shodress at their head. Not a man in that lot who had not been daily familiar with guns for many years. Not a man that did not know his horse well. Not a man that did not love a fight.

Otherwise, what would they have been doing in Yeoville among the ranks of the adherents of Alec Shodress?

He himself, mounted on a broad-hipped brown gelding, capable of bearing even his fat bulk, cantered in the lead, and his men were wild with enthusiasm at having him with them. They had almost forgotten the stories of that earlier and slenderer Shodress who had performed his share of deeds of daring along the range before increasing weight and power induced him to retire and leave his work to the hands of lighter and younger spirits.

Near Shodress went Steve Grange, with a hearty greeting from the big man:

"Steve, I'd rather have you with me tonight than any twenty men I know."

"Chief," said Steve with emotion, "I was beginning to go crazy in that jail!"

"Why, son," said the leader, "do you think that I'd ever have let you come to any harm there? No, I was simply waiting for the right time to get you out, and this is the night! What a fool Andy Apperley is. To start this business! To put his head in the lion's mouth! Why, Steve, we'll tear him to pieces!"

Steve Grange, looking back over the following host of riders that bobbed through the mist of their own dust, nodded with agreement and satisfaction, until he saw a horseman riding with a familiar lilt in the saddle.

He reined back instantly and was beside his brother, Oliver. The latter would have worked his way off, but he could not escape. He was hemmed in by the press of riders, and Steve, leaning from the saddle, shouted angrily:

"What are you doing here, kid?"

"I'm in the game!" answered Oliver. "I had to come!"

"Go back home, you fool!" called Steve. "Are you leaving Hester alone at a time like this?"

"She can take care of herself!"

"Oliver, you hear me? Go back!"

"I won't."

"Kid, there's going to be trouble before the sun comes up!"

"I'll be there for my share of it! I'm not worried!"

"You want to break Hester's heart! Go back or I'll make you!"

"You're not man enough to make me!"

For a moment, the pair glared at one another through the swirling dust, and then Steven Grange, realizing that his task was for the moment beyond his power, and that the boy was really committed definitely to this wild work, turned his horse and spurred up to the head of the procession again.

He was just in time to receive the command of a contingent of fifty men detailed to sweep down the right side of the broad valley through which they were riding. A similar number rode on the left. And with well more than a hundred men in the main body, big Shodress pursued his course along the center of Shingle Cañon.

It was narrowing rapidly, now, and soon there would be no possibility for the body under Apperley to slip through the massed horses from Yeoville.

And just now, far ahead, one of the leaders spied a solitary rider slipping rapidly over the brow of a hill and speeding away up the valley.

The news was broadcast at once.

"It's one of Apperley's outriders!" exclaimed big Shodress. "And he's turned back to tell his boss what is coming! There's five hundred dollars to the lad that rides down that devil!"

The word passed with a whoop, and a dozen of the lightest riders on the fastest horses whipped out in front and left the main body as though it were standing still.

The whole body of the men from Yeoville quickened their pace, and as they rode between the rocky, echoing walls of the gorge, they presently had a second sight of the fugitive. It was only a glimpse, but they could see their own men rapidly gaining upon the lone rider; and the next instant, as he slipped from view into a depression in the valley floor, they saw that he was not quite alone. There was another form beside the horse, a smaller, easily skimming body.

"It's the man with the wolf. It's Single Jack and Comanche!" shouted Shodress, suddenly going almost mad with excitement. "Now boys, we have him! There's one thing that he can't do, and that's ride a horse. Get him, and there's nothing that I won't give. He's worth any price!"

The tingling yells of the dozen in the lead were ample testimony that they too had recognized their quarry. They were redoubling their efforts, and being far better mounted, they gained hand over hand upon the other.

"I'd rather have that man dead than all the fools that are following Apperley, and Andy along with them. I'd rather have Single Jack dead, boys, than a million dollars in my wallet, because one of these days, either he kills me, or I kill him. I feel it in my bones!"

He did not need to talk further. All that was in the power of humans or of horseflesh was now being done to overtake the outrider who might bear the warning back to the main body of the Apperley host.

And then guns began to crack, and the ringing echoes flew back past the iron walls of the valley and clanged faintly from wall to wall over the heads of the riders.

They could see Single Jack's rifle flashing, now, and one

of his pursuers was down, and then another! It was long-range work, but such marksmanship as never had been seen in those mountains before.

"Will he get free? Will he get free?" groaned fat Shodress, seeing his leading group of hunters spread out in the shape of a fan, so that they might present a less united group target to their deadly foe.

"No," said one of Shodress' lieutenants. "Look at those boys ride. There ain't one of them that wouldn't risk his neck free and willing to have the glory of bringing down Single Jack! Look at 'em ride in!"

In fact, they went on gallantly, bending low over the necks of their horses, and now and then sending a shot after the outlaw in the hope of crippling either the rider or his horse. Luck was not with them. The distance was too great, and they were firing from the bobbing backs of galloping horses, a thing always fatal to marksmanship—except such uncanny craft as that of Single Jack.

But, brave as they were, they dared not rush in upon that deadly rifle. Instead, they pushed their racing horses to one side and then to the other in the hope of squeezing past Jack Deems and taking him from the flanks with a cross fire.

So the race was prolonged, while those in the rear checked their speed a little, and those on the sides urged their horses still more wildly forward.

A slight dimness overcast the mountains, for the moon was now blown behind a flying host of clouds which left it a dull and tarnished face, and the darkness beneath the valley walls became so great that Shodress' men could push in with little to fear from the rifle fire of Deems.

A shout of triumph came from all the riders of Yeoville. As for Andrew Apperley and his little army, they were well-nigh forgotten. This one rider was the arch-enemy.

All the rest, perhaps, might be considered velvet. And it hardly seemed to them unfair that so many should be matched against a single fighter—so enormously had the fame of Single Jack exaggerated his figure to heroic proportions!

Men said that he fired by instinct, and by instinct he could not fail to strike his target! And had they not witnessed, on this night, two spurts of flame from the muzzle of his rifle, and in answer, had not two stricken horses rolled on the floor of the valley and nearly broken the necks of their riders?

The wind scattered the clouds before the face of the moon again. Suddenly all the tawny veils were torn apart, and now the broad, yellow moon looked brightly down upon the mischief which was about to take place in those mountains.

Single Jack was indeed well back toward the others, now, but here an unexpected element was added to complicate the work. For two other riders, as the procession turned a corner of the valley, were seen to swing in beside Deems and to urge their nags along. They were the advanced outposts of the Apperley riders. Would Deems, then, gain the host in time?

A yell of disappointment and rage crashed up against the placid face of the smiling moon, and echo hurled the cry back again with a wailing close. But after that, all settled more fiercely than ever to the pursuit. For it was seen that the two new companions of Deems were upon horses which were very, very tired, or else they were of the very worst quality. No, it was far more likely that they were merely exhausted by the long march through the mountains, and therefore all the rest of the mounts of the Apperley men would be in the same condition. And the host of Yeoville was still whirled along in dust and triumph on fresh ponies.

No matter if Apperley received the warning, how could his little army escape from such a winged vengeance as this which was drawing out from the town?

Never was such a straining of horseflesh. Never was such a whir of quirts and such a jingling of spurs. Never was such a chorus of yips and yells as that procession made as it went up Shingle Cañon.

And if the fugitive three galloped hard, still they could not gallop hard enough. Faster and faster the Yeoville enthusiasts were gaining. Faster than ever, for now men marked with wonder that Single Jack did not press his mount to the limit, but reined it in to keep pace with his two new companions. Such good-fellowship was not to have been expected in him!

And yet, no matter for that. No matter what gave him into the hands of these head hunters, Heaven bless the cause! They wanted blood, and the blood money that went with it. And they were on the right trail.

Then a yell of horror passed through the whole band.

Upon the right hand, urging a fleet horse, some young cow-puncher was riding for fame and fortune so successfully that he had gained far before his friends and was drawing up fast upon the trio. He had unlimbered his rifle and was about to fire at point-blank range when a shadow swept behind him, and horse and rider rolled head over heels in the dust.

And the shadow loped away.

Comanche!

And what was it to the wolf dog except the easy ham-stringing of another horse?

31. Besieged!

If that deed of Comanche's seemed rather the work of the devil than of a mere dog, it put wonderful heart into the three riders down the valley. For here were Charley Johnson and Les Briggs, each on a horse that had been badly fagged by the hard work through the mountains, and particularly because they had had to push on ahead of the rest of the band. They were failing at every stride, now, and Les Briggs had just called to Charley that he could not keep going and kill his horse uselessly.

"I'll get in the rocks, there, and hold 'em back—"

"Talk sense, man," interrupted Charley Johnson. "They'll ride right over you!"

And then the shadowy Comanche had clipped in from the side and bowled over one of the leading riders of the pursuit.

It gave fresh heart to Johnson and to Briggs. Even their horses seemed to realize that a wonderful thing had been done in their behalf and they appeared to gallop a little more lightly.

But as they swung around the next curve of the long cañon, where the walls grew narrower and narrower, still the long vista ahead of them gave them no sight of the wished-for fighters of Apperley.

Yet, for that matter, what could Apperley and all his tired men have done against this horde from Yeoville? No, the essence of all success to the scheme of Andrew Apperley had been the silence and the secrecy of a surprise attack by night, and now that opportunity was hopelessly thrown away.

That overthrow of a horse and a man by a sneaking wolf, a mere gliding shadow, had checked the rush of the pursuit for an instant only. There were still nine men, and the odds were three to one in their favor, so they closed resolutely again, gaining at every jump of their straining ponies. In vain Johnson and Les Briggs wheeled in their saddles and emptied their repeating Winchesters. They struck no target but air and ground. Then, with the long arms of the Shodress riders fairly circling around them, Single Jack turned, and a lash of fire spurted from the end of his rifle.

There was a difference between this shooting and that of his two companions. One of the pursuers reined in his horse suddenly, cursing at the top of his voice with disappointment and fury and pain, for the rifle slug had whipped through his arm.

From the remaining eight there was a crashing volley in response, and the horse of Les Briggs sank to the ground.

He himself rolled staggering to his feet, and the next moment an arm strong as iron jerked him from his feet and drew him across the pommel of the saddle.

He looked up, amazed, into the face of young Jack Deems. Where had the strength been hidden in that slender body— where the power of hand which rendered the outlaw strong enough to perform such a feat?

But Single Jack was calling: "Johnson! Charley Johnson!"

"Aye!" yelled Johnson.

And the wild yells of the heartened pursuers rang in their ears.

"Ride straight ahead. Forget us. Go on and save yourself!"

"Never!"

"Apperley's men will all be lost then! Ride for their sakes! Get out of here!"

Charley Johnson called: "Briggs?"

"Go on, boy!" answered Briggs. "Go on, and God bless you! We'll take care of ourselves!"

And Charley Johnson urged his tired pony away from the horse of Deems, now staggering under a double burden, with the men of Yeoville pushing boldly up, closer and closer.

In the saddle, Deems turned, and pitched his rifle to his shoulder, and Briggs, looking back, saw the eight brave riders wince away and veer to either side before the leveled gun. "I've played tag with them up to now," said Deems calmly, "but after this, I mean business, and they know it!"

And he flogged his reeling horse straight for a little shack which stood in the center of the valley, with the narrowing walls descending close on either side of it.

Behind them, the leaders of the Yeoville men had rallied to their best riding again, and swiftly tore over the intervening space as Deems drew rein before the shack and dropped upon his belly, on the ground, rifle ready.

Twice he fired. There was a screech of pain from one of the charging riders, and then the party split away to either side and rode for dear life. For it is too much to expect men to rush down on an expert marksman who fires from a rest.

So that pair of shots brushed the van of the Shodress army aside and scattered them, and Single Jack said quietly, as he rose to his knees: "Take the horse and ride, Briggs. I'll hold them here, for a while. Get back to Apperley and tell him to get for cover. He could never handle this mob!" he concluded.

"I get out and leave you here?"

"One's as good as ten," said Single Jack, peering down the

157

valley at the mass of riders who came boiling up it, with the dustlike steam floating above them in the moonlight. "They won't rush this place. Besides, they want me. They want me bad!"

"Not me, old fellow," answered Briggs, hastily refreshing the magazine of his rifle from his cartridge belt. "I'm not much from the back of a horse, but I can shoot straight enough to scare 'em when I've got a rest."

"Is that final?" said Single Jack. "Because I've got no time to argue!"

"That's final. I won't budge."

There was a little silence, except for the approaching thunder of the many horses.

"I think," said Single Jack, "that you're what they call a white man, in this part of the world. Well, no man can guard both ends of this shack! Come inside! Here, Comanche!"

The wolf dog entered at their heels, and the tired pony, released by its riders, staggered off up the valley at a mechanical lope to get away from the sweeping danger which approached.

They found the shack a poor enough refuge. The walls were half rotted away. Many a year had passed since it had been used, and the mountain winters swiftly make the weight of their hands felt.

"They won't be able to spot us—and that's all," said Deems, tearing down a board which had been nailed across one of the windows, so that this opening would serve them for their firing. "These walls would never stop a bullet. Drop a few shots among 'em, Briggs, while I scoop out a trench here."

Briggs, accordingly, from the door of the shack, began to place long-range shots among the onsweeping horsemen from Yeoville, and those gallants scattered rapidly. Behind scattered rocks, trees, fallen logs, and in the depressions of the valley floor, they found their shelter and gradually they began to work around the shack from either side. Some, too, climbed to the top of the cliffs, and from these points of vantage they could open a plunging fire upon the men in the shack.

In the meantime, with a broken board as a shovel, Single

Jack scooped out in the floor of the shack a shallow trench in which they could both lie and so get protection from the bullets which were already beginning to shower at them.

For big Alec Shodress was desperately impatient. Farther down that valley, and probably not so far away, was Andrew Apperley and many a man behind him. If he could push ahead, he could overtake the tired horses of the Apperley contingent, even if they tried to flee, and at a blow, he could wipe out his only great opponent on the range. More than that, if there was ever a chance to commit a crime with impunity, this was it, for he could prove that Apperley had started with his armed mob first.

There was only this one small obstacle in the way—a little low-shouldered shack in the midst of the cañon, with merely a pair of men in it. But those men were sure shots, and they were firing at everything that showed itself. It was possible enough to sneak a few men past the shack on either side and surround it with bullets. But the horses could not go by, which seemed an insurmountable difficulty.

"Try the cliffs!" called Shodress in rage. "There's bound to be some way of getting horses up them. Then we can leave a dozen sure hands to watch that pair, and go on with the rest to eat up the crew of Mr. Apperley. By the Eternal, I'll make this the greatest night that was ever known in the mountains—but not unless we can get by that cabin. Boys, find a way up those rocks!"

32.   Single Jack Drives a Bargain

It was a simple enough matter to find places where the rocks could be climbed by men, but quite another matter to locate any spot where the horses could climb. And so the little shack remained in the throat of the valley to check the sweep and the surge of Alexander Shodress' ambitions.

He flew into a vast passion.

"Smash that shack flat! There's enough of you to blow it to bits. Wash it out of the way with lead! Hose it with bullets!"

More than two hundred men instantly prepared to obey. From every shrub near the little house, from behind every rock, and sometimes lying flat in holes which they had scraped in the dirt, and from the edge of the tall cliffs, they turned loose a storm of fire. A thousand fireflies seemed to be winking all at once, and a thousand hornets were rushing down the wind in repeated droves through the shack where the two had taken refuge.

Those hornets stung away in at one wall and out at another. They knocked the boards to dust, and filled the interior of the little house with tiny flying splinters.

They plowed up the floor of the shack. They filled the air with danger. And the two inside, working their safety trench deeper, lay quiet, or talked through the rattle of the guns.

"But what can he do? What can all of 'em do?" asked Les Briggs. "They can't blow us out of the shack, can they?"

"They can sneak up in rushing distance, however," said Deems quietly. "And that's what they're doing now. Down, boy!"

The wolf dog, feeling its master stir, lifted its head, but it immediately crouched again under the command of Single Jack.

"Coming to rushing distance!" exclaimed Briggs. "They wouldn't risk that!"

"They're getting a little wild and out of hand," said the other calmly. "Listen! They're coming closer. They've done all the talking, so far, and I think that I'd better show them that we're not dumb, either!"

He was out of the trench before Briggs could stop him. And crouching beside the wall of the shack, regardless of a fresh crash of musketry that combed the little house with bullets once more, he took deliberate aim and fired.

Instantly a shout of pain rang through the night, to be followed by a fresh roar of fury from the men of Yeoville.

"You got one of 'em, Jack!" cried Briggs.

And he in turn left the trench, and took his place at the opposite wall of the house.

"Come back!" called Deems angrily. "That's enough done. You'll get yourself killed, Briggs!"

"They've had their turn. If you could tag them, so can I!"

Lying flat on his belly, he peered through a rift in the wall against the moonlight. It was not a natural crack in the wood. That opening had been made by half a dozen rifle bullets of big caliber clipping through the board close to a single spot. On the outside Les Briggs could see the valley spotted with the vivid flashes from the hot rifles of the Yeoville men. All were firing from good cover. And if any had been taking risks a moment before, the last shot of Deems' had sent them back to close hiding.

So Briggs waited and poised his rifle, vainly hoping for a favorable target, because he was ashamed to return to his place before he had done something.

"Briggs, you're acting like a fool!"

"Perhaps I am. Look here, old-timer. What makes you go through with this deal?"

"What deal?"

"The war with Shodress. What's the money to you—I mean, the money that Andy Apperley can pay you? Can he pay you for the scalp that Shodress will sure lift off of your head, one of these days?"

"Never mind me, but get back into shelter. I tell you, I'm not in this for the money, but for the fun, and because I owe Apperley one good turn."

"What's that?"

"Don't you know?"

"No."

"Apperley hasn't talked about how he first met me?"

"No."

"He was on a boat in the East River when I broke jail and

swam for it. I was nearly done, and they were hunting me up and down and across the water with boats, when this Comanche saw me in the water and dived in and brought me out. And after I had been carried onto the Apperley boat, the police came to search it, and I would have been turned over to them, except that Andrew Apperley told them that he'd never seen me. And that's why I'm here."

Mr. Briggs whistled softly, scanning the plain before him, and then, seeing a shadow move, he took aim and fired. There was only a quickly concentrated burst of fire in response, and he crawled back into the trench.

"I missed," said Briggs gloomily. "And oh, how I'd like to tag one of 'em before I'm out of this job. Only— Why is it that you haven't let people know that you're in this out of kindness and not for money, old-timer? People around here are reading you wrong!"

"What they think of me makes no difference," declared Deems. "Particularly now. This is the finish of us, Briggs. So there's no good of thinking—except with a rifle!"

"Maybe not the finish, either. If that moon ever gets behind a cloud, we might try to sneak out—"

"And be filled full of lead while we run? No, I'll take mine here! And they'll pay for me in full."

He laughed a little, and an uncanny thrill quivered up the spine of Briggs.

At the same time, bullets began to smash through the roof, angling sharply down toward the floor. Someone was on the rim of the cliff just above them and the firing at that sharp angle made the trench in which they lay a most inadequate protection.

A puff of dust raised by one slug got into the eyes of Briggs. He shifted his position.

"They should have started that long ago," said Deems calmly. "I've been waiting for it—"

There was the distinct sound of a bullet spatting into flesh, like a fist struck against a palm, and then a groan came from Briggs.

"They've got you?" asked Deems.

"They've got me!" gasped his companion.

"Where?"

"Through the body. I—can't—talk or—"

And Briggs collapsed.

As for Single Jack, he remained quiet for a moment, whistling softly to himself. Then he leaned over, fumbled for the breast of the other, and found the heart. Yes, there was a perceptible beating of the pulse, and now he cursed grimly to himself.

He made up his mind swiftly. Crawling to the door of the shack he shouted: "Shodress! Shodress!"

A spurt of flame answered from a neighboring shrub, where two rifles had opened fire in response.

"Shodress!" he shouted again.

"Stop the guns!" called a voice near at hand. Then: "Shaw and Hammond, stop shooting!"

"All right."

"Hello in the shack!"

"Where's Shodress?"

"Where he can't hear you."

"Hello!" called a more distant voice, in the unmistakable accents of the fat man. "Here I am. Have you been peppered enough, Deems?"

"Briggs is bored through the body, and he's bleeding to death," said Deems frankly. "I'll surrender—on terms!"

"Terms nothing. You walk out with your hands over your head!"

But Single Jack merely laughed.

"Let Briggs die, then," said he. "I'm not his murderer."

"Open up on 'em again!" shouted Shodress with a torrent of oaths. "No—wait a minute! What terms do you want, Deems?"

"I want a fair trial, and your promise that I'll not be snagged during the night!"

"You've held me up tonight and spoiled my game. You'll pay for that. And what sort of a trial do you expect?"

"One chance in ten. That's all I ask. Think it over. I'll have your word of honor and one man sent in here as a hostage. Otherwise, I don't go a step with you. And if you want to come and take me—why, I'm waiting!"

There was a rapid confusion of voices, and then Deems could hear a younger man saying: "I'll go in there as a hostage and come out with him. Once you get him in Yeoville, what'll his trial amount to?"

"Maybe you're right, Steve. Will you really take your chance with him?"

"Sure I will."

"Deems."

"Yes?"

"I'm sending in Steve Grange. He'll stay with you all the way to Yeoville until you're in the jail there. Is that fair enough?"

"That's fair enough. Send him on—fast—if you want to do anything for Briggs."

Suddenly he saw a tall form striding toward the cabin, hands in the air.

"Are you Grange?"

"Yes."

"Stand there right in the front of the door. I'll bring Briggs out."

He picked up the body of the wounded man and went to the door with him, Briggs gasping: "Don't mind me, partner. I'm finished anyway. Don't mind me. Don't trust yourself to 'em. They ain't men. They're devils!"

He fainted again, and Jack Deems, kneeling by his body, called: "Come get him, Shodress. And you can get me, too!"

33.   Shodress Raises His Quirt

A storming column of a hundred and fifty men poured down Shingle Cañon and scattered through the rough hills at the farther end of it in the hope of finding Andrew Apperley and his little army. But the warning had come to Apperley from Charley Johnson in time, and he had withdrawn his forces from the field. To surprise an outlaw town by night was one thing; to meet odds of two or three to one in open war was quite another.

So the hundred and fifty rode here and there in vain, and at length coming upon a band of a few score of cows which wore the Apperley brand, they made off with these, feeling that their day's work had been brief, but that it must serve!

And in the meantime, the cream of the Shodress forces went back in triumph toward Yeoville. Behind them followed a rudely improvised litter in which poor Briggs, badly hurt but not in danger, was carried to the nearest ranch shack. But he was left there to recuperate and go his way, unmolested, when he should be able to ride. He was not looked upon as a prize in comparison with his more famous companion.

Perhaps some of the men in that armed party would have considered the capture of a single fighting man not a great accomplishment, but they were convinced by the manifest joy of Alec.

At the first moment of the surrender, he rode up to Single Jack and shook his fist in the face of the younger man.

"This is the first step, Deems!" he had shouted. "But I'm going a long way with this."

"Of course you are," said Single Jack, and smiled in his face. "In the meantime, I have a hostage here. Keep back from me, and if you shake a fist in my face again, I'll shake a gun in yours."

This was said not with any fierce emphasis, but with a perfect self-control that made the rage of Shodress seem childish and wild.

And Shodress, though his mingled joy and fury still surged and boiled in him, kept a safe distance from his armed prisoner thereafter.

They formed in a loose column. At the head rode Shodress like a returning conqueror. And behind him cantered a sufficient number of his warriors. In the center, with an open space before and behind, came Steve Grange and young Jack Deems. Others followed to the rear to shut off all chance of escape, and though there were shouts of insult and many a ringing word of abuse, no one ventured to lay a hand on Single Jack. Partly because of the awe which he inspired in them, and still more because he had Steve Grange beside him, Shodress' men considered that the first move against their prisoner would mean a bullet sent by him through the body of Grange.

So that strange cavalcade rode back and entered the streets of Yeoville, and all the way, in the distance, they were followed by the weird cry of a wolf, skulking in the distance, and that cry was the voice of Comanche.

There had been an armistice, of a kind, with the master, but it did not follow that there was any quarter for this man-killing beast. So they had tried for him with vicious eagerness, only to find that they were shooting at a skulking shadow which darted here and there and avoided them and their bullets, at last, by streaking off through the thick of their press and so getting to safety.

"That's your death song, Deems!" called Shodress over his shoulder. "That's your soul, callin' for you!"

And he laughed hugely at this poor jest.

For he was in the highest good spirits, and as they streamed through the streets of Yeoville, the whole party was filled with the same exultation which was in the breast of their leader. They reached the jail. They passed through the shattered doors which the jailer had been vainly striving to patch up, since they were burst earlier in the evening. And in the strongest, safest room in the building, loaded with irons on arms and feet, Single Jack Deems was finally brought to the end of his journey.

It was an old house which had been appropriated for the purposes of the law. The windows of the first floor were heavily barred, but for other security, there was none except such as the heavy irons that were kept on the prisoners afforded, together with the guard which was maintained over them.

And as the strength of that guard depended almost entirely upon the will of Shodress, it was a well-known fact that that jail could hold his friends from liberty no more than a sieve can hold water from the stream, whereas, on the other hand, he could make the place as secure and adamant for his foes.

"And now," said Alec Shodress, slashing at his riding boots with his quirt, while he leaned one fat hand on the table in the room where Deems had been lodged, "and now, kid, who wins?"

"I win," answered Deems instantly. "I win, because I've badgered your whole town, and you've chased me with all your men, and I've blocked you from Apperley and made a fool of you!"

"You win!" shouted Shodress, choking with rage. "You win! You win when you begin to dance on air, which ain't going to be so long from now!"

"Are you going to wait for the law to hang me?" asked Deems curiously, his nerves apparently as steady as ever.

"Law? There ain't nothing in this town for law except me! What I want is law, kid! And you and the Apperleys and the rest of the fools that don't understand that, are gonna to pay heavy for being blockheads!"

"All right, all right," said Deems. "But what's the thing you're going to charge up to me? What's the murder?"

"What's the murder? The murder of Westover! Ain't that good enough?"

"Murder?" Single Jack smiled.

"Look at him grin!" shouted Shodress. "Confound him, he enjoys this! Yes, I say the murder of Westover! Didn't you sneak up in the dark and shoot him down?"

"All right," agreed Deems. "And the four men that were with him—they ran away so they could be witnesses against me, I suppose?"

"They're witnesses that'll hang you, Deems. That's the fact. How does it make you feel?"

"It makes me more certain of one thing than I ever was before!" said Single Jack. "I'm going to live to get out of this jail and put a bullet through your head, Shodress. I've always felt I would do that, ever since I first laid eyes on you. I never felt surer of it!"

The face of Alexander Shodress turned purple and swollen with his passion. He sprang forward, the floor bending under his weight, and straight across the face of the prisoner he swung the biting lash of the quirt.

"You murdering rat!" shouted Shodress.

The quirt was torn suddenly from his hand. Much as he was feared in this town, a little gasp went up from the ruffians who had followed him into the room, because, after all, that blow was delivered to a helpless man.

It was Steve Grange who had snatched the quirt away, and now he stood over the livid Shodress, saying savagely:

"No more of that, Alec! He can't hit back and you know it."

Shodress glared at the youth as though he would willingly have thrown him to the tigers, but the next moment, seeing the solemn faces of even his best retainers, he realized that he had gone too far.

"You're right, Steve," said he. "I forgot myself. All that I could remember, just then, was that I was in front of the sneak that had murdered poor old Westover! But he ain't a man and he don't deserve to be treated like other men!"

He made a pause, breathing hard. All the others stood motionless, not speaking, for they had been chilled with horror at what they had just seen. So that, in the pause, they were able to hear the far-off bay of a hunting wolf, as it seemed.

Shodress snatched at the clue.

"That's it!" he cried, pointing through the open door. "That's what he is, and that's where he belongs, out there with the rest of the wolves!"

And there was a sudden nodding of heads. The little incident had come in so pat that it really seemed that there was something more than mere chance in it.

All eyes turned back to the prisoner.

He had not moved, either under the whip, or afterward. A great red welt ran across his face, beneath the left eye and running across the bridge of the nose and down the right cheek. And a thin trickle of blood had run down and encrimsoned his lips.

But all the while his dark, large eyes dwelt steadily and without expression upon the face of Shodress.

"What are you thinking of?" gasped Shodress suddenly, giving back a little before that fixed stare. "What are you seeing in me?"

"I'm seeing you dead in the street," said Deems slowly.

And he nodded, as though the picture were being revealed gradually and with wonderful clearness to his eyes.

Shodress loosened his collar and said hoarsely: "He's crazy! But I'll tell you what, kid, if you get out of this joint, it'll be because I've gone to sleep. Because right here in this jail I live and sleep and eat and wake, until the day when I'm gonna have the pleasure of seeing you dance at the end of a rope!"

He turned and stamped out of the room, and only Steve Grange remained behind, looking down into the dark eyes of the prisoner.

"I'm sorry," said Grange at last. "I'm sure sorry. It was the trick of a low hound! The trick of a low hound!"

He added suddenly: "Deems, I don't care what they say about you. I've been with you and I know what I saw in you tonight. You're white! You're a square shooter! You tell me what I can do for you, and I'm your man!"

"Are you the brother of Hester Grange?" asked the prisoner.

"I am."

"Then there's nothing you can do."

"Why not?"

"Go ask her, and she'll tell you!"

And so Steve Grange, utterly baffled, obeyed, and left the jail.

34.   Manners of a Toad!

In the jail, every precaution was taken to secure the prisoner. Shodress himself exhibited his pride and joy in the capture by living constantly within the building. He had had himself appointed a special deputy for this purpose and he had with him, to make doubly sure, Dan McGruder. It was known that McGruder understood the formidable nature of the prisoner by bitter experience of his prowess, and therefore it was to be taken for granted that he would never relax in his vigilance. As for the irons which weighed down Single Jack, they were doubled, both upon his wrists and upon his ankles. And attached to his feet there was a heavy iron shot which had seen service on the battle front, and was now degraded to a prison duty of this humble sort.

But though he was loaded with iron chains and weights, and had to keep upon his hands every day and all day the burden of two pairs of handcuffs, in other ways, Single Jack was treated well enough.

He had to see a number of people every day, for not only were the townsfolk never satisfied with staring at him, but cowpunchers were riding in from all parts of the range to have a look at him and say a few words. He amazed them with his

good nature. It did not bother him to have them stare him out
of countenance. And he was not in the least averse to talking
with them a little. So that the reputation of Deems lost some of
its unearthly quality. He was no longer considered an uncanny
phantom but rather a subtle and marvelously clever man, who
had united courage and gun skill to the highest possible point.

"As fast as Single Jack," became a simile which might be in-
terpreted to mean lightning fast. "As brave as Single Jack"
meant simply a man without fear. And to "shoot like Single
Jack" was simply a superlative to be applied to the mythical
marksman who cannot miss.

When it was seen that he was not exactly a poisonous creature, even women came and brought their children to look at
him, and they stared and laughed and gaped and pointed at
him while he smiled back at them with an unshakable good
nature.

His trial came quickly.

The very evening before it was supposed to begin, Steve
Grange came into the jail and found the prisoner playing poker
with Dan McGruder. For that was their occupation all the time
that Dan was on duty. They used to sit at the table near the
windows in the front room of the second story. And there,
with the sun streaming in and washing far across the floor,
Single Jack would sit on the edge of the table, so that the
heavily manacled hands would be comfortably above the
cards. Dan McGruder, sitting opposite him in a chair, did the
shuffling and dealing.

And Steve Grange found the two at this pleasant occupation as he strolled into the chamber. It was long after the hour
when visitors were admitted to the jail, as a rule. But Steve
Grange was a fellow of such proved importance that he could
go and come very much as he chose to do.

He watched the game for a moment and then sat down on
the windowsill, just as Shodress came back from his dinner.

"Hello, Steve," said Shodress. "What's the news from your
house?"

"No news."

"Apperley ain't changed any?"

"Apperley is getting better every day. He's all out of danger, now."

"Look here, Steve. What makes Hester work her head off over that fellow, will you tell me?"

"You ought to know," said Steve Grange. "It looked as though she'd asked him to come down to our house just so's she could keep him in the reaching distance of your gun fighters."

"My gun fighters?"

"Why, Shodress, you don't deny that the three of them were all your men."

He turned to Dan McGruder at the table.

"Tell me, Dan, if I'm talking through my hat."

Dan McGruder shrugged his shoulders. "I dunno nothing except what the teacher tells me," he said with a grin. "That's all that I know. And sometimes I forget even that!"

Alexander Shodress laughed largely and comfortably. For nothing pleased him more than the feeling that his followers were completely in his hands. And that his trust in them could be absolute, he knew.

"Well, Steve," he said, "you see that nothing could be proved against me. But as for Apperley, what difference does it make what he thinks? The less thinking the better; the less living the better, so far as Mr. Apperley is concerned. I wish him no luck. And you might let Hester know it. I see no reason why she should slave over him. Or does she plan on marrying a good house and a good position back East? Or maybe she has the corner of her eye fixed on the coin of old Andy Apperley. Is that it?"

And he laughed again, for he was very proud of the keen eyes with which he saw through the motives of many people.

He was greeted with a cold eye by Steve.

"Hester'll never marry for money, and she'll never marry for a house and a position in society," he declared.

"Hello!" exclaimed Shodress. "And why not?"

"Why, for one reason, because she's my sister."

"Is that a reason?"

"That's enough reason for any man," declared Steve Grange, and he thrust out his formidable fighting jaw as he spoke.

At this, Shodress turned sharply around and stared at his young adherent. It was not exactly a revolt on the part of young Grange, but it could not be taken for anything other than a declaration of rights. And that was abhorrent to Mr. Shodress. For where he was master he wanted to be absolute master.

There had been so much point in the tone and in the words of Steve that even Single Jack, who rarely seemed to pay much attention to those who were around him, now lifted his dark eyes and let them dwell on the youngster, and Grange, meeting that glance, nodded slightly, and let Single Jack see him thrust a fold of paper into a deep crack between the dobe bricks which composed the wall.

Then Jack went on with the game of cards.

For one instant angry words had swelled in the throat of Shodress at the thought of such a youngster as Grange daring to raise head against him. And then he saw that with a single syllable he could alienate that youth forever. And though it would be easy to drive Steve away, he could never be won back again.

So he pondered the matter back and forth and instantly made up his mind that it would be better by far to let matters take their own course than to press this boy into a corner.

It left a surplus of rage in his heart as he turned from Grange toward the pair at the table, and he snarled savagely at Dan McGruder.

"You're at the cards again with him, Dan!"

"There's nothing else to do with him," said McGruder regretfully. "What's wrong with the cards?"

"What's wrong? Everything is wrong! Look at him sitting up above you on the table, for one thing. All that he's got to do is to throw himself down on you. Ain't even a baby able to see that?"

Dan McGruder looked up quickly to the outlaw on the table. And then he could not help smiling.

"At the idea of anybody just falling down on me!" he explained to Shodress.

He touched one of the guns which hung at his hips. For, after all, Dan McGruder had a record behind him that was long enough to satisfy the most meticulously critical in matters of gun fighting.

"And him with his feet and his hands in irons!"

He could not help breaking into laughter, and even Shodress smiled a little, but it was a sour smile.

"You act like a young fool, not like a man that's had a few lessons already from this same gent," he declared to McGruder.

"Never mind that!" exclaimed McGruder flushing. "He had me on the run, for a while. I've admitted that to everybody. Why harp on it?"

"Because here you sit putting your head into the lion's mouth! By the powers, I'm going to change you for another guard!"

"I wish you would!" cried Dan. "This sort of fence riding ain't pleasing to me. I'd be happiest away from it. But I ask you this, Shodress. What could he do? Just what could he do, except he did try some such fool thing as falling on top of me—"

He broke off and smiled at Single Jack, and Single Jack smiled back, frankly, with no apparent malice in his eyes.

"And if he did that," said McGruder, "he'd be throwing himself right to destruction, because that's where I'd blow him! You know that, kid! You know that, Deems? Sure he knows it, Alec. He sees that I'm decent to him, but that don't mean that I ain't watching him all the time!"

Alexander Shodress leaned both his fat hands on the table, and in this manner he diminished his height until his eyes were on a level with those of his prisoner.

"Well, kid," he said, "I ain't decent to you, am I?"

"You have the look of a toad, Shodress," said the prisoner

calmly. "But I never knew before that you had the manners of a toad as well!"

Mr. Shodress started as though a spur had been driven home in him.

"You gutter rat!" he yelled.

"Because," exclaimed Deems, apparently with a naïve desire to explain the reasonable grounds for his remark, "you deal with poison, Shodress!"

Mr. Shodress glared and then recoiled.

"You lie!" he shouted.

"You see?" said Single Jack to McGruder and Steve Grange. "He has to take it seriously. I've touched him on a sore spot!"

35. Single Jack Receives a Note

At this point, Steve Grange turned and stared fixedly at Shodress, but that gentleman was unaware of anything in the world with the exception of young Jack Deems. From the first moment of the appearance of the outlaw in Yeoville, the boss of the town had dreaded him. That dread had turned into a frantic fear and loathing combined. And the more efforts he made to get rid of Deems, the more profound became his hatred of him. He had wronged Jack Deems just enough to make himself a fanatic enemy. What maddened him more than all else was the quiet manner of the prisoner. And day by day he worked with a violent concentration to break through the nerve of the younger man. But most of his efforts ended as had this one, today. The more brutality he exhibited, the more Single Jack smiled, as though he were in the possession of mysterious knowledge which made all of the efforts of Shodress futile and foolish.

Sometimes he would sit down with Deems and quietly urge him to be prepared for the worst, to think of the future world, to consider the hell to which he was surely going; and again, he would confess with a jovial outburst of good nature that he had never in his life enjoyed so much pleasure as he was now receiving from the spectacle of the younger man in the jail. Sometimes, also, he would dwell upon the trial, but since the verdict at the trial was apparently a foregone conclusion, he spent his best talents in calling up before the eyes of Deems the picture of the last fatal moment when the hangman's rope would be around his neck and his feet would be treading the thin air.

He returned to that theme over and over again.

He returned to it even on this occasion, since he could think of nothing better to say:

"Do you remember, Deems, that you said you would put a bullet through me, one day, and drop me in the street?"

"I remember that I said that," said Deems.

"I'll think of that," said Shodress, "when I see you kicking! But what about the trial tomorrow? Have the Apperleys sent you a lawyer to defend you?"

"I'll do without a lawyer," said Deems. "Do you know what you remind me of now, Shodress?"

"I don't want to hear you," said the fat man.

"You remind me of a mad dog, too fat to do as much harm as it wants to do. But looking for a few other curs to help it bite and fight."

"He calls you a cur, McGruder. Do you hear that?" snarled Shodress.

But McGruder shrugged his shoulders and listened curiously. He had overheard too many of these wordy brawls before. And the noisy rage on the one side and the coldly concentrated malice on the other always fascinated him.

Steve Grange, having started to go out, turned and lingered in the door. And in the excess of his fury, Shodress glared sidewise at his young lieutenant, as though only the presence of Steve kept him from throwing himself headlong at Single Jack.

"Lock him up in his room, McGruder," said Shodress. "And no more cards, today! I'll come in and relieve you in an hour!"

So poor Deems was marched away to his room, though it was still far from bedtime. He was not left alone there. Day and night there was always a guard over him and in the room with him, and even the strong security of the fetters was not trusted for an instant.

For new stories about Single Jack had drifted from the East. They told how deftly he could slip handcuffs, and with a bit of watch spring undo the most intricate locks. And they related many another interesting particular, until the people of Yeoville began to feel that they had a veritable will-o'-the-wisp in their midst.

At any rate, he was never left for a single instant unobserved, and it was felt that his exploits in Eastern prisons had thrown down a gauntlet of challenge to Yeoville. If they kept this dexterous fellow safely through the time of his imprisonment, they would be accomplishing more than the tallest of stone walls and the stoutest of steel bars had been able to do in the more civilized portions of the community.

That was not all. It seemed, indeed, as though the affair of Single Jack was literally putting Yeoville upon the map. There suddenly appeared in the town the emissaries of the police of many states. Could Yeoville keep her prisoner? Did she desire to spare herself the expenses of his trial? In that case, here were the legal departments of so many states only too ready, too anxiously willing to take up the matter! If only Yeoville were to be persuaded to give over her prize! Into how many penitentiaries might he not be slipped frictionlessly and easily!

But Yeoville had no desire to give up her prize and the fame which he was bringing to her. For nearly every day, someone turned up from the far Eastern states to see this criminal, and look into his dark eyes, and strive to connect him with other crimes in distant parts of the country. But while they remained in town, they could not help seeing something of the ways of that wild little village, and by every mail fat letters departed, describing what had been seen, such as the random parties of cowpunchers who, for the mere joy of living, rode through the place with guns spitting fire and lead; and the growing cemetery where there was always a fresh grave to be seen. It was the proud boast of Yeoville that three out of every four men buried there had died with their boots on, gun in hand. In one detail about Yeoville all these strangers agreed, and that was in praising big, blustering, good-natured, open-handed Alexander Shodress, who extended a broad welcome to all comers.

But to go back to the moment when Single Jack was taken from the room to his bedchamber by McGruder. It must be pointed out that the eyes of both McGruder and Shodress were earnestly upon him, and moreover, his movements were seriously restricted and hampered by the heavy double manacles. Yet when he left the room, up one sleeve was tucked the fold of paper which young Steve Grange had stuffed between two of the dobe bricks.

Presently he lay on his bed and pretended to sleep, but under that masking pretense, little by little, soundlessly, he drew forth the paper and spread it out against his raised knee and read through the lowered lashes of his eyes:

Deems: Hester has told me all about that hound, Myers. It's enough to make me see what Myers is, and what Shodress is for using methods like that.

I've ridden out and gotten in touch with Andrew Apperley. He's willing to do anything that he can. I've told him how you kept his brother from being poisoned, and he'll mortgage his whole estate to get enough money to save you if that's possible, but none of us know how we can get a lawyer into Yeoville, now that Shodress is running amuck.

Can you suggest anything?

You have the confession of Myers. Where did you hide it? If we can have that, we may be able to bring up a case against Shodress that will keep him so busy that he won't have time to bother about you.

Tell me what you want us to do. I'm your man to the limit.

Hester wants me to tell you again, what you wouldn't believe before, that she had nothing to do with the scheme to get Apperley away from you so that he could be shot up by the gang. If you knew her the way I do, you would never have suspected her of such a trick.

Steven Grange.

That letter he read twice, and then folded it and conveyed it back into his sleeve.

He could not help smiling faintly when he thought of the heedless recklessness which had induced Steve Grange to put down such things in black and white and in a place where there were great chances that the paper would fall into the hands of Alec Shodress. And if Shodress had seen it, there was no reasonable doubt as to what he would have done. Myers, Grange, and Deems himself would all have fallen.

However, that bad chance had not fallen out, and now in what manner could he use this offer of help?

He pondered it carefully, but the more he thought it over, the stranger it seemed to him. His opinions of men and women were most definite. They were the coldly selfish creatures who lived in a universe of suspicion and distrust such as he had always known. Only one thing in all his life had half startled him out of his old conceptions, and that had been the kindness of Andrew Apperley. To repay that man, he had worked and fought until his own life seemed about to be laid down. The manacles which held him were a partial token of the payment which he had made.

But with Hester and Steven Grange the matter was different. They belonged to the camp of the enemy. Steven Grange himself still lay in danger of a prison sentence which had been imposed upon him by the skill and the courage of David Apperley, backed up by the commanding guns of Deems himself.

And yet yonder was Hester Grange working day and night to draw back young David from the shadow of death. And here was Steven Grange risking his life boldly and silently in the determination to do something for the prisoner. He realized that it was no easy task he had set for himself. But he never had been a man to shrink from the unpleasant things that came up. "Life was like that," he reflected, "and you sometimes had to trust to your instincts to guide you." So now he was, without fear or regret, determined to help the prisoner.

It was enough to cause a mighty revolution in the mental world of Deems. It was a conception which ripped out old ideas and planted in their place an idea of human kindness and generosity that brought sudden tears stinging into his eyes.

He could only shake his head and decide that he would let the matter adjust itself with time. For these were ideas so great and so new that he could not comprehend them at once.

His thoughts turned on Steven Grange, young, bold, careless, reckless of himself and of others, but apparently with a heart of gold. But if Steve Grange were of the right stuff, then what of his sister? What of Hester? Suppose, then, that she also had the gold in her, that she was not merely scheming, cool, crafty, clever, and ready to take advantage of all opportunities?

If that were the case—

And all at once, he stopped thinking altogether, and in the place of thought the face of Hester blazed across his mind. He saw her smile. He felt her eyes resting upon him with gentle kindness. And the heart of Single Jack almost stopped with wonder and with joy which was the very brother of sadness.

36.   A Condemned Man's Dream

It was an extremely brief trial, as might have been suspected beforehand.

The witnesses of the "State" against the prisoner were Pete and Sam Wallis, Lefty Mandell, barely recuperated enough to be carried into the courtroom, and Dan McGruder himself.

And the story which they told could be inferred from the summing up of the judge to the jury at the end, for he said in part:

"Here we have, apparently, a lover of blood and guns who sneaks up on a peaceful party of five young friends, foregathered in a quiet home, and tearing open the door shoots in upon them without warning, and then, when the lamp has fallen, rushes in with his devilish wolf dog beside him—"

The verdict was guilty. Guilty of murder in the first degree.

And the next day Mr. Deems stood before the same judge and heard him pronounce the fatal words:

"To be hanged by the neck until dead."

He walked out from the courtroom past faces which had already turned grave, and past eyes which were filled with horror, though with sympathy.

And to Single Jack himself the thing had a bitter meaning. For he had barely come upon the discovery that there might be in life and human nature such possibilities of happiness as he had not dreamed in the old days. He had just walked by Hester Grange, crystal pale from the long watches of the sick room, and seen the tears in her eyes. He had gone past Steve Grange, beside her, dark red with anger at the course which the law had taken.

To die—why, that was a little thing, an idea which he had

looked upon with indifference all of his days. But to die and leave these possibilities of friendship—and of more than friendship—

He passed out into the sun, but though it fell burningly upon his body, it could not reach his heart, for that was gathered in the deepest darkness.

And then a heavy voice said beside him:

"It begins to mean something, kid. Eh?"

He looked up and found Shodress striding near—Shodress red with heat and with triumph.

"But this here is just the beginning," said the boss of Yeoville. "Every day, now, you can spend your time thinking about the gallows, kid. And I'll help you think!"

He broke into savagely exultant laughter, and for the first time, Deems was unable to smile calmly in return. Instead, he felt a bitter resentment.

That new feeling startled him, for he knew that it was a sign of weakness, and he dreaded lest that weakness should grow upon him.

Shodress, with a devilish intuition, saw that he had gained his first ground against this enemy, and he was filled with ardent happiness, and he called the attention of McGruder to the prisoner the instant they were in the jail.

"He looked pretty strong and confident, Mac," he said. "But take an eyeful of him now. Oh, he's weakening fast enough! He's weakening, Mac! And now that he's started going downhill, who can tell how long it'll be before he crumbles altogether? He throws a bluff until the pinch comes, and then he yelps like a dog that's been kicked! What a sneakin' puppy you are, Deems!"

And he leaned and shook his fat fist in the face of Single Jack.

The latter had recovered some of his poise, by this time. He had not spent in vain a lifetime of effort to control his nerves. They were as a rule his perfect servants.

Now he leaned back in his chair and composed his shackled hands comfortably upon his knees.

His eyes were half closed, and a contented smile hovered upon his lips. No matter what Shodress might suspect was in the mind of the younger man, he could not help asking:

"What's the matter with you?"

"It's an odd thing. Something that you wouldn't understand," said Deems.

"What!"

"And even if you did understand it, you wouldn't believe it. What about a game of poker, McGruder?"

"The deuce with poker!" exclaimed Shodress. "Let's hear what you've got to offer!"

"Did you ever hear of mediums?" asked Deems.

"You mean the gents that talk to spirits—except that mostly they're women, and not men! What about 'em?"

"It's very odd," said Single Jack, "but I've always had a little touch of that in me."

"Blamed if I don't believe you," said McGruder. "That accounts for the spooky look that you got, half of the time."

"Don't let him make a fool out of you, Mac," cautioned Shodress, but nevertheless his eyes were intent with interest. "Go on, let's hear the yarn!" he urged.

"I'll tell it to McGruder," said Deems, "because why should I waste my time on a fat-face like you, Shodress? You want to hear it, Dan?"

"Of course."

"Well, you see, ever since I was a youngster, I've been seeing things that my eyes had never rested on. A dozen times I've been in places where I never was before—and recognized them!"

"D'you mean that?"

"It's a fact, Dan."

"Yes, I've heard of things like that happening," said Shodress, forgetting his hatred of the man in the interest of the idea. "Matter of fact, it's sort of a common thing, I believe."

"I could tell you about a time when it was very useful to me," said Single Jack. "I was running down an alley in a town where I'd never been before. All I knew about its geography was that it stood about twenty miles from the sea and that it had a railroad running into it. And I had a lot of need for knowing that place well, the night that I'm speaking about, because I had a pocket more than half filled with uncut diamonds; and behind me there were about a dozen people running. And off in the distance, I could hear a horse galloping closer and closer toward me, so that I knew I'd have to run as fast as a horse, pretty soon, unless I wanted to be caught—or shoot my way out. And I always hate to do that."

"Now look here, kid, why don't you give us a chance to halfway believe you?"

"I'm talking to McGruder," said Deems gently. "This is stuff that you're not even expected to understand."

"Go on!" put in McGruder. "And leave him alone for five minutes, Shodress, will you?"

Shodress rolled himself from side to side in his seat, disturbed with hatred for narrator and interest in the story which he was hearing.

"What happened, anyway?" he asked.

"All at once," said Single Jack, "I felt that I'd been in that street before, and that I knew all about it, and it seemed to me that once before I had been down that way and that along that street there was a little alley mouth opening, next to a fruit store, and that if I turned down that alley beside the fruit store, I'd come to the river—"

He paused, and shook his head.

"Go on!" growled Shodress. "I suppose that you want us to believe that you did come across the fruit store and that you went down the alley and got to the river and dived in and got away that way?"

"It's very odd," declared Single Jack, "but now it seems that even a fool can guess the truth, because that's the only reason that I'm here tonight. I did find the fruit store, and beside it, however, there was no alley mouth but a big pile of rubbish behind a tall fence. But I had faith in my dream. I had to have, or else be caught by that mob behind me.

"When I headed for the fence, they thought that they had

me, and they yelped like dogs. I got over the fence, with one of the policemen taking pot shots at me. I staggered through the junk pile, and there I saw the little black alley ahead of me.

"When I headed down it, I could see the glimmer of the water ahead, and I guessed that my dream would save me. It did save me, and here I am!"

"You might better have died like a drowned rat in the water that night," said Shodress, "than wait to be hanged like a dog here in Yeoville—except for the pleasure that I'm gonna take in seeing you die!"

It seemed that the prisoner did not hear him, for he continued dreamily:

"And several times since I've known you, you've been in one of these dreams of mine, Shodress!"

"The devil I have!" gasped the fat man, his credulity showing instantly through his pretended contempt. "And what sort of a dream was it?"

"I seem to see you running across a street," said young Deems, squinting his eyes hard. "And when I see you, I'm leaning out from a window. I call to you, and you look up—and it's a very sick face that you make when you see me above you, Shodress!"

"Go on!"

"That's all that there is to it!"

"Do you mean that?"

"Yes."

"It's a fool dream, then, with no meaning!"

"Maybe, maybe," agreed the prisoner without passion. "But it's a dream that I like to think about."

"You're half-witted!" yelled Shodress, losing his temper completely. "What is there about it to please even a fool like you?"

"It's your face in the dream," said Deems, smiling upon the fat man, "because you always look as if you were about to die!"

185

37.   Messenger of Steel

But what of Steven Grange and his offer, during these days? Indeed, he was often in the mind of the condemned man, but he did not know what use to make of him. For there was always the constant surveillance of the sharp-eyed McGruder and the omnipotent malice of Shodress to embarrass him.

So he waited, wondering what he should do, and every day Steve Grange came to see him.

Steve had adopted an attitude of bitterest hatred toward Single Jack, and never missed an opportunity of upbraiding him. He accused Deems of having laid a plot against the life of his younger brother, Oliver. He swore that if the gallows spared Deems, he, Steve Grange, would certainly take the first opportunity to fight the old quarrel out with him.

He was so rabid that even Shodress was sometimes a little surprised, and McGruder was even a little bit horrified.

"Look here, Steve," he said one day, "I got no cause to love Single Jack. I know that he's no good, and that it'll be a fine thing for the world when he's polished off, but just the same, what call have you got for coming here to damn him black and white, every day of your life? He's gonna hang soon enough!"

"Shut up, Dan," snapped Steve Grange. "I don't need any lessons in politeness from you. But I hate a mean hound. I hate him, and I'm gonna tell him about it when I get a chance to!"

At that very moment he had passed behind the chair of the prisoner, and something cold and sharp slithered down the back of Deems between his skin and his shirt.

He had been half convinced that the recent attitude of young Grange had been real, but when he had his first chance to examine what had been dropped into his clothes, he found that it was the chiefest treasure that can be given a prisoner. It was a file of the finest quality of steel, specially adapted for eating through the best of opposing steel.

And those old-fashioned chains which held him were far from the finest quality! At every touch of the beautiful shark teeth of the saw, the steel in the links would give way.

If he had had a few minutes to work boldly, and freely with that file, he told himself that he would be a free man. But he did not have those few minutes.

During the day, it was impossible for him to do anything. The broad sun and the constant attention of McGruder and Shodress, to say nothing of the others, made it ridiculous to attempt anything. But during the night there was a little difference.

To be sure, he was never unwatched, and to be sure, his guard never slept, because every man in Yeoville dreaded him like death itself, and even Shodress and McGruder had not lost any of their awe by their constant association with him. But while he lay on his bed, he could effect a little progress with the file every night. But he did his best.

To attempt anything upon the strong double chains which controlled his hands was impossible, under such circumstances. But he could lie doubled up on the bed, with his knees drawn high, and his face toward his guard, watching through the long, dark lashes of his eyes the slightest change of expression upon the face of the other man in the room. And, while he watched, with his hands thrust far down and the file prepared, he ground it stealthily into the chain that tied his feet together, and the chain that held the heavy shot.

He had to use strong pressure, and yet he dared not let his fingers be chafed until they bled. He had to use strong pressure, and yet he dared not let the file make the slightest sound. And yet now and again his energy became a little greater than his caution, and the file would emit a slight scratching against the steel.

Once, when Shodress was on guard one of these sounds brought him to his feet with a bound.

Single Jack pretended to waken that instant.

"Can't you put me in a place where I can sleep without having rats run all over me?" he demanded in disgust. "Is this such a mean little town that it can't afford even a decent death cell?"

Shodress stood over him. In his hands was the double-barreled shotgun which never left his side, night or day. The sawed-off barrels carried in them enough fragments of lead and enough powder behind them to blow twenty men to the devil in small bits. Every day, in the afternoon, when Shodress came back from the hotel after his lunch, he was in the habit of unloading that terrible weapon and loading it again in the presence of the prisoner, and after it was loaded, he would always say with a dreadful and yearning wickedness in his eyes:

"Why don't you try to break and run, one day, Deems? Why don't you make a break for liberty, Single Jack? Oh, don't I just wish you would, so's I could have a fair excuse to drive both charges in this gun through you!"

This idea tickled the fancy of the boss of Yeoville immensely and he was constantly referring to it.

Now, as he leaned over the bed of the prisoner, he said savagely: "What're you talking about, rats? That wasn't any rat that squeaked. What was it?"

"Oh, confound your fat head, and all the fool ideas that are in it!" exclaimed Single Jack, and turning on the bed with a violent clinking of all his chains, he pretended to compose himself sullenly for sleep.

The shadow of the watcher remained in a great shapeless splotch against the wall.

"Oh," said Shodress in a whisper through his teeth, "how I would love to do it now—both barrels against the back of your neck, and both of the triggers pulled at the same time."

"I'll tell you, Shodress," said the prisoner, turning over on his back and looking up dauntlessly into the face of the other, "I'll tell you. You missed your happiest chance in life. You've made a little money and you've landed in a place where you have a good deal of power over fools that aren't quite as completely crooked as yourself. But at the same time, you haven't lived up to your possibilities!"

"What do you mean?" asked Shodress, half guessing at a compliment. "What are you driving at?"

"I mean, you ought to have worked in a slaughter house. That would have kept you happy."

A torrent of oaths broke from the lips of Shodress. He stormed up and down the room, cursing volubly, and as he cursed he threatened the prisoner with every torment. But as his storm of words reached an end and he sank into his chair again, breathing hard, once more the prisoner lay in his accustomed position upon his side, with his knees hunched up high —tying himself into a knot, much after the fashion of a young boy.

And watching the grumbling, furious Shodress, he resumed his dexterous work at the fetters.

It was a very slow progress that he made, though he pretended to more weariness than he felt and insisted upon going to bed early at night and lying late in the morning.

For, early and late, while the sun lasted, he was really sleeping, but through the heart of the night, he was lying apparently utterly relaxed, but really working with uncanny patience and a dogged resolution.

Those cramped and stealthy motions of the fingers, repeated for endless hours, and hours, began to accomplish results, at last, and a great gash began to eat up into the under side of the chain which secured his feet. This chain was never examined, but lest it should be even casually glanced at, he always finished his night's work by rubbing a little dobe dust into the crease which the file had made in the steel.

And so the days drifted past, not slowly, any longer, but with a dizzying speed toward the day of execution.

Two days before the date set for the execution, he gave up

his plan, as utterly hopeless, because there was still remaining too much of the thickness of the chain for him possibly to cut through it. But that very night he struck a veritable air bubble in what remained on one side of the link on which he was working, and when he cut into it, he ground away almost the very last of the steel on that side.

With a renewed heart, he set to work on the other side of the link, and though the steel remained as strong there as ever, yet such a fiery power had hope given to him that, despite the growing dullness of the file, he was eating rapidly through it, and by the time the morning came, there was left only a thin, brittle shell of steel on each of the links which he wanted to break.

When the daylight came and he stood up from his bed, he regretted keenly that he had worked so boldly, because he had left the link in such a depreciated condition that the slightest concentration upon the chain would show that it had been cut through, and that the veriest tissue of thin steel still connected it.

However, he trusted that such an examination would not be given. The day of his execution was literally just around the corner, and men would be thinking of his death, not of his escape.

At least, to that he must trust, and pray that no real observation came the way of that chain.

When he stood up, he walked with short steps, or steps shorter even than the hobbling chain compelled, because he knew that at the first sharp strain, the chain would snap.

And so he entered upon his last twenty-four hours, according to the verdict of the law.

But even if the cutting of the links were completed, there were still the double manacles on his hands.

However, he had made one single stride toward the distant door of liberty, and now he was ready to take every opportunity, or any opportunity, with the cool resolution of an absolutely desperate man. For one thing at least he knew—

which was that he would not die under the rope. Rather even the double-barreled shotgun of big Shodress!

38. "I Love You!"

Early that morning Steve Grange and Hester herself came and asked to see the prisoner. Shodress admitted them, and remained on guard in person, with Dan McGruder in the corner of the room with his repeating rifle across his knees.

"I've tried to keep her away from him," said Steve, "but she wanted to have a last look at him. Let's stand back and let her talk a minute alone with him."

"Not a second!" insisted Shodress. "She ought to hate him. Everybody around here ought to. But you never can tell about a woman. They do the things that are most foolish."

So he stood close by, with his ever-present shotgun dropped over the crook of his left arm and the muzzles turned toward the prisoner.

He was much amazed, now, watching Single Jack, for that man of the steady nerves had first grown red and then very pale as the girl entered the room.

She would have gone up to shake hands with him, but the harsh voice of Shodress warned her back.

"I'll have nobody touch him," said Shodress. "There's all sorts of things can happen, and even a hatpin, in the hands of a trickster like him might turn into a gun with which he'd blow all our heads off. You keep clean away from him, Hester, on the far side of this here table!"

So she paused by the table with her hands clasped together and her eyes fastened upon the face of the criminal.

"I had to come to say good-by to you," murmured Hester.

"Louder!" barked Shodress. "I ain't gonna have no whispering around here!"

There was an ominous growl from Steve Grange, at this brutal remark, but Shodress did not even notice it, and as for Single Jack and the girl, they seemed unable to notice the others in the room.

"I had to come," she told him earnestly, "because I know that you've hated and despised me, and now I can swear to you that I had nothing to do with McGruder and the others when they laid their trap for David Apperley!"

She turned with a caught breath.

"Alec Shodress, will you tell him that I had nothing to do with it?"

"Hello!" snarled Shodress. "Look at your sister, Steve. Blamed if she ain't got tears in her eyes! Say, have you let her fall in love with that crook? Tell me that."

"What's that to you?" asked Steve Grange savagely. "Did you hear her ask you a question?"

Shodress stared first at Steve Grange and then at the girl and the prisoner. Then he stepped back and made his shotgun ready.

"Dan!" he called. "Get ready. There's something queer about this. I dunno what. But you cover Grange. I'm taking no chances. Jack, if you've framed something—why, start it!"

He presented the double muzzle straight at Deems.

"I don't need his word for it," said Single Jack to the girl. "Yours is enough for me. And if you really want to know, I'll tell you that I've stopped doubting you. If I hadn't been a fool, I'd never have questioned you in the first place. But that's finished and can't be helped. It's what's to come that's worth thinking about now—"

"What's to come? The rope, d'you mean?" broke in Shodress, laughing loudly.

"It's what's to come," agreed the girl eagerly. "And I hoped that you'd let me say that no matter what happens, you'll never be forgotten!"

"Listen!" Shodress grinned. "Look if she ain't making love to him right in front of our eyes!"

As for Steve Grange, he was white with emotion. But he hardly seemed to hear the boss of Yeoville, so intently was he watching the two on the opposite sides of the table.

Even Dan McGruder seemed to feel that the rôle which his chief was playing now was most unworthy, and he stood up, his rifle across his arm.

"Leave 'em be, Shodress!" he asked. "Can't you leave 'em alone for a minute?"

"Sure! Let her work on him!" exclaimed Shodress. "She's weakening him fast! Look at him begin to shake, Dan! I never expected really to see that. But a crook and a sneak is always a coward, down in his heart. If you can only put him in the right place to bring it out!"

"He's right," said Single Jack. "I'm shaking, Hester. I'm weak as a rag. But I've got the strength to say one thing. Will you let me say it?"

"Yes!" whispered the girl. "I want you to say it!"

"Do you guess what it is?"

"I think that I guess what it is. I hope that I do!"

"It's this. If I get out of this tangle I'm coming to you in spite of the devil. I won't even wait to kill Shodress. I'll come to you to tell you I love you, Hester!"

"Hey, he's gone crazy!" cried Shodress. "I leave it to you, boys, if he ain't gone crazy! Listen to what he's saying. A gallows bird telling a girl that he loves her——"

"Shodress!" yelled McGruder in a savage burst of fury. "You leave them alone!" And so amazed was Shodress at this act of rebellion on the part of an old and proved henchman that he could not help stopping to stare at Dan McGruder.

She had stretched out her arms across the table.

"I thought I hated you, Jack. I thought that I just hated and feared you. But now I know that I've loved you from the first moment!"

"Ah," cried Single Jack, "if I die tomorrow, I'll die the happiest man in the world, knowing that——"

"Get her out!" bellowed Mr. Shodress at Steve Grange. "Did you bring her here to give him heart like this and buck him up to the very end? Confound it, Grange, you've spoiled everything! You've ruined everything! Take your sister away from here! I wish that I'd never laid eyes on her!"

Steve Grange stepped beside his sister. One arm he passed around her. His free hand fingered the butt of his revolver fiercely.

"I'm taking her away because you're the boss of this place, Shodress," he said. "But at the same time she leaves, I leave. I'm through with you and your ways. I'm done!"

"I can't go yet, Steve!" pleaded the girl. "There's one more thing I've got to say!"

"Not a syllable!" roared Shodress. "I won't have another word out of her. As for you, Grange, I'll see that you pay for daring to talk back to me like this! I'll show you who took you out of jail, you low-down cow thief, and I'll show you who can put you back!"

"Steve," said Single Jack quietly. "I understand, and I'll never forget. Take her away. Hester, good-by for a little while!"

She burst into tears, and Grange, his savage glance fixed on Shodress, led her from the room.

They left Shodress in a towering passion, stamping up and down the floor.

"I'll ruin him!" bellowed the great Shodress. "I'll smash him flat! I made that kid a man. I'll make him nothing, now! I'll show him what I am! I'll teach him who runs this town! It's time there was an example made of him! McGruder, can you believe that we've seen and heard it all these last five minutes?"

Poor Dan McGruder, baffled, and bewildered, made no reply. He could only gape at Single Jack. For it was a side of the prisoner's character which he had not even dreamed of before. Still he could not believe it. But his senses told him that Hester Grange had come to the jail and told a man already legally dead that she loved him, and he had told her that he loved her.

It was too much for McGruder. It turned the plain world of the senses into an airy, fairy place where a man knew not what to think or do!

The rest of the morning was a stormy scene in the jail. Shodress, savage beyond belief, alternated between taunting his prisoner and damning the entire Grange family.

"I'm gonna leave you hanging for twenty-four hours on the gallows," he told Single Jack. "But say, have you seen it, yet?"

"You mean the gallows?"

"Yes."

"I hear the hammers working," said Single Jack. "It's down the street, isn't it?"

"Lean out the window," said Shodress, "and you can see it."

Single Jack walked obediently to the window and leaned out. He could see the tall skeleton of the gallows rearing its gaunt head, and its long shadow lying awkwardly upon the white dust of the street.

"I'll be high enough for them all to see me," said Deems. "I'm glad of that. I hope that they have a well-stretched rope, Shodress."

"It's one that'll do for you," replied the boss of Yeoville.

He considered the smiling face of Deems with a scowl.

"I got an idea," he said, "that you still think that you ain't gonna hang tomorrow!"

"How can I?" said Deems. "Because that leaves me hardly time to put a bullet in you, Shodress. And that has to happen first, you know!"

"Man, you talk like a fool!" declared big Shodress. "I didn't have any idea that any grown man could have such an empty head. McGruder, tell me if you ever heard any such talk before? Partly crooked and partly crazy—that's him!"

But Single Jack merely smiled.

And, as it was noon a moment later, Shodress prepared to go across the street, to the hotel for his lunch.

"Watch him like a hawk, Dan," he said to McGruder. "I

hardly like to trust him to you, even. Though I know that you ain't got any reason for loving him. But keep your eyes on him. Remember that he does things that ain't possible. He turns my best men, like Grange, into blockheads. Keep your guns ready, and if anything happens—if you should have to sink a pair of bullets into him—why, I wouldn't have many questions to ask you, old man!"

39.   A Broken Link

In the door he paused for a final shot at Deems.

"What pleases me the most," he declared, "is that I do it all so safe and easy. I use the law for the hanging of you, Single Jack. And while you're about to swing, you ain't gonna be able to tell yourself that you'll ever be revenged on me! My hands are clean. It's the law that does it."

He laughed with huge enjoyment.

Afterward, when he had closed the door, they heard his steps go down the hall, and there followed the opening and the closing of another door.

"That's the armory, isn't it?" asked Single Jack.

"Yes. He always leaves his cannon there."

McGruder eyed his prisoner intently, as though eager to talk, but Single Jack seemed in no mood for it. He even settled himself deep in his chair and closed his eyes as though for sleep, but all the while, through the lowered lashes, he was watching the nervous state of his guard.

"Hell!" said Dan at last. "You sleeping?"

"If you don't mind, Dan, I'll have a nap."

"How can you sleep, man, after what's happened to you?"

"You mean Hester?"

"Of course! The finest and prettiest girl that I ever laid eyes on—and she loves you enough to come here and talk about it in front of us all!"

"I have to forget about her, now."

"Forget about her!"

"Yes. There's only one thing for me to prepare for, and that's to keep my nerve as strong and steady as ever, so that I'll be able to go up tomorrow without shaking."

"I understand what you mean. But you don't have to be afraid of yourself. How many times have you come next door to death?"

"A hundred times, I suppose. But dying under a gun or a knife is not the same thing as dying under a rope."

"Well, of course, I'll admit that. But look here, Jack, I'm as nervous as a cat!"

"What's wrong?"

"It's because I'm thinking things over. I never guessed what a hound Shodress was until this morning. No man has got a right to talk to any girl the way that he talked to Hester! And her crying, too! That's what beat me!"

"This is Shodress' big day," said Single Jack, "and let him make all that he can out of it. You can hardly blame him for wanting to run amuck a little."

"Tell me, Jack. Do you think that I'm like Shodress?"

"Not a bit, old fellow. You and I have had it out together. You played fair enough, as far as I'm concerned. I don't even hold Apperley against you. Because you stood up to him fair and square. It was the other pair that stood off to the side and put their lead into him. Westover—he's gone. And Mandell— I wish that I'd finished that rat off!"

Single Jack stretched his arms until the chains rattled loudly.

"We're what you'd call friendly enemies, Dan. If I make a move to escape, you'll squirt lead at me enough to kill a whole company of soldiers. And if I had a chance to get away, and you tried to stop me, I'd kill you if I could and never think about it again."

McGruder nodded with a little shudder at the thought. His

prisoner, with a yawn, composed himself again for a nap in the chair.

"Hold on," said McGruder. "I'd like to be doing something until the boss comes back. I'm sort of hungry and I need something to keep my mind from settling on the emptiness of my stomach. How about a game of poker?"

"Shodress don't like to have you play poker with me. He says that it's dangerous."

"Shodress is ten kinds of a fool about you, Jack. I admit free and easy that you're a faster and a straighter shooter than me when it comes to a stand-up fight, but with your arms weighted down with chains, and not even a pin for a weapon, what have I got to fear from you?"

"Nothing. I'm saying what Shodress always talks about. Not the facts!"

"Well, Shodress ain't here. It may be our last chance for a game, old boy."

"I don't feel like the cards, Dan."

"Well, you're nearly fifteen dollars up. I suppose it ain't so bad to quit a winner!"

"If you really feel that way about it, I'll play a hand or two with you."

"That's good! I'm nervous as a cat, and I need something to steady me."

"Deal 'em out, then!"

The prisoner took his place on the side of the table, his fettered feet swinging a little back and forth—and for a very good reason. For while those feet were on the floor the chains were not apt to be scrutinized very carefully. But now that they were well raised into the light, it was most probable that even an unsuspicious eye would be able to detect the cuts through them. So he kept his feet in motion back and forth, and the chain swung, of course, in the same rhythm.

Even so, it was a most perilous position. He could only hope that the attention of McGruder would be fixed intently upon the cards, throughout the play.

So McGruder, smoking a cigarette and dealing the cards, won the first hand with three sevens.

"It's my lucky day!" he exclaimed. "Every time that I've scored heavy, I've begun with three sevens! What do you say, old-timer! Do we bet free, or are you going to hedge a little?"

"I'll bet what I have to," said Single Jack. "I feel that my luck is out."

And he edged a little closer along the table.

The second hand, he received three kings in the deal, but it was not his purpose to win, if he could help it. He deliberately threw one of them away, and when he drew two aces, he let himself be weakly bluffed out of the bet which had been placed.

Dan McGruder joyously exposed an incomplete straight.

"Even bluffing works on you today, Jack!" he exclaimed. "I'm in, old boy, and I'm going to trim you! Well, it might as well come to me as to anybody, eh? You won't have long to enjoy your money."

"That's perfectly true," agreed the prisoner, and hunched himself still closer along the table.

He was fast working himself into the position that he desired. Now, with a hard strain of the right leg pulling down and the left leg straining up, the filed link in the chain burst with a sharp snap.

"What's that?" cried Dan McGruder, and gripped the butt of his revolver, letting the cards flutter from his hands to the floor. And his keen eyes fixed upon the face of the prisoner as grimly as a hawk from mid-air spying a field mouse far below him. No, there was no doubt that Mr. McGruder meant business.

"What's that?" he echoed again. "Lemme see that chain on your feet!"

"Sure," said Single Jack, "take a look!"

And swinging himself lightly around, his right hand resting a great part of his weight upon the surface of the table, he drove a heel straight at McGruder.

Fast as light that blow drove home, but not too fast for

McGruder to draw a Colt. He had it clear of the holster, but before he could level it and pull the trigger he was kicked back, his chair toppled over, and he crashed upon the floor.

The fall and the blow did not stun him. In his chest there was a stabbing pain, where the kick had broken a rib, but nevertheless his wits were about him, and he fought desperately to regain his feet in time to drive a bullet at the coming danger.

He needed only a half second, but he had not that time. Single Jack was off the table to follow his advantage, moving fast as a curling whiplash. His feet were free, except for the heavy, dangling chains. And that lent him almost his full speed.

He turned himself into a doubled-up knot, a sort of human projectile, and threw himself bodily at the man who was toppling to the floor.

Dan McGruder, in the act of lifting himself on one hand and grasping for his fallen revolver with the other, was struck a second time, and the gun torn from his fingers. So there was Single Jack armed!

The terrible thought gave an hysteria of strength to Dan McGruder. He whirled to his feet with a gasp, but only in time to see Single Jack bring up against the wall in the corner of the room, with the Colt leveled.

McGruder did not pause to ask questions. He made not the slightest effort to get at his other revolver. But he straightway tossed his hands into the air.

"That's finished, then," said Deems, getting slowly to his feet. "Turn around to the wall, Dan."

"Jack, are you going to murder me?"

"Turn around."

Slowly McGruder turned his face to the wall.

"Now hear me talk," said Deems, as he took the gun from the hip holster of the guard and dropped it into his own coat pocket. "I'm playing this game to win. Win life. Win Hester Grange. And I make every move as sure as I can. Do what I tell you, and you're as safe as if you were in your own home.

Try to double cross me, and it may make you famous, but it won't save your life!"

Poor McGruder nodded.

"I want to get to the armory, first of all. You lead the way!"

McGruder walked slowly from the room with the prisoner behind him, and his arms still high in the air.

They turned out into the corridor. A cool breath of air struck them.

"Ah," murmured Single Jack, "the only air for breathing is the free air, Dan!"

40. Chambers of Death

They reached the armory.

It was in a way the official junk shop of Yeoville. All sorts of curious odds and ends were stowed away there, from Indian war clubs to old-fashioned muskets and the latest kinds of rifles and revolvers. There were enough weapons there, as Shodress was always fond of saying, to equip every man in Yeoville with some sort of arms. And in the center of the floor stood a heavy anvil for such blacksmith's work as might be necessary without taking the tools to the regular forge.

To that anvil stepped Single Jack.

He took the second of McGruder's guns from his coat pocket and rested his manacled wrists upon the heavy iron slab. Both of the weapons pointed at McGruder.

"This is the idea, Dan," he explained. "If you take that ax over yonder, and smash away at these chains, I think that you can break 'em. I have a gun in each hand. You might be tempted to miss the chains with one of your strokes and chop off a hand at the wrist. But if you did, the second hand would surely kill you. Or you might be a little more reckless and take a swipe at my head, while the ax was in the air. But I don't think you would go quite as far as that. You're brave, Dan, but you don't really want to die for your country. Now, you start in, and swing that ax hard, but be sure that you use a good aim, all the while!"

Dan McGruder obeyed.

It was a ticklish business to heave that heavy ax up and down with the muzzles of the two revolvers constantly centered upon him. He could see that one was turned upon his heart and the other upon his head.

And wild thoughts grew up in his mind. If he struck down the hand which was directing a gun at his body, in the shock of the terrible pain and the surprise, was it very possible that the left hand would be able to shoot?

Especially because his very next movement would be to dash his ax at the head of the criminal?

With that desperate resolve in his heart, he swung the ax up for the next stroke, but at the top of the swing, his eyes flickered up and let in the keen, calm glance of Single Jack.

That glance was reading him deeply, and suddenly he knew that he had no chance whatever, against this man.

He let the stroke fall upon the first chain, and such was the ardor in it that the steel cracked open at once, and the chain fell apart.

"Very good," said the prisoner, "second thoughts are usually best, eh, Dan?"

And he smiled a little, but in such a way that cold moisture beaded the forehead of McGruder.

He found the second chain a more difficult job.

"Let it go, Jack," he advised in a gasp. "The noise that we're making will call 'em up here, and—"

"Thanks," said Single Jack. "But I like to have my hands about me!"

And he smiled again, while the shattered ax rose for another stroke.

That was the lucky blow. It snapped a central link across,

202

and now both of the hands of the archcriminal were free, except for the dangling, jangling weight of the chains.

"The best bit of work that you've ever done, I think," said Single Jack calmly. "Now walk ahead of me."

"What are you going to do with me, Jack?" asked the frightened guard.

"I won't hurt you. Not while you give me a fair show to be square with you. But no funny motions and no funny steps, old man!"

"I'll walk a chalk line!" declared McGruder with fervor, and he started down the hall again, according to the instructions of his prisoner.

"Hello!" called a voice from down the stairs. "Hello, McGruder?"

"Hello!" called McGruder, his voice a good deal broken.

"The old man sent me over to ask what is making all the noise over here?"

There was a bit of silence.

"Tell him to go fetch the old man to see for himself," said Single Jack.

"Hey, go back and tell Shodress that he can come and see for himself!"

"What! You want me to tell him that?"

"Yes."

"All right. It's your funeral, McGruder. But you must be crazy!"

There was a sound of steps crashing down the lower stairs, and then the front door of the building slammed.

"What if that messenger had come to the second floor, instead of merely calling up the stairs!"

"You see that luck is with me," said Single Jack. "Walk a little slower, McGruder, because I want you close ahead when you come to the turn in the hall."

That, and the noise of the messenger descending the stairs a moment before, gave McGruder his daring idea. If he could bound around the sharp angle of the hall wall, the stairs opened directly to the right, and with a single leap he could be down to the first landing, and whirl from it down the lower flight and out of the sight of the eye of Single Jack, and out of the possibility of his dreadful guns!

He acted on the thought, which is the best way, if action there must be, and action there had to be for McGruder. It was either a chance to redeem himself, or else eternal shame. Bad enough to have allowed a helpless, chained prisoner to escape. But ten times worse to have actually broken away the chains which bound his terrible hands!

No, McGruder could never live that down.

"How did you get the chain on your feet broken, Jack?"

"I filed 'em through at night."

"Oh, that was the rat that squeaked in the wall, now and then!"

"Yes, that was the rat!"

"I just about guessed it. Shodress will go mad when he hears about it!"

"Shodress isn't apt to hear about it. Not while he's in Yeoville, at least, but—come back, Dan!"

McGruder, at that instant, had reached leaping distance of the wall angle.

Around it he went, like a streak of light, and with a single bound he crashed down upon the landing beneath.

Single Jack followed down the hall. There would never have been the slightest doubt about what was to happen had not the chains impeded the tigerish speed of his rush in pursuit.

But as it was, only chance was against brave Dan McGruder. For when he struck the landing, he staggered with the force of his leap. If that reeling uncertainty had thrown him toward the lower flight, all would have been well. But he staggered back and to the side and as he leaped again toward safety, he saw Single Jack glide out on the head of the stairs, gun in hand.

A scream tore the lips of McGruder, but it was cut short by the roar of the gun. He fell across the top of the stairs and rolled down to the bottom. And on the wall of the landing they still point to a round hole, where the shot of Single Jack bored its way out of sight after passing through the body and heart of poor McGruder.

At the top of the steps, Single Jack paused a moment to consider.

Then another thought came to him, and turning about, he hurried to the armory which he had just left. Beside the door as he came into it he found the sawed-off, double-barreled shotgun which had been so much in the hands of Shodress since the time of imprisonment began.

This he picked up, and handled it with a grim fondness.

Then, with his chains rattling at his heels, he ran forward and down the corridor into the chamber which had served him for a jail room.

When he stood in it again, he wondered at the long silences which filled the old building.

But when he stepped to the window, he could see some signs of life, there. A dozen men were walking out from the veranda of the hotel, just opposite, and staring up at the jail, and it was plain that they must have heard the booming reverberations of the revolver shot, as it went echoing down the stair well.

Now the door of the hotel was dashed open, and big Shodress came running out. He was in a great fury, and so great, indeed, was his passion, that he had snatched out a revolver from the holster and he was shaking this on high as he ran, leaving a stream of oaths upon the air behind him.

The grinning messenger who had brought the insulting word from Dan McGruder paused at the door of the hotel.

And now Single Jack leaned from the window of the jail. From the corner of his eye, he saw a sullen and silent scattering of the men across the street, as though the weapon which he now held to his shoulder had been pointed specially at each one of them. So great was their surprise and their fright that not one of them so much as cried out, but all trusted implicitly in the speed of their feet to take them out of harm's way.

Then leaning from the window, he called, "Shodress!"

The fat man, checking himself in his running, looked wildly up into the window of the jail, and there he saw death waiting for him in the dark double mouths of his own gun, and in the sinisterly smiling face of Single Jack Deems behind it.

An expression of horror and of utter bewilderment came upon Shodress. He did not attempt to defend himself.

"You remember the dream, Alec?" asked Single Jack Deems and fired the first chamber.

Shodress was crushed into the dust as though a great foot had stamped upon him. But into his back, as he lay, Single Jack fired the second barrel, and saw the heavy charge strike home between the shoulder blades, and knock out a little puff of dust from the coat.

41.   Toward Freedom and the Grange Cottage

A bolt had been dropped into the mechanism of the town of Yeoville. The machine which had run on at such a furious rate and for so long now ran hit or miss.

Yonder, on his face in the dust, lay the vital factor, and the bravest men in Yeoville dared not step out to see whether their benefactor still lived, or was dead.

In the meantime, the prisoner in the jail tied his chains high on his legs and upon his arms and then, when they were thus more commodiously arranged, he left the room and went down the stairs.

Even from outside the building, there was not a voice. One would have thought that the heat of the noon sun had put the place to sleep.

Yeoville had not yet recovered the use of its wits, and how long would it be before Yeoville did recover?

That was something else, also, that no man could tell.

No one was more aware of all these possibilities than was Single Jack Deems. But he did not hurry.

He went out the back way from the jail, and in the adjoining pasture were a dozen horses running about. An old man hurried from one wing of the building toward the other.

"Hello!" said Single Jack.

The old chap whirled, saw him, and then dropped upon his knees.

"My God, Deems, don't kill me!" he cried.

"I'm not going to touch you," said Jack Deems. "But I want you to catch me a horse in that pasture. I don't care which one. Get me a horse and put a saddle on its back. The saddles are in that shed, aren't they?"

The other ran to obey this order with trembling haste.

In the meantime, why did no one come? What had happened to the brave and true men of Yeoville? Why did they not pour out and sweep down upon the dare-devil?

There was no sight of them, but telltale sounds began to sweep up and down through the village.

When the work was done, Jack asked of the old fellow:

"What's your name?"

"Jay Greenfield."

"Greenfield. I'm a thousand times obliged to you. Remember me kindly to all your grandchildren. So long!"

He climbed into the saddle rather awkwardly, because there was a burden upon each hand and upon both feet. Also, because he had never managed to become a really good horseman.

And he turned his back upon Greenfield, and jogged the horse past the jail and straight on out into the center of the street.

Greenfield himself followed at a run, not able to believe his ears because they did not hear a universal roar of weapons at the first sight of the bad man.

But there was no roar of guns. No, not a glimmer of steel was exposed to the sun of the early afternoon, and even the whispers of talk died away as Single Jack rode up the street calling out gravely and quietly as he went:

"Gentlemen, there'll be fame enough even for the man who has the nerve to shoot me through the back! I think that you all need a little encouraging. I hope to see a bit more action from you, my friends."

He maintained a running streak of talk, in this manner, as he went up the street, until when he was opposite the blacksmith shop upon one side and the vacant lot on the other, a young calf in the lot threw up its tail, flourished its heels, and ran bawling to the other end of the lot.

The roan horse gave one sharp, quick buck, and even that bit of unruliness was enough to drop Single Jack in the dirt!

Now was the time for the guns to roar! Now was the time to revenge on Single Jack the language and the deeds they had endured from him on this day!

He himself surely expected it, and dropping his rifle, he landed on his knees in the dust with a revolver flashing in either hand. There were a dozen gleams of metal up and down the street—but no one quite dared to shoot.

They allowed him to catch the horse, to mount again—and to ride deliberately toward that side of the town where the Grange cottage stood!

42.   A Friend at Court

Neither did they pursue Single Jack. Not a single rider left the town to win money or glory at the expense of the famous outlaw. So he rode unmolested through the streets, and reached the Grange cottage. There he was met by Steve Grange who rushed out from the house and shouted with joy at the thing which he saw.

They did not have much time for congratulations.

In a little trench, under the apple tree in the Grange garden, Deems exposed the paper which he had made Doctor Myers write out and sign.

"Where's Hester?"

"You'd want to know that, of course. She's gone uptown to buy some groceries. But wait a minute—I thought that I heard shooting. Jack, aren't you going to tell me what happened?"

"Shodress is dead. That's what really matters. I did what I told him I'd do, and with his own gun. If I have to die tomorrow, Steve, I'll think that I've done enough good by killing Shodress to make up for all the wrongs I've committed. How's young Apperley?"

"Sitting up in bed. Looks halfway like himself. He's a fine fellow at heart, Jack. But you can't wait to see him. They'll be after you—"

"I don't think that they'll be after me," said Single Jack gravely. "I think that they've had enough of me for one day. I'll see the face of Dave Apperley before I go on."

"Go on in then," said Steve. "You'll find Oliver in there. Oliver says that you're the greatest man that ever lived. I'm going to get a saddle on my Winnie mare, and when you ride off, I'm going along with you, if I may!"

"With an outlaw?"

"I've got a jail sentence over my head, anyway, and I'll never serve it unless they catch me with a trap. You and I together to fight out the rest of this game, Jack!"

He ran for the barn, and Single Jack went across the veranda and stood in the window and looked in upon David Apperley.

At the sight of Single Jack, he uttered a great shout.

"Jack! Jack Deems!"

Single Jack slipped through the open window and stood beside the bed.

"Don't ask questions. I'm in a hurry; you can guess why. Shodress is dead, though. That's the main thing. And that'll leave the rest of the people that hate the Apperleys—and me

—without a leader. I want a justification for what I've done, and this is the confession of Doctor Myers. You keep that. You're a lawyer and you'll know when and where to use it. In the meantime, I cut for the mountains with Steve. So long! I'll see your brother and let him know what's happened!"

So he rode from Yeoville and went with Steve Grange in perfect safety down the roads and across the mountains until they came to the home grounds of Andrew Apperley.

In the dusk of a long summer evening, they stood together outside the house in the new garden, where the little sapling fruit trees were daintily silhouetted against the sky and the rising moon.

"Listen to me," said Andrew Apperley, "you have done enough for me to make me want to use every power in my control to help you, Deems. If you'll only tell me what I can do—"

"I used to think," said Deems gravely, "that I could never be anything other than a wild man. But Comanche taught me different. Nothing was ever any wilder than he. But he finally met me, and I tamed him. And then I met someone who was able to tame me—or make me want to be tame."

"No man, though," suggested the rancher.

"No. You've heard the facts from Steve."

"I've heard them."

"Well, Apperley, I'll go straight now if the government will give me half a chance. If they push me to the wall, it'll cost them a good many lives, and a great many thousands of dollars to capture me. But if they'll give me a chance to be good, they'll never have trouble with me again. You have friends in Washington. You can talk to them. Talk to them over the telegraph. Get me half a chance. Because I want to settle down!"

"Where, man?"

"Right here. This is going to be the most peaceful part of the West, now that Shodress is dead and his gang has been scattered. It will be a good place for me to settle—with my wife."

Affairs at Washington moved slowly, and for months Jack Deems led a wretched life of suspense.

But at last suspense ended like all bad things, however long, and the countryside buzzed with the news that Single Jack Deems had been pardoned for all offenses, East and West.

"Good sense!" said friends.

"Crooked politics," said enemies.

But Single Jack did not care to listen to their criticisms. He had headed south and west for the Apperley range where a ranch house had already been built on the knoll by the river and where Oliver and Hester Grange had already opened the place to wait for his coming with Steve, and with Comanche.

OLD MASTER OF
THE OLD WEST
MAX BRAND

Thundering action that never quits—Max Brand
lets you have it just the way you want it.
For the very best in Western entertainment, get
these Max Brand titles, available from
Pocket Books:

ZANE GREY

WESTERNS THAT NEVER DIE

They pack excitement that lasts a lifetime.
It's no wonder Zane Grey is the bestselling
Western writer of all time.
Get these Zane Grey Western adventures
from Pocket Books:

_____	83102	BORDER LEGION $1.75
_____	82896	BOULDER DAM $1.75
_____	82818	CODE OF THE WEST $1.75
_____	82692	DEER STALKER $1.75
_____	82883	KNIGHTS OF THE RANGE $1.75
_____	82878	ROBBERS ROOST $1.75
_____	82076	TO THE LAST MAN $1.75
_____	82879	UNDER THE TONTO RIM $1.75
_____	82880	U.P. TRAIL $1.75
_____	83022	ARIZONA CLAN $1.75
_____	83105	BLACK MESA $1.75
_____	83309	CALL OF THE CANYON $1.75

POCKET BOOKS
Department ZG
1230 Avenue of the Americas
New York, N.Y. 10020

Please send me the books I have checked above. I am enclosing
$_____ (please add 50¢ to cover postage and handling for each order,
N.Y.S. and N.Y.C. residents please add appropriate sales tax). Send check
or money order—no cash or C.O.D.'s please. Allow up to six weeks for
delivery.

NAME_____

ADDRESS_____

CITY_____ STATE/ZIP_____

ZG 11-79

Clair HUFFAKER

Westerns

"Move Huffaker onto your list of great storytellers!"
—*Chicago Tribune*